Praise for

New York Times and USA Today Bestselling Author

Diane Capri

"Full of thrills and tension, but smart and human, too. Kim Otto is a great, great character. I love her."
Lee Child, *#1 World Wide Bestselling Author of Jack Reacher Thrillers*

"[A] welcome surprise… [W]orks from the first page to 'The End'."
Larry King

"Swift pacing and ongoing suspense are always present… [L]ikable protagonist who uses her political connections for a good cause…Readers should eagerly anticipate the next [book]."
Top Pick, Romantic Times

"…offers tense legal drama with courtroom overtones, twisty plot, and loads of Florida atmosphere. Recommended."
Library Journal

"[A] fast-paced legal thriller…energetic prose…an appealing heroine…clever and capable supporting cast…[that will] keep readers waiting for the next [book]."
Publishers Weekly

"Expertise shines on every page."
Margaret Maron, Edgar, Anthony, Agatha and Macavity Award-Winning MWA Grand Master

HARD MONEY

by *DIANE CAPRI*

Published by: AugustBooks
http://www.AugustBooks.com

ISBN: 978-1-942633-94-5

Original cover design by: Cory Clubb

Hard Money is a work of fiction. Names, characters, places, and incidents either are the product of the author's imagination or are used fictitiously, and any resemblance to actual persons, living or dead, business establishments, events, or locales is entirely coincidental.

Published in the United States of America.

Visit the author website:
http://www.DianeCapri.com

ALSO BY DIANE CAPRI

The Hunt for Jack Reacher Series

(in publication order with Lee Child source books in parentheses)

Don't Know Jack • (The Killing Floor)

Jack in a Box (*novella*)

Jack and Kill (*novella*)

Get Back Jack • (Bad Luck & Trouble)

Jack in the Green (*novella*)

Jack and Joe • (The Enemy)

Deep Cover Jack • (Persuader)

Jack the Reaper • (The Hard Way)

Black Jack • (Running Blind/The Visitor)

Ten Two Jack • (The Midnight Line)

Jack of Spades • (Past Tense)

Prepper Jack • (Die Trying)

Full Metal Jack • (The Affair)

Jack Frost • (61 Hours)

Jack of Hearts • (Worth Dying For)

Straight Jack • (A Wanted Man)

Jack Knife • (Never Go Back)

Lone Star Jack • (Echo Burning)

Bulletproof Jack • (Make Me)

Bet On Jack • (Nothing to Lose)

Jack on a Wire • (Tripwire)

Tracking Jack • (Gone Tomorrow)

The Michael Flint Series:

Blood Trails

Trace Evidence

Ground Truth

Hard Money

Dead Lock

CAST OF CHARACTERS

Michael Flint
Kathryn (Katie) Scarlett
Alonzo Drake
Carlos Gaspar
Spencer Lyman
Ward Lyman
Emily Royce
Anthony Boldo
Naomi Wagner
Bartholomew Trawler

For the readers who have supported me and enjoyed my books and asked for more.

I couldn't do this without you.

Thank you.

HARD MONEY

"It's not how much hard money you make, but how many generations you keep it for."

—*Robert Kiyosaki*

CHAPTER 1

Las Vegas, Nevada

MICHAEL FLINT STOOD ON the Las Vegas strip outside the sprawling Venietio casino, reviewing the situation before moving ahead with his plan. The influence of organized crime in Las Vegas was not a myth. Extreme caution was required.

Although the Venietio rested on the quieter end of the Las Vegas strip, it dazzled with the bling for which these casinos were famous.

Venietio's central building housed two floors for gambling, forty-five floors of hotel rooms, and a top floor of penthouse suites. Tropical plants, choreographed lighting, and swimming pools spread a couple of hundred yards in all directions. Occasional access paths crossed the scene to keep numerous bars, restaurants, and cabanas supplied.

Running such an establishment was like managing a small city. The logistics required constant attention.

But the most treacherous path every casino owner in Las Vegas had to navigate was the one between legal business operations and unscrupulous grifters exploiting every angle, legal or otherwise, attempting to amass and keep their fortunes.

Nick Kodinsky and Dayton Whyte had been two such grifters. Years earlier, they'd begged, borrowed, and cajoled to raise half a billion dollars to break ground on the Venietio casino.

Kodinsky had been the voice of reason to investors and banks, and Whyte had the balls to repel the mobsters before they had a chance to get their hooks into the fledgling operation.

Operating a casino in Vegas that, one way or another, wasn't controlled by crooks and killers had always been an impossible challenge. Kodinsky and Whyte believed it could be done.

They were wrong.

Over time, Kodinsky ran the operation on the right side of the law, albeit barely. While organized crime kept chipping away at Whyte, who was, without a doubt, the weakest link.

Businesses in Vegas, legal or not, were owned and operated by those who took the long view. Which meant a constant struggle to keep Venietio on the legal side and out of the mob's hands.

Inevitably, weak men like Whyte fell under the mob's control.

Which was the very moment, Kodinsky's wife said, her husband became expendable, living on borrowed time.

Exactly who killed Nick Kodinsky was never clear, but they dumped his body forty miles from the strip. All forensic evidence was destroyed before the body was found.

Nick Kodinsky's will gave his half of the casino to his wife, Dolores. But Whyte challenged the will in court, and his delays and legal maneuvers had kept it there for three years. So far.

A thorough investigation by the Las Vegas homicide unit turned up questions but few answers. So few that Delores Kodinsky had finally turned to Michael Flint.

Flint's investigation had turned up a string of anomalies. For a casino on the strip, the business didn't look so healthy.

Staff had been cut and suppliers were clamoring to be paid. Croupiers were shopping their skills to other casinos, and several had already left.

Flint's client, Delores Kodinsky, was being systematically cheated by her husband's business partner. No doubt about it.

Yet, every time Flint had checked the place out, the slot machines and the tables were always full. Where was the money going?

When Flint confronted Whyte with these facts, he denied and deflected. Which ticked Flint off and made him dig harder.

Hanging out in a small bar off the strip the previous evening, Flint had hit gold. The bar was a popular meeting place for Venietio casino staff. After a bit of eavesdropping and heavy tipping, he found a cook with an interesting story.

All casinos had a vault. Usually underground, the vaults stored the hard money. Cash accumulated in casinos, even as they tried to encourage payment by plastic.

A steady stream of cash flowed to the banks daily. Some banks specifically allowed casinos to deposit money over the weekends. Casino cash handling was a well planned and executed process.

Except at Venietio's, the cook claimed.

The armored car that collected the money hadn't been seen for a month, and the cash had stopped flowing to the banks. According to the cook, Venietio's vault was full of cash.

Delores Kodinsky's cash.

Flint had checked the Venietio's floor plans. He'd located the underground tunnel to the vault.

He had two options. He could watch and wait to confirm that Whyte planned to disappear with Kodinsky's fortune in cash. Or he could act now.

Flint considered both options fully. It was the right thing to do. Weigh the pros and cons. The risks, the benefits. But the answer was obvious.

Which was why Flint's finger was now poised over the call button on a burner cell phone. It was time to disturb Whyte's cozy scheme. He pressed call.

Whyte answered on the third ring. "Who's this?"

"Michael Flint. I'd like a meeting."

Whyte scoffed. "No chance. Talk to my lawyer."

"Two minutes. I'm in Vegas."

"Go have fun. Somewhere else."

"You've been reading too much Mickey Spillane."

"Get lost."

"If you've got any sense, we should talk."

"You step on my property, I'll have you arrested."

"I've got an offer you can't refuse, as Mickey would say."

"Who the hell's Mickey?"

"I know what you're doing with the money the casino generates."

Whyte paused. "My business has got nothing to do with you."

"Has a lot to do with Dolores Kominsky."

"The ex-croupier Max kept on the side? She doesn't deserve squat."

"They were married."

"In Vegas? You think that counts for anything?"

"Married's married. Seven years."

"She's a gold-digging b—"

"You don't like her because she turned you down."

Whyte's voice dropped an octave. "You watch your mouth, you—"

"Let's discuss this in person."

"No chance. Go back to whatever hovel you crawled out of. Now. Because my security has been alerted, and we've called the police."

Flint snorted. "You? Called the police? Right."

"I'll see you put away for the rest of your life. A very short life."

"You threatening me?"

Whyte laughed. "That would be like threatening a roach. Because I can step on roaches. And I do."

"So I've heard. People like Clyde Beatty."

Whyte didn't speak for three full seconds. Over the phone, his breathing sounded irregular. Forced. Like he was holding something back.

"You weren't charged with murder," Flint said. "But I have a photograph that could change that."

Whyte remained silent for another full second. "You're a piece of work."

"I'm a hard worker. That's why I'm on the phone with you now."

Flint heard a single click. Distinct. Crisp. He heard no breathing from the other end of the phone, but the call remained connected. A moment later, another click sounded, and Whyte came back on.

"All right. Two minutes. Come up and show me what you've got. Penthouse elevator."

This time the line went dead.

Flint placed a second call to Bradley, a Las Vegas PI he'd hired for backup. "We're on. I'm headed up to his penthouse. You don't hear anything from me five minutes after I get up there, call the cops."

"You got it."

"And call the cops if you see anything being moved out of the tunnel. Anything at all. A bicycle comes through there, call the cops," Flint said, to be clear, as he moved through the casino toward the elevator.

"Roger that."

CHAPTER 2

FLINT PUSHED THROUGH A door marked *Penthouse Visitors Only*. Which led to a small room and a second door. This one was solid oak with no handle. A girl in a short and clinging dress sat behind a reception desk. Behind her, a camera stared down from the corner of the ceiling.

"Michael Flint. Meeting with Dayton Whyte."

The girl nodded and typed on a tiny laptop. "You're early."

"Sue me."

"Mr. Whyte has authorized a single visit." She looked up, stared a moment, then raised her eyebrows with a smug smile. "Two minutes. Precisely."

"Won't be a problem. Even a single minute's going to put me off my feed for a week."

Whyte never had combative visitors. The girl's mouth opened and closed a couple of times as she searched her brain for a snappy comeback. She waved toward the elevator.

Metal scraped against metal and a moment later the oak door opened a few inches. The setup must have had a crude metal brace bolted inside the dignified oak door, effectively blocking intruders.

"Enjoy your visit," she said snidely and busied herself on the computer.

Flint pulled the oak door open. It led to a second room where two large men in dark suits stood on either side of shiny brass elevator doors.

Arms by their sides, eyes locked straight ahead. Barrel chested. Casino name badges, unlikely to be real names, but Flint noted that Rick had a goatee and Cuba a buzz cut.

"So this is where you either beat me to a pulp," said Flint, "or you wait until your mob boss has seen what I have to show him."

"We identified you when you started poking your nose where it doesn't belong," Cuba said. "We could have buried you long ago."

Flint scoffed. "Obviously you don't think so. Because you haven't done it."

Cuba stepped forward, lips pressed into an angry thin line.

Rick intervened and beckoned Flint forward. "Arms out. Legs apart."

Flint took a breath. This was it. He lifted weights, ran marathons, and trained to stay sharp.

But this pair were disciplined fighters, not backstreet brawlers. Solid muscle, and plenty of it. Probably trained as well as he was.

If they'd been instructed to work him over, they'd coordinate. In the confines of this six-foot square room, they believed he wouldn't stand a chance against the two of them.

Flint stepped forward, raising his arms as Cuba reached for Flint's torso to pat him down for weapons.

Flint grabbed Cuba's lapels and spun around, catching the man off-balance. With one thrust, he shoved Cuba out of the small room, slammed the door, and rammed the metal brace into place to keep it closed.

Rick lunged forward, leading with his fist. Flint dodged and shoved him to one side.

"I'm not here for a fight," Flint said reasonably. "But two against one didn't seem fair."

Rick steadied his feet and prepared to land the second blow.

Flint held his hands up, fingers spread to show he meant no harm. "He's not hurt. You can open the door to check once I'm in the elevator."

Rick adjusted his fist, clearly considering Flint's comment. After a moment, he lowered his arm. "Against the wall. Spread 'em."

"I'm not armed. Against casino rules."

"Shut your mouth. Against the wall."

Flint stared a moment before turning to face the wall. He kept his muscles taut. Rick roughly patted him down and pulled the burner phone from his jacket pocket.

"I need that," said Flint. "If your boss wants to see what I have."

Rick pushed a button on the wall and tossed the phone back. Flint caught the phone in his left hand.

Half a moment later, Rick attempted a solid punch, planning to hammer into Flint's back and side.

Before the punch landed, Flint twisted swiftly out of reach.

Rick's knuckles landed hard against the wall.

A nasty sounding crunch resounded. Rick yowled loudly and jerked his fist back to his chest for protection.

The elevator doors slid open silently and Flint stepped inside.

"Better get some ice for that hand," he suggested as the elevator doors closed between them.

The smooth ride up started slow and accelerated relentlessly. The speed decayed as quickly as it grew, but the stop was easy and then the doors slid open again.

Flint stood to one side and waited. Whyte's goons didn't show up. Which was a bad sign.

Pausing a moment, Flint peered around the door's edge. Mirrors and modern art hung between Doric columns in a hallway that led to what looked like the living area. A flickering mixture of neon light from the strip, forty floors below, bounced in reflection from floor-to-ceiling glass and back again.

Flint stepped out into the unoccupied room and the elevator doors closed behind him.

Where was Whyte?

Flint's every step echoed on marble flooring. In the opposite direction, the hallway led to a kitchen. He walked into the living area.

The interior reflected the designers' taste for the modern. Simple shapes defined the furniture and light fixtures. The chairs and sofa bowed to magazine covers and geometry more than comfort. The glossy white baby grand piano was devoid of embellishments.

The living area occupied the corner of the building and spanned seventy feet in either direction.

There was no sign of Dayton Whyte.

"Whyte?" Flint called.

The hard surfaces bounced his name around the empty room and the hallway and would have been heard in the kitchen. Easily. But the silence that followed had an edge. Something beyond the lack of voices.

Flint moved to the wall, collecting a crystal statue on the way. Eighteen inches high with good heft, it was a reasonable weapon against anything but a gun.

He covered the hallway into the kitchen, which was a giant affair with appliances ringing the walls, an island in the center, and a breakfast area that overlooked the rear of the building. A vast array of stainless-steel saucepans hung from a rack above the cooking island.

Flint circled the room, calling for Whyte, but no one responded.

From a drawer beside the enormous range, he swapped the statue for a knife. Japanese steel with well-honed edges. It had a sheath, so he tucked it in his belt.

Retracing his steps along the hallway, Flint found a door artfully disguised as a giant gilt-edged mirror. The oversized panel swung inward to reveal a massive bedroom. Flint wondered if he'd find a bloody body draped across the sheets, but this room, too, was unoccupied.

He checked the en suite as he dialed Bradley again.

Bradley answered on the last ring. "Yo."

"He's not here."

"Where are you?"

"In his penthouse."

Bradley whistled. "Didn't think you'd make it inside."

"Thanks for the vote of confidence. What do you see down there?"

"Nothing special."

"Anyone in or out?"

"Nope. Nothing."

"Sure?"

"Of course I'm sure. What kind of question is that?"

"It's a big place."

"And I'm watching it all. No excitement. Keep looking up there. The penthouse is a big place, too."

Flint frowned. "I checked the living area and kitchen thoroughly. But I can't find the bedroom," he lied. "So I'm coming down."

"No, wait." Bradley paused a moment. "Try ... like big pictures and mirrors. Rich people love that. Hiding stuff. Makes them feel special. Like they're the only ones who know the secret."

"Yeah. Them and you."

Bradley paused again. "What d'you mean, them and me?"

Flint sneered. "You know where to find the bedroom."

Bradley didn't speak.

"How much is he paying you?"

Flint heard heavy breathing before the line went dead.

CHAPTER 3

FLINT LOOKED AT THE empty bedroom. Damn. Whyte had skipped out. Decided to take his money and run. Which meant there was another way out of the penthouse.

Whyte had attempted to trap Flint here.

How long had he been gone?

Could Flint catch him before Whyte disappeared?

He raced from the bedroom to the elevators, found the call button, and stabbed it. The light didn't illuminate.

He pressed the button several times. Nothing happened.

He shoved his ear against the metal doors but heard nothing.

Opposite the elevator door were the emergency stairs. But he couldn't open the door.

He hammered the sole of his shoe against the door by the closing mechanism at the doorknob.

The door didn't give.

Flint ran to the kitchen. He collected three saucepans with steel handles tapering to an elegantly narrow tip.

Flint approached the narrow glass window beside the stairway door. He pounded the window with repeated blows from one of the heavy pans until the glass broke. He wiped the spiky shards away and reached into the stairwell to unlock the door.

But the latch refused to turn.

Flint rammed the end of two saucepan handles into the doorframe at the locking mechanism.

Alternating, he used them to jimmy the gap between the door and the frame, attempting to widen the gap.

The oak trim splintered off and the pans fell to the floor.

He pounded the handles deeper into the gap, straining against each one before adding the next. More wood broke off and he kept using the same technique.

Finally, one of the handles pierced through the side of the door. A few more moments of pounding and the door swung open.The saucepans clamored to the floor as Flint pushed through into the stairwell.

The concrete steps were jarring next to the modern luxury of the penthouse, but Flint barely noticed. He took the stairs three and four at a time, using his shoulder against the walls to slow his pace at each one-eighty turn.

Four floors down a fire door opened into a corridor.

Flint ran through and along the hallway. Apartment doors led off on each side. The corridor turned a couple of times. Finally, he found an elevator.

This time, when he pushed the call button it illuminated, and the digital counter marked the car's progress toward him.

When the car arrived, two well-dressed women shuffled to the rear as he stepped in.

This elevator was glacially slow compared to the one for the penthouse. Flint spent the minutes that felt like hours during the slow descent creating his plan of attack.

Whyte must have used the time between Flint's phone call and his arrival to disappear with Delores Kodinsky's money. A hundred million at least. If Whyte succeeded, Flint's client would be broke. Whyte would hide the money where Kodinsky would never find it next time.

Whyte's plan to cheat Nick Kodinsky's widow from what was rightfully hers was way too close to succeeding. Which Flint absolutely would not allow.

The casino complex had three lower levels. Kitchens and guest services filled the first two floors. Access to the main vault on the third level was strictly controlled.

Whyte was moving cash from the vault. He'd be forced to exit at the rear of the building through the tunnel. It was a hundred feet underground. At the end was what looked like a normal roll-up garage door.

Behind it was a second door. This one was a steel-reinforced airlock style, fabricated with metal and concrete.

The guest elevator doors eventually opened onto a casino entrance. Flint hustled quickly across the floor and burst outside. At the base of a dozen steps out front, lines of cars and taxis alternated dropping off and collecting departing guests in a loading area.People milled around in every direction.

The whole casino complex covered several acres of land. Running flat out, it would take several minutes to reach the tunnel exit. He needed faster transportation.

His gaze scanned for one of the golf carts he'd seen transporting gamblers earlier.

Before finding anything suitable, he locked eyes with a man he recognized standing across the road from the entrance.

As soon as the face registered in Flint's mind, he started moving. Rick, Whyte's elevator guard, hurried away, too. Fast. Oblivious to the screeching of car tires and honking horns as he ran in front of the traffic.

Rick was speaking into a walkie-talkie. Which meant he had backup. Possibly the casino's security muscle. They'd have weapons and comms.

Quickly, Flint turned and ducked into a crowd of gamblers entering the building.

The casino was a few steps below grade from the entrance which was meant to impress visitors with the scope of the spectacle. It also gave Flint a wide view.

Throngs of people packed the casino floor. Hardcore gamblers at tables, tourists at slot machines, and gawkers everywhere.

On Flint's left, two men in black suits cut a path through the crowd headed directly toward him. He spun on his heel and hoofed toward the shopping gallery. His pursuers picked up the pace.

Dodging, weaving, and a judicious use of his elbows gave Flint the advantage. He reached the far side of the gallery two dozen steps ahead of his pursuers.

An archway separated the casino from a larger food court and shopping mall combination. The mall security guards wore gray short-sleeved shirts instead of black suits. Which probably meant they were a different team. Flint steered clear of them anyway.

At the exit, Flint leaned against the wall beside a fire alarm. He rammed his elbow backward to smash the glass and then swiftly yanked the handle down.

Instantly, sirens whoop-whoop-whooped. A recorded voice instructing people not to panic while the reason for the alarm was being investigated sounded from speakers in every direction. Followed by the same whoops and then a repeat of the voice.

Flint's pursuers were just twenty feet away. He turned toward the shopping mall's long, wide hallways and pumped his speed.

Just as he started to run sprinklers opened up above the crowds. People screamed and ran for cover.

His pursuers were slowed by the mass as they tried to power through.

Flint ran along the hallway until he reached the end of the sprinkled zone and once again found dry pavement. The faces he passed looked perplexed by his drowned appearance, but no one was heading for the exits here.

He followed the walkway as the mall zigzagged through the building. He was out of sight, but he'd also lost sight of his pursuers.

Moments later, he saw them.

Directly ahead.

Dripping wet.

One on either side of the twenty-foot-wide corridor. They'd found a shortcut.

One man placed his hand inside his jacket to suggest his gun rested there and motioned toward the side of the corridor.

Flint pretended to take the warning seriously.

He feigned a move to one side. Then he pivoted and ran flat out into a designer clothes shop. He kept low, dodging left and right between the racks and shoppers. He crouched down behind a row of jackets, squeezing against the side wall. Easing the jackets back into place and keeping down to wait.

Seconds later, the two men ran through the center of the store, swiveling their heads.

CHAPTER 4

FLINT COUNTED TO FIVE before easing out from the cover of the jackets. Bent double, he raced for the exit and took a left. Moments later, he found a set of double doors marked MAINTENANCE.

He slipped through and found himself in a narrow concrete corridor.

He located the stairs and headed down.

Exiting the stairwell beneath the casino, he found mechanical equipment roaring and rumbling. This was the home for air handling, water treatment, and power for the whole building.

He ran along the narrow spaces between the equipment, looking for a route to the vault on the floor below.

He turned a sharp corner around a massive air handling unit and stopped short. He ducked back into the crevasse to figure out where he was.

A blockhouse sat in the middle of this section of the floor. A solid concrete block structure within the building. Probably some sort of office and break room. Sanctuary from the deafening noise for the workers.

CCTV cameras were posted on all four sides of the blockhouse. Which meant they might have seen him step into the open or running through the equipment already.

Flint backed around the corner out of camera range and then stood up and turned to find another route.

The moment he turned, Rick somehow appeared out of nowhere, positioned and threw his body behind a straight arm punch to Flint's face.

With lightning reflexes, Flint barely managed to rotate his head a fraction. Angling his mouth and nose away from the impact in order to preserve bones and teeth.

Which didn't diminish the impact's force.

Rick's knuckles smashed into Flint's cheek, ramming his jaw backward and pummeling the bones in his face. He staggered back, placing a hand on the wall of machinery to stay on his feet.

He heard a noise. Shuffling, scrabbling. Behind him.

He swept his arm back hard and fast with his elbow at head height. He made soft contact.

Choking and gagging, Rick's sidekick, Cuba, fell to his knees, hands around his throat, trying to breathe.

Flint bobbed to his right.

Rick faked a second punch.

Flint sidestepped.

Cuba, from his position on the floor, launched a low kick to the back of Flint's knees.

Flint's knees gave out.

He collapsed and looked up.

Rick swooped down, leading with his elbow, making solid contact with Flint's temple.

Pain shot through his head as his balance swam. He reached to break his fall to the floor, but his arm didn't work. He hit the pavement face-first.

Rick's patent leather shoe with the sole of a heavy boot stamped down on Flint with his whole weight.

The impact hit Flint's ribs. He felt them flex until his kidney's searing pain overwhelmed his senses. He lost consciousness.

Sometime later, when Flint opened his eyes, he was in a white-painted concrete room. Harsh fluorescent lighting made him squint.

Residual pain welled up from his side. He clenched his teeth to keep himself from groaning.

He couldn't move his arms. Zip ties held them behind his back and cut into his wrists.

He realized he was in a cheap plastic garden chair on a bare concrete floor.

In front of him sat a huge white pickup truck. A Chevrolet Silverado. The enormous, flared arches around the rear wheels indicated it was the top of the range, easily capable of carrying several thousand pounds.

A Ford Explorer SUV was parked behind the truck.

Beyond both vehicles, stainless steel gleamed.

The casino vault with the door wide open.

The Silverado's tailgate hung down for loading.

Cuba pushed a two-foot-long box onto the bed. The man was sweating. He disappeared and returned a moment later with an identical box and loaded it on the truck.

Given the size and obvious effort and where they were coming from, the boxes likely held cash. And lots of it.

Flint knew that one square foot would hold a couple of million dollars in carefully stacked hundred-dollar bills. Which meant Delores Kodinsky had been right all along.

Someone grabbed Flint's jaw and yanked his head around.

Rick sneered down at him. "Sleeping beauty wakes up."

"Master raconteur, aren't you?" Flint jerked his head free.

Rick frowned, obviously missing Flint's sarcasm.

Flint leaned forward, lifting his wrists. "Loosen these zip ties while I can still feel my fingers."

Rick sneered. "Not a chance."

Whyte walked around the truck and gestured to Rick. "Get the rest on board. We've gotta move."

Rick walked off to help Cuba heft boxes from the vault.

Whyte threw Flint's phone into his lap.

Whyte said, "We used your fingerprint to open that burner while you slept. You don't have squat."

"You think I'm stupid enough to have the evidence only on that phone?"

"You were stupid enough to walk into a trap."

Fair point. "I had a legitimate business proposal."

"How is blackmail legitimate business?" Whyte sneered.

"You didn't hear the proposal."

"So tell me."

Flint tilted his head toward his bound wrists to show the ties.

"Absolutely not," Whyte said.

"Can't exactly enter passwords on my phone like this, now, can I?"

Whyte walked away. Eventually he came back with a pair of wire cutters from a toolbox on the side of the truck.

Cuba and Rick loaded more boxes as Whyte cut through the sturdy nylon binding Flint's wrists.

Wiggling his fingers and flexing his hands, Flint gave an exaggerated sigh as if he were still feeling extreme pain. Couldn't hurt if Whyte assumed Flint was unable to fight.

Rick and Cuba loaded four more boxes, restrained them with cords, then secured a tarp across the top of the Silverado's bed.

"Ready," Rick said when they had secured the payload.

Whyte grunted his approval and turned back to Flint. "Show me your evidence."

Flint pushed a few virtual buttons on the burner to bring up a webpage and beckoned Whyte closer to see.

When Whyte leaned down, Flint drove a fist straight up into his chin. Square on. Ramming the jawbone back. Smashing it hard into a bunch of nerves around the ears.

Whyte groaned. His eyes rolled up. He staggered sideways.

Flint braced his feet apart and swung his arm around, smashing his elbow into the side of Whyte's head.

Whyte went down like an imploding building, all knees and hips and shoulders, eventually landing on the concrete.

Flint leaped for the Silverado's cabin, jumping into the cab behind the steering wheel. He started the engine while Rick and Cuba remained in the back, securing the boxes of cash.

Rick must have felt the big engine start up. He ran to exit the rear of the bed, but Cuba leaned over the edge with a hammer in his hand.

Flint grabbed the tool with one hand and Cuba's jacket with the other. Using Cuba's momentum, Flint yanked him over the edge.

Cuba fell. Face first onto the concrete. Flint stepped out onto the running board and drove a kick into his side to make sure he remained down.

Rick leaped out of the truck bed and ran forward brandishing a gun.

Flint hurled the hammer. Rick twisted sideways to avoid the flying projectile, but the hammer hit his free hand.

Flint followed the hammer milliseconds later. He grabbed Rick's head and slammed it into the side of the truck. Once, twice, three times.

Rick's gun went off with an accidental wild shot at the far wall.

Flint twisted Rick's arm around, pried the gun from his grasp, and kicked him away. Rick rolled on the ground, hands holding his bleeding forehead.

Flint jumped into the truck's cab again. The engine was still roaring. He slid the transmission into drive.

CHAPTER 5

FLINT SWIVELED HIS HEAD to scan for exits.

Only one path led out of the room, a square tunnel barely wider than the Silverado.

There must have been a switch somewhere to retract the truck's giant mirrors, but Flint didn't bother to look for it. He gunned the engine and raced into the tunnel.

Both big side mirrors scraped the walls, screeching like a wailing animal. Flint kept his foot on the accelerator.

Fluorescent lights illuminated the way ahead and what appeared to be a solid wall.

He braked hard, stopping inches from the concrete and studied the options until he noticed large hinges protruding from the concrete on the left side. And an electrical control panel nearby on the wall.

He shoved the transmission into reverse, backed up, and stopped beside the panel.

He leaped out and punched the open button in the control box.

After a moment, an exceptionally loud horn blasted out repetitive warnings and the giant door began to move.

Behind him, Flint noticed headlights shining along the tunnel. Whyte or his goons must have recovered enough to start the Explorer. It wasn't moving yet, but it would be soon.

He checked Rick's handgun, which was a Kel Tec semi-automatic. An amazingly light and compact gun with a staggering thirty rounds. Minus one for Rick's unintended shot in front of the vault.

Flint didn't want to start shooting inside what amounted to a concrete bunker. The ricochet would be unpredictable and deadly. Whyte and his crew couldn't be counted on to realize the same.

Flint had to go. Get out in the open and away from flying bullets.

The concrete door had opened as wide as possible. Flint punched the button to close the door again before he climbed up into the Silverado.

He raced through the tunnel toward the exit. The side walls tore off the wing mirrors as the truck sped forward.

Flint stopped inches from the exterior roll up door, leaped from the truck, and stabbed the up button. The exterior door started to rise.

Racing toward the rear of the truck, he kept his head down and fired four rounds into the control box. The roll up door creaked to a halt, only a quarter open. Its controlling mechanism was now destroyed.

Back in the Silverado again, Flint hunched down away from the windows.

He inched forward, getting the truck's hood under the door until the whole vehicle would clear.

Shots sounded behind him. He shoved the truck into reverse and jerked the vehicle backward. Several thousand pounds of moving metal in a confined space would give his attackers something to think about.

With agonizing slowness, the exterior door opened fully. He gassed the Silverado's engine and raced out of the tunnel.

He'd traveled only twenty feet when a second Explorer SUV rammed into the passenger side of the truck, pushing it sideways into a palm tree.

The impact threw Flint across the seat.

Two men, guns drawn, jumped from the second Explorer. He recognized them as the men in suits that he'd outwitted in the casino with the fire alarm.

Flint reversed away. The two men fired wild shots in Flint's direction and hurriedly returned to their vehicle.

Changing gears, Flint floored the accelerator and leaped forward, glancing off the rear of their Explorer and shoving it away.

Several sirens sounded in the distance. No doubt someone had called the police when the disturbance couldn't be ignored.

People dived out of the way as he drove through palms and gardens, hoping to find the main road. He heard more shots. The second Explorer had righted itself and turned to give chase. The man in the passenger seat leaned out of the side window firing randomly.

Flint needed to get away from the populated areas before they hurt someone. He took a sharp right into a parking lot.

The Explorer, following closer now, did the same. It took a direct route to the exit and cut off his escape.

He turned left, bouncing over a grassy mound into the pool area. Towels, upturned sun loungers, and pool toys were abandoned as people fled the area.

The second Explorer followed, keeping to his right and driving him one way around the pool.

Too late, he realized their plan was to force him into a ten-foot-wide channel leading to an indoor pool.

He screeched to a halt and managed two points of a three-point turn to reverse direction, when the Explorer returned, blocking his escape.

The two men jumped out and crouched beside the engine, weapons trained on him.

The police sirens were no longer distant. They sounded twenty feet away.

Whyte appeared from the casino complex with Rick and Cuba close behind. They all had guns.

Whyte staggered to a stop, bright red in the face and struggling to breathe, ten feet from the Silverado's driver's door.

He waved an assault rifle at Flint. "Get out! Now!"

Flint breathed hard. Stepping out would leave him entirely defenseless.

Whyte had to know the police were already here. His options had narrowed. As had his focus.

Whyte had clearly lost control. Abandoned all pretense. He had a tiny window of opportunity to grab the money and get away. The only way he could do that was to commandeer the Silverado.

The pool lay at an oblique angle in front of Flint. At fifty-feet wide, there was no way to cross it, even in something the size of the Silverado.

Whyte fired. His gun rattled off three shots. A controlled burst. The Silverado's side window shattered. Flint rolled away from the glass.

Now or never.

He swept his foot from the brake to the accelerator.

The Silverado lurched forward, tires squealing.

The passenger side wheels fell over the edge of the pool.

Flint kept his foot down hard.

The truck plowed on, leaning over the edge of the pool, the underside grinding on the pool's concrete.

More gunshots rang out. The Silverado lurched. The center of its mass was hanging over the pool now.

There was no stopping it.

The whole vehicle rolled sideways into the water, toppling upside down.

Water flooded in through the broken windows.

Flint used his legs to force open the driver side door against the influx. The roof hit the bottom of the pool.

Flint swam, staying close to the vehicle.

Bullets traced white lines through the water.

He grabbed the side of the truck and forced himself under the upturned bed.

The boxes of money shifted above him, held in place by the cords and tarp.

He curled up, staying under the mass of money. Depending on it to stop the bullets that continued to churn the surrounding water.

How much longer could he wait? His lungs burned without oxygen.

Air bubbled up from the wheel wells. He breathed out and used his hands to funnel the bubbles into his mouth and lungs.

The gunfire shifted position, moving toward the rear of the truck.

He choked on the air and water.

Fighting his reflexes, he calmed his muscles, exhaled completely and inhaled another lungful of wheel-well air.

Feet appeared around the tailgate. Whyte and his goons were still coming.

Flint swam for the toolbox, grabbed a wrench, and turned to see Rick heading toward him.

Rick had swapped his gun for a knife that curved to a wicked looking point.

Flint waited for the right moment and hurled the wrench.

The water stole its momentum, but Rick weaved, suggesting the wrench had made contact.

Flint grabbed more tools, flinging them in a constant stream.

Grabbing an eighteen-inch pipe wrench, Flint pushed off from the rear of the truck's cabin and swung at Rick.

Rick attempted to twist away, but the wrench struck a solid blow to his elbow. He yelped, grimaced, and tried to brace his arm.

Flint pulled the wrench straight back and plunged it forward. Fast. Through the path of least resistance he could find in the water.

The heavy metal wrench struck Rick across the forehead, knocking him backward.

Flint kicked hard to get behind Rick and pounded the wrench into his back.

A cloud of bubbles escaped Rick's mouth. He swam and kicked wildly for the side of the truck and disappeared upward.

Flint's lungs burned like they were on fire.

Air no longer bubbled from the wheel wells.

He waited as long as he could manage but he finally had no choice. He simply had to find a way to breathe.

Peering around the tailgate, through the rippling surface, he saw lines of people staring into the water.

Either Whyte had left, or the police had taken control.

Breaking through the water into the open air, he found police on all sides, weapons ready. He released the Kel Tec and let it sink.

Choking and spluttering, he made his way to the steps and climbed out of the pool, hands raised in submission. He lay face down on the concrete.

Across the pool, Whyte was being cuffed. Rick, too. Cuba and the others were already being led away to a cluster of blue flashing lights.

An officer barked at Flint to put his hands behind his back. Flint complied.

"Call Delores Kodinsky," he said. "The owner of this place."

The officer frowned and nodded to Whyte. "He said he was the owner."

Across the pool, Whyte was dragged away to the cruisers.

"Nope," Flint said, water dripping down his body. "Not anymore."

CHAPTER 6

Kansas City, Missouri

ANTHONY BOLDO EYED THE private golf course nestled amid the rolling hills on the outskirts of Kansas City with a predatory glint in his eyes. His biggest competitor owned this particular club. But Boldo would own it soon enough.

His blunt fingers drummed impatiently on his thigh as he waited his turn to tee off on the sixth hole. The game was a diversion while he waited for the phone call that would set the evening's business in motion.

Boldo barely noticed as his crew of three trusted associates, equally formidable, exchanged friendly conversation interspersed with hearty laughter and laden with menace.

The four were members of the same criminal organization that ruled all relevant activity in Calabria, Italy. The Calabria

Mafia had expanded into most of Europe and extended throughout the US.

In Kansas City, Boldo was the boss.

A ripple of anticipation coursed through the group when Boldo's phone buzzed. With a sharp nod, Boldo silenced the device and lifted it to his ear, his expression unreadable as he listened intently.

"Meet at the site in an hour," Boldo ordered before he disconnected and dropped the phone into his pocket.

"And the package?" one of Boldo's associates inquired. The others exchanged knowing glances.

A grim smile tugged at the corners of Boldo's lips when he replied, "The package will be delivered as promised."

Boldo strode away from the tee, returned his club to his golf bag, and settled into the passenger seat of the cart. His companions followed suit, movements fluid and synchronized, like a well learned habit following years of unwavering loyalty to Boldo's empire.

They drove three luxury armored SUVs to the construction site. Marino was behind the wheel and Boldo occupied the passenger seat in the middle vehicle. The three SUVs traveled at a steady speed, one ahead and one behind Boldo's vehicle.

"Lucky Jones has always been a few bricks short of a load, Boss," Marino said casually across the cabin.

Boldo didn't reply. True, Jones wasn't the sharpest knife in the drawer. But he wasn't an idiot either. Or, at least, he'd never been an idiot before.

"After that business with his ex-wife, I thought Jones was solid," Marino said. "What caused him to go so far off the rails?"

"Only two answers that make sense," Boldo replied. "Bribes and threats."

Each passing mile seemed to stretch on indefinitely until they finally arrived. Marino followed the lead SUV as it turned off the pavement onto a gravel road.

The three heavy SUVs threw up a cloud of dust that settled on the windows and stuck there like a shroud. Marino turned the windshield washers on for a few swipes that did nothing more than muddy the view.

After driving three miles along the dusty road, Boldo saw the sprawling construction site ahead. He scanned the scene, his gaze sweeping over the skeletal framework of the courthouse beyond the survey's location for the parking garage.

Another armored SUV idled nearby. Heavily tinted windows blocked Boldo's view of the SUV's occupants. Which was okay. He already knew who was inside.

"Stop here," Boldo announced abruptly, his voice cutting sharply through the silence.

Marino stopped the SUV instantly in the middle of the road and killed the engine.

"Let's go," Boldo said as he opened the door and stepped onto the rough dirt.

The driver pushed a button and the SUV's hatchback opened slowly. Boldo strode to the vehicle, looked inside to confirm the cargo, and gestured to Marino.

"Get the package the hell out of there," Boldo demanded.

Marino leaned deep into the vehicle, grabbed two squirming legs, and yanked hard enough to slide Lucky Jones along the carpet. Jones began to kick and scream and tried to hold on to stop Marino's momentum.

Which didn't work.

Marino leaned back and continued to pull on his legs until Jones slid out of the vehicle. He plopped onto the hard ground, landing like a two-hundred-pound bag of cement.

"Stop sniveling, Jones. We're not gonna carry you. Get the hell up," Boldo demanded as he stomped forward, leading the way toward the garage site.

Marino yanked Jones to his feet and pushed him forward. He stumbled behind Boldo, twisting his neck, looking around wildly for any possible escape.

Boldo scanned the situation expertly. The stage of construction was exactly as it should have been.

A deep hole had been emptied and prepared for the thick concrete foundation the multi-level parking garage would need. The first layers had been completed perfectly.

Installing another layer would be simple enough.

Boldo's expression hardened. Marino gave Jones another hard shove to close the distance to Boldo's reach.

Boldo seized Jones by the collar and dragged the struggling man toward the deep, gaping maw.

"Let go of me, you son of a—" Jones's words were cut short as Boldo delivered a vicious blow to his jaw.

"You crossed me, Jones. Big mistake." Boldo's icy fury grew as he hoisted Jones closer to the edge of the pit. "You had one job. One simple task. You failed."

Jones, understanding exactly what was happening, struggled and fought and twisted to get away. All to no avail.

With a swift, practiced motion, Boldo grabbed his belt and flung Lucky Jones into the abyss below.

Jones screamed all the way down as his body disappeared into the dark hole.

A sickening thud silenced his screams leaving only the echo of his terror alive in the still evening air.

Boldo's men watched the murder in silence, their faces pale masks of indifference beneath the glare of sunlight. Each man knew he could easily be the one dead and broken at the bottom of that pit or another one like it. Boldo was unforgiving.

"Finish this," Boldo demanded with cold finality. He gestured toward the waiting equipment.

With a deft hand, Marino activated the machinery. The other two slipped into heavy boots and collected tools to guide the concrete's flow.

A thick slurry began to pour rapidly down the chute into the pit.

Boldo stood aside and the others worked quickly. They'd performed this ritual many times before. They were experienced and skilled. Movements were precise, methodical, and effective.

Lucky Jones was soon completely buried.

If he hadn't died when his body hit the concrete slab, he was certainly dead now. No man could breathe under that crushing gray weight.

Minutes stretched on, marked by the rhythmic pour of concrete landing in the pit.

While the work continued and his men were occupied, Boldo returned to the SUV. He approached the driver's side and rapped his knuckles on the window.

When the window buzzed down, the driver said, "Problem solved?"

"Yeah. Thanks for picking him up."

"It was easy. He wasn't suspicious at all."

Boldo stuffed his hands in his pockets and stepped back. "Okay. Well, you'd better get going."

The window buzzed up and the SUV reversed away from the garage, turned, and drove away along the dusty road. Boldo watched until he could no longer see the taillights.

Finally, the work on Lucky Jones's concrete grave was done.

While two of the men cleaned and returned the equipment, Boldo stepped forward and leaned in to survey the results. The concrete was smooth and flat, with no hint that a body was buried beneath.

He rested both hands casually in his pockets and nodded sharply toward Marino with a sense of grim satisfaction.

"Excellent," Boldo declared as he inclined his chin toward the garage floor. "Time for dinner."

CHAPTER 7

SPENCER LYMAN'S ESTATE ON the outskirts of Kansas City looked to be easily the largest and most expensive home in Missouri.

Michael Flint counted eight distinctive roof peaks atop the main building. Seventeen hundred square feet of what appeared to be fieldstone.

But Lyman's residence was all concrete construction. Which befitted the concrete billionaire who had often boasted that concrete was the best and safest building material in the world.

Whether building with concrete was the best way to go or not, supplying it to builders of all kinds had been the Lyman family's big moneymaker for decades. Not a sexy product, to be sure. But concrete was the second largest selling product in the world, after water. Which was, of course, needed to create concrete.

Unlike fashion, concrete never went out of style. Unlike vehicles, demand never declined. Unlike technology, nothing better had ever been discovered or created.

The Lyman empire and its legacy was built on the strongest foundation invented since before the first examples were discovered in 7000 B.C.E.

Flint's clients were often wealthy beyond reason, but Spencer Lyman's reported net worth was mind boggling.

Lyman's driver had collected Flint at the Kansas City airport for the ride to the Lyman Estate. Once on Lyman property, the stretch SUV moved along concrete driveways through elaborate gardens, past several ponds and waterfalls and two exterior swimming pools. All constructed of concrete.

Aerial photos that Flint had studied beforehand displayed the elaborate estate from above, but on the ground, the amenities were even more impressive.

The limo finally rolled along a wide circular drive and stopped at the grand front entrance.

"Mr. Lyman is expecting you," the driver said, making no move to escort Flint up the sweeping stairs to the massive front door. "The door is unlocked. I'll wait here."

Flint stepped out of the limo and onto the smooth, white concrete that could have been poured last week. He hustled up the steps and across the paved patio to pull the twenty-foot arched door open and walked inside.

He had studied the layout of the house, but it took a moment of scanning the spacious open foyer to orient himself and find the corridor that led to Spenser Lyman's office. His cowboy boots pounded the decorative concrete floors toward the east side of the house.

"Lyman must have one helluva view of the sunrise," Flint murmured aloud as he wandered through the winding hallway which was windowed from floor to ceiling on both sides.

When he reached the office, he pushed the heavy wooden door open and stepped into Lyman's dimly lit workspace amid the echo of his bootsteps.

Flint scanned the shadowed room and coughed as he drew in a lungful of thick, acrid air. The unmistakable scent of cigar smoke swirled lazily in the dim light filtering through the floor-to-ceiling windows.

Spencer Lyman lounged behind a huge mahogany desk. His silhouette was barely visible amid the smoky haze. The billionaire's face, weathered and worn, bore the marks of a life lived long and hard.

A handsome woman Flint didn't recognize occupied one of the chairs near the desk. She was dressed like an equestrian's idea of attire appropriate for a weekend in the country. Camel riding pants, crisp white shirt, highly polished riding boots. Flint guessed her age at mid-fifties, give or take.

"Mr. Lyman," Flint's voice cut through the smoky silence as he walked deeper into the cavernous room.

The woman turned her head and gave Flint a level gaze. Her expression wasn't warm and welcoming, but she wasn't openly hostile, either.

Lyman glanced up and squinted toward Flint with a mixture of weariness and determination.

"You must be Michael Flint," his voice gravelly with years of abuse to his vocal cords.

Flint nodded. Something about Lyman's demeanor suggested a lifetime of secrets, of battles fought and lost in the shadows.

Lyman gestured toward the woman. "This is Emily Royce, Lyman Enterprises CFO."

"Delores Kodinsky recommended me," Flint said by way of reminder as he shook hands with Ms. Royce and took the empty seat next to her, opposite Lyman.

Royce seemed both unimpressed and uninterested.

"Doro speaks highly of you," Lyman's lips twitched in a grim smile. "We travel in the same circles."

Flint raised an eyebrow, intrigued. "And what circles would those be?"

Lyman leaned back in the leather chair that creaked softly in protest. "Circles where secrets are currency and trust is a prized commodity."

Flint had dealt with enough billionaires to know that the super-rich really *are* different. Their worlds were often filled with intrigue and danger. Betrayal was common. And loyalty, to the extent it existed at all, was easily bought, sold, and destroyed.

Breaking the uneasy silence that had settled over the room, Flint said, "Mrs. Kodinsky didn't give me any details, which means I'm not sure I can help you. But I'm curious.

You have unlimited resources. You can hire anyone you want. What brings you to me, specifically?"

"Everyone else I've tried has struck out." Lyman shrugged and his expression grew more serious, aging him another ten years in an instant. In his low, raspy voice, he said, "It's my grandson. Ward Lyman. He's been missing for two years."

Flint's interest was snagged. He was the best heir hunter in the business. He could find anyone, anywhere, any time. Dead or alive.

His success rate was one hundred percent. So much so that most of his work came from other investigators who had already tried and failed.

Flint's expertise allowed him to charge exorbitant fees and his successes made clients happy to pay his prices.

All of which meant that he had to pull off a miracle every now and then to keep his legendary reputation intact. Would Ward Lyman's case require a miracle?

"Tell me more," he said, leaning back.

Lyman nodded, a haunted look in his eyes. "Officially, my grandson is presumed dead. But I don't believe that. Never did."

Flint leaned forward. Lyman was nobody's fool. He'd inherited wealth beyond measure, but he'd also doubled his family's fortune more than once.

Some said he'd supplied concrete to the mob for decades, in Kansas City and elsewhere. Flint hadn't confirmed the rumors, but he had no reason to doubt them.

If Spenser Lyman believed his grandson was still alive, his reasons were worth Flint's time. Especially since Lyman would pay handsomely for success.

Lyman hesitated as if, now that he was presented with the need to disclose his secrets, he was unsure whether to trust Flint with the truth.

Emily Royce seemed to take the hint. She stood and straightened her cardigan. "If you'll both excuse me, I have some work to do before dinner."

Without waiting for a response, she turned and strode across the room, letting herself out and closing the heavy door behind her.

After a moment, Lyman reached into his desk drawer and pulled out a bulky brown accordion file with an elastic band holding its contents inside.

Lyman placed the file on the desk between them and tapped it with his index finger. "I've hired others to find out what happened to Ward. They've gathered some useful information."

Flint reached for the file and opened it.

Inside were documents, photographs, and newspaper clippings meticulously arranged. Each item contained fragments of the mystery surrounding Ward Lyman's disappearance. Two small flash drives rested at the bottom of the folder.

"This is just the most relevant of the information we've gathered. But we're no closer to finding my grandson," Lyman said, his voice heavy.

Flint sifted through the contents quickly. Photographs of Ward, smiling and carefree, had been captured in moments during the few months before his disappearance. The rest would require closer examination later.

"And what do you think happened to your grandson?" Flint asked after he'd flipped through the pages.

Lyman gazed through the big windows to the flower garden across the koi pond, lost in memories of the past. Flint waited for his response, which was a long time coming.

"Ward was more than a little wild. A thrill seeker, some said. It wasn't his fault. Lymans have always been reckless," Lyman finally said. "More than a few have died in foolish pursuit of what they wanted."

Flint shook his head. If ever a kid had a lot to live for, Ward Lyman was that kid. The whole world was his oyster. Why give all that up for momentary thrills that might actually kill him?

Lyman pursed his lips and said nothing for a few moments. Then he seemed to make a decision. "You probably need to know this. It might make a difference."

"Know what?"

Lyman cleared his throat. "Some say that Lymans are cursed."

"Cursed?" Flint raised his eyebrows.

"You know, like the Kennedy curse? Too many people connected to the Kennedys have died over the years. Some family, some not. People like to talk. To make things up. It's ridiculous. There's no such thing as a curse," Lyman said firmly.

"But Ward believed in this curse?" Flint guessed, finally seeing where this line of discussion was headed.

"Absolutely believed it. Wouldn't even entertain rational explanations," Lyman nodded. "Lyman heirs, he said, are cursed to die before they're thirty years old. Ward's father died at twenty-seven. His uncle and two cousins also died before they were thirty."

Flint cocked his head. "So Ward thought he might as well grab as much exciting life experience as possible before he turned thirty because he was destined to die anyway? That's crazy."

"This time, Ward was on a diving expedition." Lyman shrugged. "A team exploring a sunken Spanish galleon rumored to be filled with treasure."

"A treasure hunt?" Flint mused aloud. Lots of young men would love to hunt treasure, but most didn't have the resources Ward Lyman had available at his fingertips.

"Yes, it sounds foolish. And maybe it was." Lyman nodded grimly. "But Ward was excited about it. He loved an exciting adventure. He loved diving. We've got a diving pool on the property here, even. This wasn't the first time Ward had been diving for treasure."

"Okay. So what happened this time?" Flint asked.

"The expedition ended in tragedy," Lyman said. "The submersible he was on imploded beneath the surface before they reached the sunken ship, killing all passengers onboard."

Flint frowned and narrowed his eyes. "But if everyone was killed, why do you believe Ward survived?"

Lyman hesitated, probably wrestling with his own doubts and fears. "I've had...visions," he admitted finally.

"Visions?" Flint said, keeping a lid on his skepticism.

Billionaires were odd, but usually not crazy. Still, supernatural visions were a bridge too far for Flint. He lived in the moment, the here and now, and always had. He didn't believe in the supernatural or any other kind of visions.

And Lyman was ancient. He'd lived almost a century. Could the old man have dementia?

Lyman took another draw on the cigar and nodded decisively. He would brook no objections. "Visions of Ward alive and in dangerous situations. Worrisome visions. But hopeful, too."

Flint pushed his skepticism aside to focus on the facts. "And you believe these visions are real?"

Lyman nodded solemnly. "I believe they're a sign, maybe only from my subconscious, that Ward is still out there waiting to be found."

Flint studied Lyman's face, searching for any hint of deception or dementia. What he saw was raw emotion etched in every hard-won line and crease of the old man's papery skin.

Whatever doubts Flint had about this story, he could see that Lyman was sincere and serious as a heart attack.

Which meant there was, at least, something odd going on.

Still, Ward Lyman was probably dead.

But what if he wasn't?

For a moment, Flint considered rejecting the work. Billionaires were a special breed and working for them was never easy.

But old man Lyman would hire another investigator to find Ward if Flint turned down the very lucrative job. Another investigator wouldn't conduct the search as well as Flint.

The least he could do was give the old man some closure so he could move on with what was left of his life.

"Alright, Mr. Lyman," Flint said with firm resolve. "I'll find out what happened to Ward."

"Thank you, Mr. Flint," Lyman's voice was choked with gratitude. "Find my grandson and bring him home to me. The full extent of my fortune is at your disposal. Any resources you need. And you'll be very well paid for your trouble."

"I'll do everything in my power." Flint cleared his throat. "But I can't promise I'll find Ward alive."

"I understand," Lyman replied. "I just need to know. One way or the other."

Flint nodded and rose to leave. He shook hands with Lyman and tucked the folder under his arm.

"One more thing," Lyman said before Flint reached the door. "We don't have a lot of time. We're fighting off a hostile takeover of Lyman Enterprises. The buyer thinks I'm old and weak and the shareholders would be better off with a younger man at the helm."

Flint nodded again. The shareholders might actually agree on that point. "I'll do my best. How much time have we got?"

"One week. No more," Lyman replied.

CHAPTER 8

Houston, Texas

SCARLETT SAT IN THE bleachers, her attention divided between her daughter's soccer game unfolding before her and the wriggling bundle of fur in her arms.

The schnauzer puppy was a delightful little terror named Whiskers. Maddy's seventh birthday present from Flint a few weeks ago. Of course, he hadn't asked permission to burden Scarlett's life with a puppy.

She'd reacted with outrage, but Flint had simply shrugged on his way out the door. "Maddy wanted Whiskers. You know I can't refuse her anything."

"Typical," Scarlett murmured then and now, shaking her head. She lifted the puppy to gaze into his eyes and grinned. "You're way too cute, you know that?"

Holding the squirming puppy warmed Scarlett's heart. Maddy's obvious joy on the soccer field, accompanied by cheering parents and the rhythmic thud of soccer balls meeting cleats, melted her heart completely.

Yes, she admitted privately, her life was pretty damned great these days.

Her thoughts occasionally drifted to the stack of paperwork waiting for her back at the office. But for now, she simply relished the pleasure of being present for Maddy while Whiskers snoozed in her lap.

Until a stranger approached and shattered the mood. "Excuse me, are you Kathryn Scarlett?"

Scarlett glanced at the young woman standing on the bleachers. A buzz haircut emphasized her sharp features and determined eyes. She looked about fifteen, but she was probably in her early twenties.

"How can I help you?" Scarlett replied flatly, offering zero encouragement while deliberately returning her gaze to the field.

"I'm Naomi Wagner. You've probably heard of *The Truth*, my true crime podcast," she said with absolutely no modesty, false or otherwise.

Scarlett gave her head a quick shake. "Sorry, no. I don't have time for podcasts."

Wagner wasn't deterred. "Look us up. We've been on the air for five years. We've won awards. Millions of followers."

"Sorry. Still don't know who you are," Scarlett said rudely from behind oversized sunglasses.

Wagner didn't take the hint.

"I'd like to hire you to help me with a case," she said. "I'm told you're one of the best investigators in Texas. The case is interesting, so you won't be bored. Your fees are substantial, which I can handle."

Scarlett shrugged. Wagner had done her due diligence, at least.

True crime podcasts were a fad, but Scarlett couldn't deny their popularity. If Wagner thought the case had potential, she was probably the kind of person who wouldn't give up. Scarlett could devote a bit of time to hear about the situation now instead of fending Wagner off for a few weeks.

She gestured Wagner to take a seat beside her, making sure to keep a firm hold on Whiskers, who wanted to lick the woman to death.

"I'm listening," Scarlett said, as if her curiosity was now fully engaged.

Wagner settled onto the bleachers, gave Whiskers a quick ear scratch, and got right to the point. Her first words caused the little hairs on the back of Scarlett's neck to stand at full attention.

"The case is old and cold, but my gut tells me there's more here than we know," Wagner said, settling into her story. "I've been investigating a wrongful conviction. James Arthur Preston was recently executed for the murder of June Pentwater."

Scarlett felt her nerves buzz with tension. She knew the case. Preston's conviction in the Pentwater murder had filled newscasts for several decades.

Every appeal his legal team had pursued ended in failure and had been covered extensively in real time. Still, Preston had maintained his innocence in the Pentwater murder all the way to his grave.

"The more we examine the facts, it's looking like Preston could have been guilty in another murder case. The MO was similar, but not exactly the same."

Absolutely every single grain of sand in the Preston case had been examined at one time or another. No one living in Texas during the past thirty years could have been unaware of Preston.

Wagner probably didn't live in Texas. Nor did she seem to notice Scarlett's cold reactions. Instead, she pressed on. "The second victim's name was Marilyn Baker."

Scarlett's brow furrowed and she clamped her teeth shut to conceal her involuntary gasp. Wagner's mere mention of Marilyn Baker's name sent a chill down her spine.

"You think Preston was guilty of a second murder?" Scarlett asked when she could get the words out.

Wagner nodded, her expression grave. "But here's the thing. Preston was never charged in connection with Marilyn Baker's death. There just wasn't enough evidence to connect him to the crime. And now, with Preston dead, it seems like nobody's interested any more. The Baker case may never be solved if we don't do it."

Scarlett felt a surge of unease, for reasons she would not share with Wagner. At least, not until she had a chance to discuss the situation with Flint.

"This is where you come in," Wagner continued, eyes burning with intensity and the kind of urgency only impossibly young people can muster. "I want to hire Scarlett Investigations to help me prove that Preston didn't kill either woman. Not June Pentwater. Not Marilyn Baker."

"After examining the existing evidence, several juries and several judges over the years decided otherwise," Scarlett replied. "The Pentwater case was closed and Preston was executed. The case is closed."

"They were all wrong. Someone else killed both women." Wagner was convinced as well as convincing. Which made the situation worse. She might be too enthusiastic, but she was not an idiot.

"Hard to prove, after all this time," Scarlett said. "Both murders were committed decades ago. Witnesses will have died. Evidence destroyed."

"The killer could be dead or in prison, I guess. But James Preston wasn't the killer," Wagner declared as if only she knew the truth. "An innocent man was executed by the State of Texas, and I intend to prove that, regardless. I also believe there's still a chance to uncover the real killer, but I can't do that piece alone. I need you."

Scarlett cocked her head as if she were considering Wagner's proposal carefully. She could easily turn down the work. She had plenty of cases in her office already.

But what concerned her was Wagner's dogged insistence. She wasn't the type to give up. Determination, perhaps, or a belief in the power of seeking justice, no matter how elusive it might seem.

Whatever motivated her, Wagner was like a dog with a bone.

If Scarlett turned her down, Wagner would keep looking until she found another investigator. One who might not be as concerned about Flint.

The podcast would happen, whether Scarlett and Flint were happy about it or not.

Which meant Scarlett needed to keep Wagner under control. And the best way to do that was to be on the inside with her and her team.

Scarlett nodded, her decision made. "Why do you believe that Preston didn't kill Pentwater or Baker? What specific *new* evidence do you have to back that opinion up?"

Wagner leaned in closer as if the soccer moms in the bleachers were listening and lowered her voice to a conspiratorial whisper.

"It all started with June Pentwater's case," Wagner said, excited and alight with conviction. "I've been digging into the evidence, and the more I uncover, the more convinced I become that James Preston was the patsy here. He took the fall, but he didn't do the crime."

Scarlett listened intently, stroking Whiskers and watching Maddy on the field.

"There were inconsistencies in the witness statements. Discrepancies in the forensic evidence. Other things that just didn't add up."

"Did you discuss those issues with Preston's defense team?" Scarlett asked.

"I tried. Preston had several lawyers over the years. I couldn't find them all. Some were appointed by the court, and they've moved on. A couple of his lawyers actually died," Wagner said, then looked down briefly. "The ones who are still around have refused to speak to me. I can be a bit, uh, enthusiastic for some people."

Scarlett smirked. *I'll bet*, she thought, but said nothing.

"And then I stumbled upon something that really caught my attention." Wagner reached into her bag and pulled out a bulky file, handing it to Scarlett.

"What's this?" Scarlett asked, accepting the file but not opening it.

"Police reports, witness interviews, forensic analyses," Wagner replied. "Look at the witness statements carefully. There are multiple accounts that contradict each other, inconsistencies in the timelines, and even reports of police coercion."

Scarlett's eyes scanned the soccer field looking for Maddy. Whiskers had been squirming for five minutes. He needed to pee.

"I have to take a break," Scarlett said, hoisting Whiskers into the air by way of explanation. "And the game is almost over. I don't want to discuss any of this in front of my daughter. It's not an appropriate topic for a seven-year-old."

"And then there's this," Wagner said as if Scarlett's objections had gone unspoken. She pointed to a section of one report. "The forensic evidence doesn't match. New DNA techniques have become available since Preston died.

The DNA samples recovered from the Pentwater and Baker crime scenes don't belong to Preston. And I think there's a connection between the Pentwater and Baker crimes that was not presented at any of the trials or hearings."

Scarlett's breath caught in her throat as she considered the implications.

If the Pentwater DNA evidence didn't match Preston, then who did it match?

And what did that mean for solving Marilyn Baker's murder?

Wagner continued like a child describing her first trip to Disney. "I've been doing some digging into Marilyn Baker's murder as well, and I believe there's a connection between the two crimes."

Scarlett frowned and said, "Again, Pentwater had competent lawyers. They defended his conviction for decades and ultimately lost every appeal. Unless you've got something *new*, none of this will matter."

"True," she said, not the least concerned.

"So do you? Have new evidence to support your theories?" Scarlett asked as the other parents cheered.

She looked up to see Maddy's team had scored. She applauded and whistled her support.

When the moment calmed, Wagner replied, "Yes. I do have new evidence."

Scarlett felt a surge of apprehension. If there was truly new evidence that could potentially exonerate Preston and solve Marilyn Baker's murder, she needed to hear more.

Because she couldn't allow Flint to be blindsided by all of this. They had only recently confirmed that Marilyn Baker was Flint's biological mother.

Scarlett wasn't sure what Flint's feelings were about that fact. But she was sure he wouldn't want to be the subject of anybody's podcast. He wouldn't want his mother's life and death to be exploited, either.

Beyond that, at some point, Flint would want to know what really happened to Marilyn Baker. He deserved to know first. Long before Wagner broadcast whatever dirty laundry existed to the world.

"Alright. You say you've got compelling new evidence," Scarlett said, her voice tinged with determination. "Let's hear it."

"Like I said, I've been combing through old case files, police reports, and witness testimonies," Wagner explained. "And I dug up something that was unavailable to Preston's defense team."

"What is it and where did you find it?" Scarlett was skeptical by nature, but Wagner's claim made no sense.

Preston's lawyers and the prosecution teams would have combed through absolutely everything multiple times over the years. There was very little chance that Naomi had actually found new evidence.

Scarlett wanted to chop the head off this podcast thing and kill it right now.

Wagner reached into her bag and pulled out a stained and mangled envelope that looked like it had been run over by a freight train and left to dry in the rain. She handed it to Scarlett.

"It's a letter," Wagner explained. "Written by a witness who saw something the night June Pentwater was murdered. Something never brought up in court."

Scarlett unfolded the letter and scanned the handwritten page. The witness claimed Preston was seen in a completely different location at the time of the Pentwater murder.

"What makes you think this is actually authentic or even true?" Scarlett asked, reading through the crumpled notes again.

Wagner said, "Because I've also uncovered inconsistencies in the alibi of a second suspect who had motive and opportunity to commit the crime."

"You're saying the original investigation didn't clear that second suspect?" Scarlett asked, skepticism plain.

"They say they did," Wagner replied, her tone suggesting otherwise. "I haven't followed up yet because I think we've got better evidence to chase down first."

"Who is this witness?" Scarlett said, waving the paper.

"His name is Dean Taylor," Wagner replied. "He contacted me after Preston was executed. He claimed to have served as a priest with Preston back then. Taylor said Preston gave him a key to a storage unit and told him to open it only after his death."

"What did Taylor find?" Scarlett asked, as if she were buying into the whole preposterous story.

"When he opened the storage unit after Preston's execution, he found something that could mean Preston couldn't possibly have killed Pentwater or Baker."

"What was it?" Scarlett pressed, annoyed now with Wagner's breathless delivery.

She lowered her voice to a near whisper. "Preston's calendar, detailing his movements and whereabouts on the nights of both murders. And the entries contradict the timeline presented at Preston's trials."

"You mean the Pentwater trials?"

"Of course. He was never charged with Baker's murder. Insufficient evidence, they said." Wagner nodded vigorously, the way a child might. "But they believed he killed Baker, too. One hundred percent."

Scarlett processed the implications. If Preston's calendar could prove his innocence in both cases, it would be a monumental breakthrough. But then, why didn't he offer it to prove his innocence long ago?

The soccer game was over. Maddy was already running toward the bleachers.

"My daughter is coming. I can't discuss this anymore right now," Scarlett said flatly. "I need to review this file and I need to see that calendar."

"I hoped you'd say that," Wagner nodded in agreement. "I've already arranged a meeting with Dean Taylor."

Scarlett gave her a final sharp nod and left her sitting there as she made her way to Maddy, who was bouncing with excitement. "Mom! We won!"

"I saw. How great is that?" Scarlett said with a smile as she handed Whiskers to Maddy.

She made a mental note to contact Jess Kimball—a private detective she had worked a couple of cases with—to get an insider's opinion of Naomi Wagner. Before becoming a PI, Jess had been a high-profile reporter for *Taboo Magazine* for years. She'd know Wagner. And she'd know whether Wagner could be trusted.

CHAPTER 3

FLINT SETTLED INTO HIS home office in Houston, the file of information from Spencer Lyman's estate sitting on his desk. He'd called Drake, but the call went to voicemail. He left a message.

Drake might be out with a date. He had a much more active love life than Flint did. But he'd show up when he got the message.

While he waited, Flint began to sift through the contents of Lyman's file, scanning each document and photograph briefly as he organized them into three loose categories.

The treasure hunt.

The Lyman Curse.

Everything else.

Once the piles were sorted, he began with the treasure hunt because the so-called Lyman Curse had to be pure fiction. Flint liked a supernatural story as well as anyone, but he drew the line at encouraging clients to spend money chasing a fantasy.

Treasure hunts, on the other hand, were both rooted in the real world and often deadly. Unlike the Lyman Curse, Flint had no trouble believing Ward Lyman died while risking his life on foolish pursuits like Spanish gold buried in the seabed.

Flint sifted through the treasure hunt papers until he found two detailed reports. One was authored by a private company hired by Lyman. The other was the official report of the incident from the US Coast Guard.

The Coast Guard report was classified. It might have been shared with Spencer Lyman for humanitarian reasons. More likely the old man demanded access all the way up to the president.

In Flint's experience, men like Spencer Lyman behaved badly when thwarted. Which meant it was easier to placate them than survive the aftermath of their tantrums. No doubt the Coast Guard brass had felt the same way.

When he took on a new case, Flint liked to begin at the beginning. But this time he skipped directly to the catastrophic implosion that had claimed the lives of Ward Lyman and five other passengers.

The craft lost its physical integrity and folded in on itself, crushing everything inside the hull.

No way could anyone have survived that catastrophe.

Which was why Ward Lyman was declared dead at the time. Even if his grandfather refused to accept the verdict.

Flint refilled his coffee and carried the two reports to a more comfortable chair to study more carefully.

Two hours later, he'd confirmed that the two hundred pages of reports were almost duplicates. The gist of both the private report and the official one, including the final conclusions, was the same.

The miracle was that the craft lasted almost four hours below the surface before it was destroyed. Simply put, the submersible turned out to be unfit for the scope of the mission.

On top of that, the warning systems were either non-existent or failed. Which was a blessing in one way. The passengers never saw it coming.

The implosion occurred when the craft entered deeper waters and all passengers perished. Simulations suggested that the implosion was lightning fast. The victims would have experienced no terrifying warnings and absolutely no pain. Which was a blessing, too.

Spencer Lyman didn't take solace from his grandson's quick death, and Flint could understand that.

Flint flipped through the reports to see photos of the submersible. *Galeane II* was named after a minor Greek goddess said to personify calm seas. At this point, the name was overly optimistic.

The *Galeane II* was not the first submersible to run into serious trouble nor the most famous, the reports said.

Unlike the ill-fated *Titan* that had imploded and killed all passengers aboard on an excursion to view the shipwrecked

Titanic, the *Galeane II* should have been more than capable of completing Ward Lyman's adventure.

Or so the reports claimed.

Both reports described the *Galeane II* as a sleek, state-of-the-art vessel, equipped with advanced technology and reinforced to withstand the pressures of deep-sea diving.

Unlike the *Titan's* Atlantic Ocean dive to great depths, the Gulf of Mexico was relatively shallow. But the Gulf was certainly deep enough to be dangerous. Too many souls had been lost to drowning over the years to deny the danger.

Beyond that, had there been no danger in the Gulf, the shipwreck Ward Lyman's crew sought to find wouldn't have been there to explore in the first place.

Flint knew his way around boats. He'd been a Marine, which was a part of the US Navy. He knew enough to make his own judgments.

He studied the diagrams and blueprints, visualizing the structure of the *Galeane II* and the layout of the submersible's interior compartments. The *Galeane II* was, in a word, impressive as hell.

Ward Lyman might have been a wild child, but he was no fool.

As Spencer Lyman had said, the submersible was on a mission to explore the wreckage of a sunken Spanish galleon believed to be carrying valuable treasure. The expedition had been organized by a wealthy investor seeking to recover the lost riches.

Ward Lyman was recruited to assist in the endeavor because of his experience in similar, but less risky treasure hunts.

Eyewitnesses watching the disaster unfold were interviewed and their statements were included in both reports.

According to those accounts, the submersible had been descending slowly and carefully toward the galleon when a sudden noise rocked the vessel, sending shockwaves rippling through the water.

The cause of the implosion remained unknown. Theories were thick on the ground, ranging from a malfunction in the submersible's equipment to sabotage by unknown assailants.

Flint pored over the technical specifications of the vessel, looking for any signs of structural weakness or design flaws that might have contributed to the disaster.

A sense of unease, a nagging feeling that something didn't quite add up, settled in his gut. The official explanation seemed too neat, too tidy. Flint had investigated his share of disasters. The search for truth was never so straightforward as these documents reported.

Flint stood and stretched the kinks out of his body. He took the coffee mug to the kitchen sink and grabbed a tumbler for whiskey. When he glanced at the clock, he saw he'd been staring at the documents much longer than he'd realized.

"Where the hell are you, Drake?" he murmured. He grabbed his cell phone on the way to the liquor and dialed.

After a dozen rings, the call went to voicemail again. He restated his question to the machine, followed by, "We've got a job to do, man. Call me."

Flint frowned as he poured the whiskey and took a warming sip. When Drake didn't call back immediately, he shrugged and dialed Carlos Gaspar's number.

"I've got a knotty problem I need help with. Any chance you've got some available time?"

"Where's Drake? Isn't he your go-to guy?" Gaspar asked reasonably.

"Must have a hot date or something," Flint replied.

"You know I have a wife and five kids, not to mention a job, right? I gather this request isn't coming through Scarlett Investigations," Gaspar said with a smile in his tone. "Meaning Scarlett doesn't know, and you don't want her to know."

"One of the things I like about you is your quick grasp of the obvious," Flint smirked.

"Years of practice, my friend," Gaspar replied good naturedly.

Flint liked Gaspar. He was good at his job and easy to work with. He was also reliable, which was a rare trait in Flint's world.

"I've got a missing person. Ward Lyman."

"The billionaire's grandkid? Who says he's missing? It was all over the news here in Florida when he died a couple years back," Gaspar said. Flint could hear keys clacking on a keyboard as Gaspar searched for the stories. "Lyman

Concrete Enterprises? As in the guy's richer than the King of England?"

"The very same. Except the grandfather thinks the young man is still alive," Flint said.

"And you agree?" Gaspar's tone conveyed preoccupied surprise as he skimmed the preliminary research he'd already discovered.

"Hey, if this job was easy, anybody could do it. They wouldn't need high-priced talent like us," Flint replied with a grin.

"That treasure hunt was a crazy story," Gaspar said as he continued to pound the keys. "Ever since Mel Fisher found those two old Spanish galleons in the Gulf back in the 1970s, people have come out of the woodwork thinking they're gonna do the same. It's nutty."

But the treasure hunt wasn't the only nutty thing about Lyman's disappearance.

"Yeah." Flint agreed. "I'm looking into that, too. Ward Lyman's treasure hunt was in that same area. Between Havana and Key West."

"I was living and working in Miami then. It was big news in Florida," Gaspar said. "I saw the photos when the Lyman kid died. That submersible was destroyed. No way anybody survived that disaster."

"Maybe not. But I promised to find the kid or find his body. So can you look into the submersible implosion for me?" Flint asked.

"Sure. Happy to help. What are you looking for, exactly?"

"You've got access to intel most detectives don't have. I want every detail, every shred of evidence, no matter how small," Flint said. "The grandfather's old and frail and all he wants is to know what happened to the kid."

"And he'll pay you a king's ransom to find out," Gaspar smirked.

"Yeah, well, that, too." Flint swiped a palm over his face to wipe away fatigue. His entire body felt stiff.

"One other thing," Flint said. "The Lyman Enterprises CFO is a woman named Emily Royce. See what you can find out about her, okay?"

"Lyman Enterprises employs thousands of people," Gaspar replied. "Why do you care about her?"

"She was with Spencer Lyman when I arrived, but he seemed reluctant to talk about Ward while she was in the room. It was odd."

Flint figured the old man didn't want to reveal that he'd been having visions to anybody. Bean counters responsible for the kind of money Lyman's CFO handled weren't relaxed about such things by nature. Could make shareholders antsy about his mental state. Could put a target on his back from rivals and enemies, too.

Gaspar's voice became serious and focused. "I'll start now. We might get lucky. You never know. Stay tuned."

Flint glanced at the clock after Gaspar rang off. "I'll give you another half hour, Drake."

He refilled his whiskey and returned his attention to the documents.

CHAPTER 10

FLINT'S BROW FURROWED AS he delved deeper into the history of the Lyman family. He was so focused on the story that he barely heard the back door open and close.

Before he had the chance to reach for his weapon, Drake called out from the kitchen.

"Flint! Don't shoot me, man," he said, only half-joking because he knew Flint's reflexes as well as he knew his own.

Flint heard Drake open the cabinet door and swipe a glass. His boots came down in a loud tattoo on the kitchen tile and then softer on the hardwood as he walked through to the den.

"Make yourself at home," Flint said sardonically, replacing the gun beside him as Drake filled his glass with the good whiskey.

"Sorry I'm late," Drake replied after a quick slug of brown booze.

"I hope she was worth it," Flint deadpanned.

"Jealous? You could make time to have some fun, you know. Wouldn't kill you." He tossed his Stetson onto the couch and plopped down across from Flint. "What's up? Something interesting and preferably out of town? If I have to watch Maddy's puppy another week, I'll go crazy."

"Sorry," Flint smiled, unable to contain the twinkle in his eyes.

Katie Scarlett was the closest thing Flint had to a sister. Scarlett's annoyance at his gift to Maddy was more than half the fun for Flint.

But Drake was catching the fallout.

Every time Whiskers needed a sitter, Drake got the call. Which was his own damned fault. Drake made the mistake of telling Scarlett how much he enjoyed having Whiskers around.

"Yeah, you'll be sorry after I drink all your whiskey," Drake growled in response. But his objections were good-natured.

Maddy had every adult in her life wrapped around her little finger and she knew it. The miraculous thing was that the knowledge didn't make her insufferable.

"So, again, what's up?" Drake said after he'd drained and refilled his glass and put his feet on the coffee table.

"How do you feel about curses?"

Drake's frown was puzzled. "Curses? You mean like a pissed off witch stuffing a genie into a bottle for a thousand years and stuff like that?"

Flint smirked. "Not exactly. More like a lot of members of your family have died so you're convinced the whole family must be cursed."

"I guess I'd say that's more than a little crazy," Drake replied after another swig of the good stuff.

"Right. But we've got a new case. We're treating it like a missing person. The client says the missing grandson believed the family was cursed and that's why he went missing," Flint said.

"Sounds like the kid's a few bricks short of a full load."

"The client is Spencer Lyman."

Drake's eyes widened. "The concrete king?"

"The very same." Flint gestured toward the paperwork spread out around his chair. "According to these documents, four heirs of the Lyman family met untimely deaths before the age of thirty. The grandson didn't want to become number five."

"Seems a bit unlucky," Drake admitted with an easy nod. "But then, there have always been rumors that Spencer Lyman was involved with organized crime."

"Behind every great fortune, there's a crime, as Honoré de Balzac famously said," Flint replied.

"Or a few decades of crimes," Drake grinned. "Short lifespans are common in those circles."

"Yeah. But each one of these deaths is shrouded in mystery and speculation."

"Such as?"

Flint said, "Spencer Lyman's son, Jonathan, perished in a boating accident at the age of twenty-seven. His body was recovered from the depths of the ocean."

"Okay. That sort of thing happens." Drake rolled the glass between his palms.

"Spencer's daughter, Rebecca, succumbed to illness at twenty-eight. Attributed to sudden cardiac death of unknown etiology," Flint said, reading from his notes. "*Unknown*, despite exhaustive medical examinations before she died and an extensive autopsy afterward."

Drake cocked his head and shrugged. "Western medicine doesn't have all the answers."

"Alexander Lyman met a grisly end in a car crash at twenty-five. He was Spencer's younger brother," Flint said. "His sports car careened off a cliff and plunged into a deep abyss in the Alps."

Drake shook his head and said nothing.

"Alexander's daughter, Charlotte Lyman, was found dead in her home at twenty-nine. The circumstances surrounding her death have been kept secret, which aroused a lot of speculation," Flint said. "Could have been a drug overdose or suicide, maybe."

"It's not that rare to die at home. Until recently, most people died at home. Maybe they still do," Drake replied. "If she died unattended, there should be autopsy files, at the very least."

"Should be. But if autopsy files do exist, they weren't provided to me with this pile of documents," Flint explained.

"We can ask the client. Or get Gaspar on it," Drake suggested.

"Gaspar's already searching," Flint reported after another sip of the whiskey. "Finally, our subject is Ward Lyman. He vanished without a trace at the age of twenty-three, two years ago. He was on a submersible in the Gulf of Mexico. The whole crew died. Including Ward Lyman, according to official accounts. Which brings the Lyman family body count to five."

Drake nodded. "Yeah, I remember when that submersible implosion happened. Freaky thing. Mechanical failure, wasn't it?"

"Possibly. But what the grandfather is holding on to is that the body wasn't there."

"Where?"

"With the others. In the depths of the Gulf of Mexico apparently sealed inside the wreckage of that doomed submersible."

"So you're saying Ward Lyman's body hasn't been recovered? You know that's not unusual with victims who die underwater or even in regular drowning accidents," Drake replied slowly, as if he'd exhausted his supply of easy answers.

Silence settled in for a few minutes while Drake refilled the glasses and returned to the couch.

"Well, there's rational explanations for the first four victims," Drake said, breaking the silence. "I mean, people die every day. Some under much more unusual circumstances than car wrecks and suicides and boating accidents."

"True. But that's a lot of wealthy heirs eliminated from inheriting one of the world's largest private fortunes. Which is suspicious, at the very least." Flint continued to contemplate the implications.

"What does old man Lyman say about this curse business?" Drake asked after a moment of silence.

"He said Ward's belief in the curse was unwavering. Ward was absolutely convinced he would die before the age of thirty."

"So he set out to prove his own fears?" Drake suggested. "Back when he died, I seem to remember a lot of stories about the crazy risks that kid had already survived."

"He put himself in harm's way, for sure," Flint replied. "I guess it's possible he simply ran out of luck."

"Come on. Ward Lyman died before the age of thirty, yes," Drake shook his head slowly. "But you don't honestly think there's some sort of supernatural curse at play here, do you?"

"No, I don't," Flint replied. "But I think it's possible there's a killer out there targeting the Lyman family and freaking them out for some specific reason."

"Makes way more sense to me." Drake drained his glass and set it down hard for emphasis. "But have we been hired to find that killer?"

"No. We don't have the resources for that. All five cases have been investigated sixty ways to Sunday. Although Lyman's authorized an unlimited budget for us," Flint replied. "We've been hired to find Ward Lyman."

"You know how I do love money," Drake nodded with a grin. "But that might not be easy, either. Hire a psychic to contact him in the great beyond?"

"Very funny. If this job were easy, anyone could do it. Lyman wouldn't need high-priced talent like us," Flint deadpanned. "Pack a bag. Gas up the Pilatus. It'll give us the flexibility we need. We'll leave in the morning."

"Flexibility for what? Where are we going?"

The Pilatus claimed to be the world's best super-versatile jet. It was designed to operate from short paved or unpaved surfaces, short runways, and remote fields. Flexibility was the very nature of the plane.

"You know how these things go. One thing leads to another. Field conditions change," Flint said. "We'll start in Key West. It was the jumping off point for the submersible. I want to see the area myself. Maybe find a few witnesses."

"While you're doing all of that, I'll hang out on the beach and meet women," Drake said with a grin and a wave on his way out.

CHAPTER 11

SCARLETT HAD TALKED WITH Jess Kimball. She'd said Naomi Wagner was a piece of work, for sure. But she was damned good at true crime podcasting, a growing market segment. Which wasn't necessarily a ringing endorsement.

"You're saying I can trust her?" Scarlett asked, skeptical.

"Not at all," Jess replied, dead serious. "I'm saying trust but verify."

Which told Scarlett everything she needed to know and confirmed her own misgivings about Wagner. Still, this was Flint's mother. Wagner would keep digging unless Scarlett could deflect her.

Scarlett arrived at the downtown restaurant a few minutes early. It was a trendy farm-to-table place and a line of customers had already formed at the entrance. She'd made a reservation and requested a quiet booth toward the back.

She nursed a cup of coffee while keeping an eye out for Wagner and her witness, Dean Taylor.

Five minutes later, Wagner strode in with an older man trailing behind her. His appearance was eccentric, to say the least.

Sporting round wire-rimmed glasses askew on his face, he wore a mismatched brown suit with a green shirt and bright red sneakers and carried a tattered canvas briefcase. Wispy gray hair spiked from his scalp in all directions like he'd combed it with an eggbeater.

As they approached, Scarlett noticed Wagner was carrying a laptop bag. She must have brought her records and notes.

Wagner slid into the booth first, smiling briefly at Scarlett, while Taylor took the opposite side, scooting along the bench awkwardly with effort.

"Thanks for meeting with us, Ms. Scarlett," Wagner began once they were settled. "I appreciate you hearing us out."

"Yes, thank you for your discretion in this matter." Taylor's reedy voice was tinged with weariness. He cleared his throat. "Despite James Preston's...troubles...he was a friend of mine. I'm still uncertain about sharing his private information."

Scarlett held a neutral expression. "Mr. Taylor, I'm not interested in publicizing or profiting from Preston's case. I simply want to uncover the truth, for the sake of the victims' families. They deserve answers after all this time, don't you agree?"

Taylor studied her carefully through the smudged and crooked glasses for a moment. Eventually, he gave a slight nod. "Very well. I'll tell you what I know."

He reached into the canvas briefcase and pulled out a padded manila envelope. Removing its contents with exaggerated care, he placed the charred and warped remains of what seemed to be two old-fashioned pocket planners on the table between them.

The years stamped on the vinyl covers coincided with the Baker and Pentwater murders.

"This...is what James entrusted to me before his execution," Taylor said solemnly. "He instructed me to keep these safe and private until after his death."

Scarlett stared at the partially melted vinyl covers. The pages inside were charred. She imagined the two calendars had been tossed into a fire pit and left long enough to be damaged before someone snatched them from the flames.

Could these tattered artifacts unravel two murder cases after all these years? Seemed unlikely, but she kept her expression neutral as Taylor carefully lifted a fragile page fragment.

He opened the damaged vinyl cover to display the interior pages. The calendars were identical. Three inches wide by six inches high, they contained both monthly and weekly views and a few pages for notes. Scarlett guessed they were each about 130 slender pages.

"As you can see, the calendars are James's handwritten entries," Taylor said, voice hushed with reverence as he pointed to the first page where James Preston's name was block printed in blue ink. He continued to point to the pages as he flipped them. "Quick notes, mostly. His whereabouts and activities on specific dates."

Taylor's words trailed off and Wagner leaned in eagerly to fill the silence. "The entries contradict the prosecution's timeline, which is what the jury relied on to convict Preston for June Pentwater's murder."

Taylor nodded grimly. "Precisely. According to these notes, James had an alibi for the time of Ms. Pentwater's death. He was nowhere near the crime scene."

Scarlett felt her breath catch in her throat. If legitimate, this evidence alone might have exonerated Preston decades ago. Presumably, he'd be alive today. She had to tread lightly.

"And I take it there are similar contradictions around the date of Marilyn Baker's murder as well?" She kept her voice steady.

Baker was the reason she had come to this meeting. If the evidence didn't pertain to Baker, Scarlett could bow out and get back to work for her own clients.

"Yes." Taylor carefully extracted another charred page from the second calendar. "See here? This entry shows James was in Mount Warren earlier in the evening. But later, he was performing a memorial service in another town. He stayed overnight there. All of which is inconsistent with the any case against him because the Baker murder happened during the memorial."

"Could be why Preston was never charged in the Baker murder." Wagner looked like a kid on Christmas morning.

"We knew there were problems with the prosecutions, but these calendars are concrete proof of Preston's innocence!"

"Not so fast," Scarlett cautioned. As much as she wanted this new evidence to be ironclad, she couldn't afford to get her hopes up prematurely. "These are just one piece of potential evidence that's decades old. We have to verify accuracy and authenticity."

"And we will," Wagner said, raising her chin defiantly.

"Preston was never charged in the Baker murder. But we need to know why these facts were never submitted during the Pentwater trials," Scarlett said.

Taylor frowned. "You don't trust that I'm telling the truth about how I came to possess the calendars?"

Scarlett held up a placating hand. "I'm not questioning your integrity, Mr. Taylor. But you have to understand, from an investigator's perspective, I need to vet every shred of evidence thoroughly."

She leaned back, steepling her fingers as she eyed the damaged calendars again. "However, I will concede that if this contemporaneous record from Preston himself can hold up to scrutiny, it could blow both cases wide open. We would have to re-examine all the circumstantial evidence in a new light."

Wagner was practically vibrating with excitement at the prospect. Scarlett couldn't blame her. The allure of cracking two longstanding cold cases was strong.

But she knew from hard experience that chasing rabbits too eagerly could lead you down an empty rabbit hole.

Scarlett said, "We need to go through his calendar entries thoroughly and compare them to all the evidence, testimony, and court records. We'll need to chase down both alibis ourselves."

"That sounds doable," Wagner replied. "How long will it take?"

"But even if Preston's alibis directly contradict the witnesses and prosecutors, it will still be difficult to exonerate him now," Scarlett continued as if Wagner hadn't interrupted her. "We'll need at least one expert to confirm the authenticity of the calendars. If we get the right answers, we can move forward."

Scarlett paused to make direct eye contact with Wagner.

"From there...who knows where the investigation could lead," Wagner said, with her typical youthful exuberance. "Maybe we'll finally get real answers about who actually killed both women."

The words hung heavy in the air.

Wagner fairly beamed, thrilled at the prospect of her podcast achieving such lofty goals.

Taylor looked pensive, perhaps wondering if he'd chosen the right path after remaining silent for so long.

Scarlett's paramount concern was Flint. Because if the truth about Marilyn Baker finally came to light, skeletons could come tumbling out of the closet in the process. Flint could be damaged, professionally, and personally.

Scarlett wanted no part of that. Flint was the only family she and Maddy had. She wouldn't jeopardize the bond between them for any reason.

The decision should be Flint's call.

And he'd made that call every time they'd talked about that in the past.

He'd baldly stated his position about Marilyn Baker.

His answer was no. Flatly. Definitely. Simply. No.

Which left Scarlett in an impossible position.

She couldn't ignore Flint's wishes on this score, even though she thought he was wrong.

He'd never forgive her. And Maddy wouldn't forgive her, either.

Hell, probably even Whiskers would be unforgiving, at least until she apologized with the treats he loved.

"Mr. Taylor," Scarlett began, her tone measured but firm. "I need you to walk me through exactly how you came into possession of these calendars."

The older man fidgeted slightly under her steely gaze. "Of course, Ms. Scarlett. You have every right to be skeptical."

Scarlett waited without comment.

He took a sip of his water before continuing. "I first met James Preston when I was serving as a prison chaplain. Perhaps because he'd been a priest, we developed an unconventional friendship, I suppose you could say, over the years that he was incarcerated."

Wagner watched Taylor with rapt attention, hanging on his every word.

Scarlett realized the zealous podcaster had not heard Taylor's full story before. She'd made assumptions and leaped to conclusions when she'd pressured Scarlett to hear Taylor out.

Which meant Wagner's candor and ethics should be viewed skeptically at all times.

"In the months leading up to his execution, James made arrangements to ensure a small cache of his personal effects would be preserved after his death. Including these two calendars." Taylor gestured to the burned remnants on the table.

"Why these specific items?" Scarlett pressed. "What's so significant about them?"

"You already know." Taylor's eyes grew somber. "James insisted that these calendars proved he couldn't have committed those murders."

"Yet he never produced this supposed exculpatory evidence during any of his trials or appeals?" The skepticism dripped from Scarlett's words.

Taylor chuckled dryly. "You know how the justice system grinds people down, Ms. Scarlett. James had been declaring his innocence for more than thirty years. Plenty of evidence and witnesses were rejected, ignored, or covered up along the way. Lawyers came and went. Judges, too. Some were more sympathetic than others. James had little faith that his alibi evidence would be accepted when nothing else had ever been good enough."

Scarlett had to concede the point. The criminal justice system, including its flaws and failures, could be daunting, for sure. But that didn't mean Preston or his lawyers should have simply stopped trying.

Taylor continued, "He entrusted the calendars to me secretly a few weeks before his execution. With instructions to preserve them safely and take them public only after his death, when the truth could no longer be buried or dismissed."

Scarlett nodded. Wagner practically rubbed her palms together with glee like a Munchkin.

Taylor's eyes grew haunted. "Part of me wonders if I made the right choice by keeping the calendars hidden away. Maybe they really could have helped him after all."

Wagner immediately jumped in. "But now we finally have the chance to prove his innocence and get to the bottom of what really happened."

Scarlett shot her a quelling look, throwing a damper on her excitement at least momentarily. Wagner closed her mouth and Scarlett turned back to Taylor.

"How can we verify the authenticity of these calendar pages?" She tapped the calendar with her index finger. "That the calendar did, in fact, belong to Preston, and the entries are legitimate and can be confirmed as having taken place as noted here?"

Taylor opened his hands, conceding her point. "You'll have to examine the handwriting, the materials used, anything that can tie it incontrovertibly back to James. I kept it preserved properly for just that purpose."

"It looks like someone tried to burn these. How did that happen?" Scarlett asked.

He shook his head. "James didn't tell me anything. He just said to keep them safe."

Scrubbing a hand over her face, Scarlett took a moment to process everything. She wanted to believe they were on the cusp of major revelations about not just one but two horrific murders. But Taylor's story was unlikely, at best.

Scarlett had been a private investigator for a long time. None of this was remotely normal in her experience. Which didn't make Taylor's story untrue, exactly. But it did raise suspicion.

"Alright," she said at last. "First, we'll have these calendars and everything else you've got examined by experts."

"How long will that take?" Wagner asked.

Scarlett shrugged. "We want it done right. So it'll take as long as it takes."

"And then what?" Wagner prodded, frowning.

"If the calendars and their contents are genuine," she locked eyes with Taylor, "then we may open a new chapter. We'll move on from there. I'll let you know as soon as I have anything to report."

Taylor looked relieved, while Wagner could barely contain her excitement.

Scarlett remained stoic, her mind already working through contingencies.

What really happened to Marilyn Baker? If Preston didn't kill her, then who did? And why?

And if she answered those questions, how would Flint cope with the knowledge? Would he simply accept it and move on? Or would he kill the messenger?

CHAPTER 12

Key West, Florida

DRAKE FLEW THE PILATUS with his customary skill and precision while Flint glanced at the ominous clouds on the horizon.

"Looks like a storm's brewing," Flint remarked into the headset's microphone.

Drake nodded and adjusted course. "It's a way's off yet. We might hit some turbulence on descent. Nothing we can't handle, though."

Flint's thoughts were already focused on their arrival at the executive airport in Key West. "Once we touch down, we need to move fast. There's no telling what we'll find at the launch site."

Drake arched an eyebrow. "Anything specific you're chasing?"

"Mainly, we need to get comfortable with the surroundings and the situation on the ground," Flint said. "Gaspar found a couple of amateur videos posted to social media. People who were at the site when the submersible launched."

"What did those videos show?"

"They were consistent with the written reports and the news broadcasts at the time," Flint replied. "The launch seemed to go smoothly. There were no immediate alarms of any sort."

"The implosion didn't happen for several hours after departure, right?" Drake asked. "And even then, no one saw or heard it happen. They're just guessing."

The wind had picked up, buffeting the aircraft. As the Pilatus approached Key West International Airport, the jet bounced like a basketball. Drake's attention tightened on the controls as he navigated through the turbulence.

"We're coming in too hot," Flint said as he tightened his harness and braced for a rough landing.

Drake kept his attention on the challenging conditions. "Hold steady. We're almost there."

Half a moment later, the Pilatus plummeted straight down, fast, as if a child had dropped it like a toy from a skyscraper.

"Woo hoo!" Drake yelped. Giving the task his full attention, he worked to level out and continue a controlled descent.

Drake guided the jet toward the executive runway through the harsh, gusting winds. Twice more, turbulence battered the Pilatus from its path.

A few minutes later, the aircraft touched down expertly and rolled along the runway to stop near the private terminal building.

Riding his own surge of adrenaline, Flint unfastened his harness and gave Drake a grin. "Nice work."

Drake nodded, hands still steady on the controls. "Told you we'd get here in one piece. But we might not get out again before morning. That storm is pushing this way fast and hard."

"There are worse things than spending a night in Key West," Flint replied. "Let's tie the plane down, just in case."

"Definitely," Drake said.

Flint disembarked from the aircraft onto the warm tarmac and Drake followed. The tropical breeze gusted hot air. He felt like he was standing in front of a blast furnace.

Quickly, they secured the plane and hustled to the open Jeep Flint had reserved which was parked nearby.

He glanced skyward, assessing the approaching storm. "We're gonna get wet."

"Yeah." Drake climbed into the driver's seat while Flint settled in beside him. The Jeep's engine sputtered to life, and they rolled forward.

The submersible's launch site was on the northeast side of the island. Following Flint's directions, Drake turned left onto Florida A1A, avoiding the throngs of tourists downtown. At US-1, they made a right.

"The launch site is three miles ahead," Flint said, gaze drifting to the brightly colored buildings and palm trees going by. "Near the Naval Air Station. Watch your speed. They'll be monitoring approaching traffic."

"Roger that," Drake said, slowing the Jeep and keeping the vehicle steady in its lane.

After another mile, Flint said, "Turn right here. The driveway is a block north."

The dark clouds had moved rapidly across the sky blocking the sunlight as effectively as a total eclipse.

As Drake drove the Jeep along the driveway and into the main parking lot, the bottom fell out of the sky, cascading rain with the pressure of a firehose.

Both Flint and Drake were drenched instantly. The rain poured down with renewed force. Wind gusts battered the Jeep, threatening to flip it over.

Drake turned the windshield wipers to their fastest setting and tried to peer through the vanishing view.

"Park there, near the main building. We'll dash inside. See if there's anyone we can talk to while we wait," Flint said with a quick glance at Drake's scowl. "Florida thunderstorms are famously fierce, but usually blow over quickly."

Without comment, Drake parked the Jeep, turned everything off, and cut the engine. They hopped out and hustled toward the building, heads down, feet splashing through accumulating puddles that bordered on mini lakes. The wind whipped at their clothes, turning their sprint into a battle against nature's fury.

Inside the building, they shook off the assault like wet dogs, droplets flying. Flint raked a hand through his soaked hair, the moisture adding a darker shade to its already deep brown color. Drake's eyes flicked to the sign across the room.

"Coffee?" Drake gestured with a nod toward the aroma of freshly ground beans.

Flint checked his watch. "Yeah. This storm's not letting up any time soon."

The woman behind the counter wearing a bright tropical shirt, greeted them with a worn smile and a handful of paper towels. "Rough weather for driving. You guys are soaked. What can I get you?"

"Two coffees, black," Flint ordered, accepting the paper towels with a smile.

"And a couple of those blueberry muffins," Drake added, wiping the rain from his face and neck.

They found a clean corner table. Flint sat with his back to the wall, facing the entrance. An old habit hard-wired into his psyche. Drake sat next to him, relaxing into the chair with a sigh as he surveyed the nearly empty terminal.

"Can't believe how fast that sky turned nasty," Drake said, blowing on the steaming coffee to cool it.

Flint nodded. "I've seen sudden storms, but this one came up like a mobster's vendetta."

Drake took a careful sip. "Now, about the launch site..."

Flint leaned forward, his voice low. "We're looking for a guy named Bartholomew Trawler. Supposed to be some kind of freelance tech wizard. He hangs out around here."

"Why do we think he could be helpful?"

"He was freelancing with the *Galeane II* team at the time. And he had access to the submersible before launch, according to the reports."

Drake raised an eyebrow. "You think he was involved with whatever caused the implosion?"

"No evidence of that. Not so far," Flint's gaze didn't waver. "Seems he still lives here, on Key West. We'll find out more when we talk to him."

Drake nibbled on his muffin, considering. "We find this Trawler, then what? If he's got anything to hide, he's not just going to spill his guts because we ask nicely."

"We'll have to persuade him to do the right thing," Flint said, his tone as hard as steel.

A sudden flicker of lights heralded a struggle between the storm and the power supply. Flint's attention snapped to the front door as it burst open.

A man wrapped in a rain poncho staggered inside, fighting to close the door against the wind.

The stranger's gaze landed on Flint and Drake. For a heartbeat, there was a silent exchange, a sizing up of sorts, before the newcomer made a beeline toward them.

Flint's hand subtly shifted closer to the concealed sidearm resting against his hip.

The man pulled back his hood, revealing salt-and-pepper hair matted against his forehead. Flint recognized him from photos in Layman's reports.

"Are you Flint?" His words were urgent, tinged with an accent Flint couldn't immediately place.

Cuban, maybe? Key West was close to Havana. The populations were comingled. Ernest Hemingway famously traveled to Cuba from his home in Key West regularly. Back in the day, it was an easy thing to do if one had access to a boat.

Drake straightened up, palming a napkin to dry his hands. "Who's asking?"

The man's eyes darted to the storm raging outside before settling back on them. "Bart Trawler. We need to talk." He glanced around nervously. "But not here. Too many eyes and ears on this place all the time."

Flint and Drake exchanged a quick look.

Trawler's concern was well founded. Every port of entry in the country was constantly under surveillance of all types. Especially airports and naval air stations close to foreign soil.

"Lead the way." Flint's reply was low and controlled.

The power flickered again, casting shadows across Trawler's face, deepening the weathered creases etched into his skin.

Which was when the lights went out completely, plunging the windowless building into total darkness. The storm's roar seemed to magnify in the silence.

A few seconds later, a generator kicked on somewhere and emergency lights flickered to life. Drake's hand brushed his sidearm and Flint's gaze searched the dimly lit room.

Trawler was gone. As if he'd been swallowed by the shadows.

His abandoned poncho lay puddled on the floor where he had been standing, and a note, hastily scribbled on the back of a crumpled coffee receipt, rested on the adjacent table. Flint picked up the note, read it, and passed it to Drake.

Meet me at the Southernmost Point. Two hours.

CHAPTER 13

THE STORM ABATED, SLOWING and then stopping as quickly as it had begun. Flint and Drake left the building and returned to the Jeep, which had been thoroughly washed, inside and out. They left the vehicle to dry out and walked toward the launch site.

As they approached, the scene crackled with activity. Technicians scurried to unload a cargo boat that had probably docked just before the storm.

Flint said quietly, "Let's split up. Get a feel for things. Be careful asking about Trawler. He's nervous about something and we don't want to spook him more than he already is."

Drake set his jaw and plopped a baseball cap on his head. "I'll start by talking to the workers."

Flint watched him approach a group of technicians and engage them in conversation. When he was satisfied Drake was on track, Flint scouted the docks.

The two reports he'd received from Lyman, along with the amateur videos and television news footage he'd studied, gave the scene a familiar feel, even though he'd never been here before.

He replayed events in his head as he walked from one side of the site to the other.

The gravel parking lot had been full the day the *Galeane II* launched. The videos and photographs chronicled the festive celebration. He'd estimated at least five hundred curious spectators and supportive groupies had arrived early to tailgate until the time the crew boarded the submersible.

Which should have been good news. With that many people watching, at least one person should have seen any crimes committed.

But nothing untoward happened on the day of the launch.

The spectators were happy and supportive. No fights broke out. No accidents occurred. Nothing untoward either before or after the launch. Everything seemed to go along as planned.

All of which meant that law enforcement had no reason to attend the launch. Because no cops were there, the spectators were not identified. No statements were taken. Not until much later.

Once the *Galeane II* left the dock on its way to the gulf, the crowd had dispersed. Because *Galeane II* had dived beneath the surface, there would have been nothing more to see even if they'd hung around.

Galeane II imploded several hours later. It was well below the surface when the disaster happened. The destroyed *Galeane II* wasn't actually located for another two days.

Which gave the spectators and supporters time to scatter to the four winds.

Afterward, authorities had tried to locate witnesses. But the effort was futile. Most of them had already departed. They found a few regulars who worked at the launch site. A few more called local cops to volunteer what little information they had. None of it added up to much.

On his third trip across the docks, Flint's gaze landed on a surveillance camera he hadn't noticed before nestled high in a corner opposite the dock where *Galeane II* had been. The camera was newer than the others and the shape of it suggested a wider lens.

From that position, had it been in place at the time of the launch, the camera would have recorded aft of *Galeane II* and probably captured most of the spectators who lined the gangway. Each of the five treasure hunters would have been recorded as they climbed aboard.

He didn't recall seeing video shot from that vantage point among the footage he'd reviewed already. Was there more footage somewhere?

Flint pulled the bill on his cap lower to shield his face from the glaring sunlight and approached the identified camera. He slid his phone from his pocket and snapped several shots of the camera and its location, zooming in and out until he'd covered the entire field.

After he'd pocketed his phone, Flint looked around again, this time seeking the surveillance monitors. No point to all of the high-tech cameras if no one ever reviewed the video. But the monitors could be located off site.

Flint approached a pair of technicians clustered around a set of monitors, their attention focused on the intricate details displayed on the screens.

"Excuse me, gentlemen," Flint began. One man glanced up, but the other kept his focus on the screens. "I'm investigating an incident involving a submersible that launched from this site a while back."

The technician seemed wary but cooperative. "The one that imploded? *Galeane II*? Investigators have been dogging that incident since it happened. Can't be any stone left unturned, surely. But what do you need to know?"

"You're right. I've read the reports," Flint said in a friendly tone. "I'm looking to find anything that wasn't covered before. Anything unusual or unexpected or out-of-the-ordinary happening earlier on the day of the launch? Or later, after the *Galeane II* left the dock?"

"The whole situation was unusual, man," the second technician said without looking up from the screen. "Treasure hunting is a fairly normal activity around here. Spanish galleons, you know? Since they found the Atocha in eighty-five, hunters have flooded the place. Amateurs with their metal detectors and snorkel equipment. Pros with sophisticated tech. And everything in between. Most hunters don't really expect to find anything. It's a gas, you know? Something to have fun with."

"What about the *Galeane II*? Were the hunters in the submersible expecting to find something?" Flint asked.

"They were so damned sure they were on their way to fame and fortune," he wagged his head sorrowfully.

The first technician scratched his bearded chin. "There was that one guy who seemed kind of nervous. Kept checking his watch like he was running late for something."

Flint said, "Can you describe him?"

The technician shrugged. "Just your average Joe, really. Medium build, dark hair. Nothing too remarkable about him. I just had the feeling he was impatient. Like he was expecting something or someone."

Flint pulled up a photo of Ward Lyman on his phone and showed it to the technician. "Is this the man?"

He studied the photo a moment and handed it back, shaking his head. "Dunno. I didn't get that good a look at him. Cops might have found him after the *Galeane II* imploded. They were asking the same questions."

"Thanks. I'll do that," Flint said, pointing to the high camera across the way. "Do you have the video from that camera on the day *Galeane II* launched?"

The tech looked at the camera and shook his head. "That camera's newer. It belongs to Homeland Security. It's not one of ours. You'd have to ask them."

Flint nodded. "Okay. I'll do that. Can I get a copy of all the footage you do have for the day of the launch?"

The second technician shook his head. "Sorry, man. We turned it over back then. We didn't keep any of it."

Flint pulled a business card out of his wallet, handing it to the technician. "If you think of anything else that might be helpful, can you give me a call? And especially if you see that guy again, the one you thought was impatient. I'd really like to talk to him."

Drake had worked his way through the opposite side of the site. As Flint approached, he heard Drake talking with a forklift driver loading equipment onto a nearby truck. "Mind if I ask you a few questions?"

The man paused, wiping sweat from his brow. "Sure. How can I help you?"

"I know it's been a minute, but were you here the day the *Galeane II* launched?" Drake asked.

"Yeah, that was a couple of years ago. There was a lot of excitement. The *Galeane II* team was well known and regarded around here. People wanted them to succeed, you know?" He frowned and gazed into the distance as he tried to recall the events of that day. "But there was this one guy who seemed to be in a hurry to get away for some reason. Kept glancing over his shoulder like he was afraid someone was following him."

"Can you describe him?"

"Sorry." The man shrugged. "Can't say I got a good look at him. But he definitely stood out. Mostly because he wasn't watching the dock or the *Galeane II*. He was rushing in the opposite direction. Like a salmon swimming against the tide."

Flint walked up just as he finished. He showed the same photo of Ward Lyman on his phone. "Was this the guy you saw leaving the area?"

He took the phone and squinted to see the snap. He manipulated the screen to enlarge the photo and then stared at it a couple of moments before he handed the phone back.

"Possibly. I mean, I didn't see the guy up close. And really, I didn't see his face at all. That guy has a similar build. Could've been him," the man said. "I've got to get back to work. Sorry I couldn't help more."

Flint handed him a card and requested a call if anything else came to mind. Then he turned to Drake. "Let's go."

Before Drake had a chance to agree, a sudden commotion erupted. A loud crash followed by shouts of alarm.

A group of workers gathered quickly around a collapsed section of scaffolding, frantically trying to free a man trapped beneath the debris.

"Clear a path! Give them some space!" Flint barked, his authoritative voice cutting through the chaos as he and Drake approached.

The workers scrambled to obey, creating a makeshift perimeter around the fallen scaffolding. Flint and Drake wasted no time, pushing through the crowd to reach the center of the scene.

The man lay on the ground beneath the rubble. His leg was pinned beneath a heavy beam, and blood seeped from a gash on his forehead. His face was twisted in pain as he struggled to free himself.

"Help me!" he pleaded, his voice hoarse with agony.

Flint heard sirens in the distance heading toward them. He and Drake began working alongside the others, carefully removing the debris piece by piece.

They toiled in silence punctuated by the injured man's groans and the clang of metal against metal. Finally, they managed to free him from the wreckage.

He lay on the ground panting and clutching his injured leg. Flint used his forearm to wipe sweat from his face and knelt beside the man to assess the extent of the damage.

"Paramedics are on the way. Can you tell us what happened?" Flint asked, trying to keep the injured man's mind occupied.

He grimaced, "I was doing my rounds when the scaffolding collapsed out of nowhere. I didn't see it coming."

"Was anyone else around when it happened?"

The man shook his head. His breathing was more labored now. Skin clammy. He was already in shock and getting worse.

"It all happened so fast," he croaked.

Two EMS units rushed up and parked close to the injured worker. Paramedics jumped out and began to work with practiced efficiency.

Soon, the man was loaded onto a gurney, slid into the back of an ambulance, and headed to the hospital.

"Think they'll save the leg?" Drake asked quietly.

"We can hope," Flint replied. "What the hell happened?"

"Dunno," he shrugged. "But this place seems to be unlucky, don't you think? Wonder how many incidents and injuries they have around here?"

"Good questions. Add them to the list," Flint said, headed toward the Jeep. Drake fell in beside him. "Let's get a shower and a meal and a cold beer. In that order."

"Good plan," Drake said, stepping around the potholes. "Nobody I talked to mentioned Trawler. You?"

"No. We might have to come back for that if he ghosts us." Flint sent the photos of the Homeland Security camera to Gaspar with a quick text asking him to take a look.

The Jeep was where they'd left it. The rain had evaporated on the outside, but the interior would need another few hours to dry out.

"Guess we'll see how waterproof this thing is," Drake grumbled as he climbed inside.

Flint took the soggy passenger seat. "It rains almost every day here in the summer. Safe bet that this Jeep has been drenched before."

"Next time, rent an SUV with doors and a roof," Drake replied sourly.

As Drake turned the key and the engine actually started, Flint said with a grin, "I'll keep that advice in mind."

CHAPTER 14

Kansas City, Missouri

THE PENTHOUSE SUITE WAS rich with the scent of leather and aged wood, a testament to the luxuries Anthony Boldo never denied himself. He sat behind a modern mahogany desk, sunlight casting tall shadows through panoramic windows.

Marino, his silhouette bulky and imposing, lounged silently in a club chair placed on Boldo's left side.

The two soldiers fidgeted in their chairs across from Boldo.

Boldo's fingers danced across the laptop's keyboard before he slammed it shut. The sound echoed through the hushed atmosphere.

"So, it's simple," Boldo said quietly. "We use the information our mole feeds us, play the stocks like a damn fiddle until Lyman Enterprises is ripe for the picking."

Paulie, a lean man with a nervous twitch, leaned forward. "Boss, the Lymans won't know what hit 'em."

Boldo fixed him with a steely gaze. "The Lymans are not our concern right now. It's the other investors. We need to convince them we're doing them a favor."

Marino's deep bass voice rumbled, "And the SEC? They sniff around when the market stirs like this."

Boldo smirked and shared a small fraction of the plan. "That's why we're smart about it. We're buying Lyman Enterprises stock in small moves, undetectable, until we're ready for the kill."

The second soldier, the one called Romeo because he imagined every woman on the planet was enthralled by his good looks, chimed in, "We got people in place to throw 'em off the scent. Ain't that right?"

"Exactly," Boldo confirmed to shut down the conversation.

These guys didn't need to know the full extent of Boldo's reach or the people on his payroll who shielded his activities from government interference. He was the boss. They followed his orders without questions. Simple as that.

Boldo stood and walked to the serving station for a drink. He glanced in the mirror to confirm his bespoke gray suit was unwrinkled and fit him perfectly. Bench-made brown shoes were polished to a high sheen. The timepiece on his wrist and the signet ring on his pinky had belonged to his father.

In short, Boldo looked like what he was. A successful businessman from a long line of high achievers. Men who did whatever they had to do to get what they wanted and make success happen.

"We've got this mapped out. Our mole gives us the layout and we follow the plan to the letter," Boldo said, feeding them only what they needed to know. "By the time Ward Lyman's little escapade comes to light, Anthony Boldo will be at the helm. Lyman Enterprises will be folded into Boldo Construction."

Marino nodded, the ghost of a grin on his face, "To the new King of Concrete."

They all stood, and Boldo clasped each man's hand firmly. Their loyalty to Boldo was as thick as the tension they all felt at the audacity of his plan.

With a single nod, Boldo dismissed them. The two soldiers left. Marino, as always, stayed.

Boldo walked to the window and looked out over the kingdom he was poised to conquer.

"Marino, wait outside," he said while still facing the glass.

Without a word, Marino did as he was told.

Boldo ignored the city sprawled out below and returned to his desk. He flipped open a hidden compartment and extracted the sleek phone reserved for conversations that would never be traced.

He dialed a number he memorized and discarded after one use. The call connected after the first ring.

"Report," he demanded, foregoing pleasantries.

"Sending now." The voice on the other end was distorted, a digital mask for security.

A soft buzz signaled an incoming message on his laptop. Boldo opened it to see a new self-destructing email with the latest financial reports and projections. He scanned the figures, noting the subtle indicators that would go unnoticed by most.

Lyman Enterprises appeared stable, but Boldo saw cleverly disguised instability. He finished skimming the financials, and the email disappeared into the ether.

A moment later, the door to the suite opened again and Marino reentered, a silent question in his posture.

"Everything's in place," Boldo said with the certainty of a man who believed in his destiny. "Lyman Enterprises will be ours soon."

"And the other matter?" Marino inquired, ever vigilant to the scope of their operations.

Boldo set the glass down, his gaze never leaving the screen. "Progress is being made."

Marino nodded, standing by the door like a guardian of the realm. "And the detective, Michael Flint? Old man Lyman hired him to find the grandson. Flint's been asking questions, poking around where he shouldn't."

A flicker of annoyance crossed Boldo's features. Flint's arrival on the scene was a nuisance, a variable he needed to neutralize discreetly. When the time was right.

"Keep an eye on him. All men have weaknesses. Find his."

"Already on it, boss."

The conversation dwindled and Boldo's focus returned to considering the financial forecasts no longer on his screen. He drafted a reply email with clear and precise instructions. Each move had to be calculated, each play had to be perfect.

Marino waited silently by the door.

Boldo's gaze was once again drawn to the city below.

"Let's keep the pressure on," he said, his tone sharp as a blade. "And turn up the heat on Flint if he gets in the way. Let's see how he reacts when things get a little... uncomfortable."

Marino's grin was the last thing to fade as he closed the door, leaving Boldo to savor his planning.

Boldo pulled the phone from his pocket and pressed the redial. The altered voice answered promptly again.

"Message received."

"And the hostage?" Boldo demanded.

A longer than acceptable pause sucked the oxygen from Boldo's lungs. Finally, the voice replied, "The situation is under control."

Which was not what Boldo wanted to hear. Before he could draw breath to reply, the call was terminated.

The situation is under control. Situation. Under control.

What the hell did that mean?

CHAPTER 15

Houston, Texas

A BURLY MAN EYED Scarlett suspiciously as she approached the dilapidated house on Raven Street. She'd parked a couple of blocks away and advanced on foot. This was Alvarez Gang territory. No one was safe here. The burly man was a lookout. He slouched against the building as if it might fall down when he stepped aside.

Scarlett paused at the intersection of the main sidewalk and the broken concrete leading to the front door. She gave him a quick glance, noticing the big lump of tobacco he had stuffed between his lower lip and his gums.

He saw her hesitation.

"You sure you want to be pokin' around in Benny's business, lady?" His gravelly voice carried an unmistakable edge of threat. He punctuated the question with a long stream of brown spit projected onto the bare dirt near her feet.

Scarlett stepped closer, expression impassive, hands firmly in the pockets of her jacket. "Tell Benny I'm here."

"Why would Benny care?"

"He knows me. I have reason to believe he's got information I need," she said, simply to get her foot in the door.

The thug slipped one hand into his pocket for a cell phone. He punched a single button and lifted the phone to his ear. After a moment, he said, "Some broad says she knows Benny. Wants to come up."

Scarlett had been here for information before. Benny Alvarez managed his own crew. He was also well connected to Houston's crime networks. Which meant he lived in a constant state of combat readiness.

Almost every weekend, Benny's crew shot up a couple of his archrivals and the Sanchez Gang shot up a few of his. A couple of times a month, crew members were killed.

But Benny knew things. Sometimes, he'd spill what he knew. When she saw his name in Naomi Wagner's file materials, she'd grabbed the lifeline.

After a bit of quick research, she'd discovered that Benny had served his last stint in prison at Huntsville, Texas. Which was where Preston spent the last few years and where he was executed.

It was the same prison where Dean Taylor served as chaplain. She was hoping Benny might know something useful that he hadn't told investigators before.

Benny's security was tighter than all the oil tycoons in Texas. But she wasn't worried. The last time she'd seen Benny, they'd parted on friendly terms. Benny wouldn't kill her. Not right here or right now, anyway. She hoped.

The grungy sentinel grunted, disconnected the call, and dropped the phone into his pocket. He gave her a single nod and moved away from the door.

Scarlett brushed past him up the crumbling front steps. Taking a fortifying breath, she twisted the tarnished metal knocker and rapped it firmly against the door's peeling green paint. A couple of paint flakes fell to the concrete stoop.

A few muffled thumps sounded from within and then the door creaked open three inches. One beady eye peered out, barely visible in the shadows.

"Whaddya want, Curly?" Benjamin Alvarez demanded.

"Let me in, Benny," Scarlett said.

"Why?"

"We need to talk about James Preston."

"You alone?"

"Yes."

"Anybody follow you here?"

"No."

A tense pause, then the eye disappeared and the door swung inward.

Scarlett found herself staring up at an absolute mountain of a man. He had to be pushing seven feet tall, built like a grizzly bear. Prison tats covered nearly every visible inch of skin on his bald head, thick neck, and bulging arms.

"Yeah, okay," the beast of a man rumbled, unsmiling. "Heard you been sniffin' around that executed killer's old business. That a fact?"

"It is." Scarlett held his gaze steadily. "Preston may have been wrongfully convicted. New evidence has come to light that could exonerate him."

Benny's lip curled in a sneer. "Wagner been fillin' your head with garbage too? Figures."

Wagner's searching had come to Benny's attention, then. Scarlett filed that intel away for later.

He jerked his head toward the gloomy interior. "Get in here before one of Sanchez's crew takes you out."

Scarlett stepped across the threshold into a surprisingly spacious room. It looked like a drug den, with various shady characters lounging around smoking and playing cards. Some gawked, leering as she passed. Others were laid out on the floor, eyes open and fixed on something no one else could see.

The stench of body odor was overwhelming. Scarlett clamped her teeth together to avoid gagging.

Benny led her toward a smaller room at the back. He kicked aside debris and garbage, then pulled up a ratty recliner and collapsed into it with a growl.

"Siddown," he commanded Scarlett, gesturing at a stained armchair across from his seat. "And start talkin' before I lose my patience."

Squaring her shoulders, Scarlett took the proffered seat, keeping her body angled toward the exit just in case. She quickly outlined the basics about Dean Taylor's claims. She leaned on Preston's supposed alibi calendar that contradicted the timeline for June Pentwater's murder.

When she finished, Benny leveled a menacing stare for several heartbeats. "And you're actually buying into this crap?"

Scarlett bristled. "I'm doing my due diligence. It's my job."

Benny scoffed. "Preston's defense team? Bunch of ambulance chasers looking to make a name off a sensational case."

He leaned forward, the armchair creaking ominously under his immense bulk. "Listen up, Curly. I knew Preston back in the day before the Pentwater thing. He was a twisted, greedy son of a bitch. The exact type to pull that sick stunt."

"That so?" Scarlett said.

Benny's gaze bored into hers. "You really think if he had some magical calendar that proved his innocence, Preston wouldn't have shoved it down everyone's throat decades ago?"

Scarlett held her ground. "So you say the calendar evidence is fabricated?"

"Preston was a piece of trash. He raped and killed that Pentwater girl just like the courts said," Benny growled. "And if they say he helped himself to any other innocent girls, that tracks too. Outside of prison, he'd have been dead twenty years earlier. He had plenty of enemies."

Benny scratched idly at his wrist, riding up the sleeve of his stained T-shirt to reveal a glimpse of another frightening tattoo. Scarlett recognized the numerical sequence of digits as an inmate ID from the Texas prison system.

Her heartbeat quickened. She'd expected to get intel from Benny. Now she was sitting across from an extremely dangerous ex-convict with some kind of personal grudge against Preston.

This scenario could turn ugly very fast.

"Look, I appreciate you sharing your perspective on the matter," Scarlett began carefully, already starting to inch her way out of the chair. "But I've been hired to get the facts."

Benny's eyes narrowed dangerously, one beefy hand clenching into a meaty fist. "Maybe you shouldn't go pokin' your pretty head where it ain't wanted."

Scarlett stood slowly, muscles tensing in preparation for a fight. But before either of them could make another move, a deafening crash shattered the quiet.

In the stunned beat of silence that followed, Scarlett and Benny stared.

His eyes widened with sudden rage. "Sanchez," he spat.

Whatever had just kicked off outside, she was trapped in the thick of it now.

Her hand strayed toward the pistol holstered under her jacket. Benny lumbered to his feet, his massive body radiating the menace of a thousand thugs.

"Stay put," he snarled at her.

CHAPTER 16

AS BENNY STOMPED AWAY toward the disturbance, Scarlett strained to make out sounds that could clue her in to what was happening out there. She gripped the pistol, ready to fire at a moment's notice.

Seconds ticked by in a tense silence. Then she heard a thump and a guttural grunt of pain. Shuffling footsteps came nearer.

She pivoted, sidestepping quickly to put the armchair between her and the entrance just as the door burst open.

Benny staggered into the room, a crimson bloodstain running down his chest and spreading across his shirt from a nasty gash along his collarbone.

Two goons wearing Alvarez gang colors shoved their way in after him brandishing wicked-looking blades. Scarlett automatically leveled her weapon directly at the threat.

"They followed you here!" Benny roared, spittle flying from his bloodied lips as he charged at her.

"Nobody followed me. Your location isn't exactly a secret." Scarlett stared directly at him, holding his enraged gaze as she waited until the last possible second.

She dropped to a crouch just as Benny's meaty fist swung through the space where her head had been. He'd put all his weight behind the punch, throwing himself temporarily off-balance when he missed.

Benny staggered to one side as he tried to stay on his feet.

Scarlett used the opening to drive her shoulder hard into his torso.

The blow stunned him long enough.

She followed through by slamming the grip of her pistol across his face.

Benny went down in a heap with a teeth-rattling crash when he hit the floor. Blood from his knife wound spurted into a growing puddle near his shoulder.

She turned quickly, slightly off-balance.

Benny's two goons were on her in a heartbeat, moving with surprising speed despite their bulk. Scarlett squeezed off a couple quick shots that sent them diving for cover.

Shouts and more pounding footsteps echoed from the hallway. Reinforcements? Or Sanchez? Either way, she was trapped.

Her gaze fell on the small window across the room. Maybe just big enough to squeeze through and escape.

Two Sanchez thugs rushed in. One took a wild slash at her with his blade.

Scarlett deflected the clumsy strike and fired again.

The muzzle flash lit up the room.

His head snapped back, spraying a grotesque crimson arc across the void. He crumpled bonelessly, landing with a hard plop that shook the floor.

From her periphery, Scarlett glimpsed another Sanchez goon scrambling low and fast, looking to catch her from behind.

She spun toward him. His revolver was leveled and aimed squarely at her gut.

"Lights out, lady," he snarled. "You're done here."

The deafening gunshot seemed to echo endlessly. Scarlett flinched, bracing for the burning impact that never came.

He went rigid as his face slackened in shock. Blood spread across his chest and he toppled backwards, unmoving.

Scarlett spun around to see Benny lumbering upright, the front of his shirt now completely soaked in blood and dripping onto his shoes.

In his massive, shaking hand, he gripped the pistol that had dropped from the Sanchez thug's hand.

His gaze met Scarlett's across the room, expressing both rage and satisfaction. "Sanchez will send twenty more. Get out. Now. While you can."

More street thugs from both gangs were drawn inside by the raucous gunfire. Benny closed the door and shoved a wooden brace across it.

Benny must have believed her. And he was right. Scarlett needed to find an exit. Fast.

She pivoted and sprinted toward the window, leading with her shoulder and tucking her chin close to her chest.

She felt the glass shatter around her as she hurtled through the narrow opening in a shower of razor-sharp shards.

Gunshots echoed from the house behind her. She tumbled without grace onto the overgrown lawn.

Scarlett scrambled upright, broken glass raining from her clothes and hair, and sprinted away, ignoring the pain in her side where she'd landed on the hard ground.

Rapid footsteps gave chase behind her, accompanied by shouted curses and threats. Scarlett took a quick glance over her shoulder. Two more armed thugs piled out of the busted window, weapons raised to take aim.

With a growl of desperation, she put on an extra burst of speed and ducked around the corner of a garage. Her vehicle sat untouched at the curb up ahead.

More gunfire roared out behind her, peppering the wall and pavement in her wake.

Scarlett willed her body forward those last agonizing yards to her SUV. Mercifully, the locks popped with a press of the button on the driver's side door handle.

She jerked the door open and flung herself into the safety of the vehicle just as a lucky shot from one of her pursuers blasted the right passenger window.

Scarlett ignored the gunfire and took off in a screech of spinning tires as more bullets spanged off the vehicle.

In her rearview, she saw Benny and his thugs charging outside through the front door, guns blazing, faces twisted into animalistic fury.

Fighting to catch her breath, Scarlett sped around the next corner and floored the accelerator to put as much distance from that nest of vipers as possible.

From the bloody way the encounter had escalated, she figured she'd stepped into the middle of something unrelated to Preston. But Benny Alvarez knew the guy and detested him. Which was not a reaction she'd expected.

Scarlett didn't slow her SUV until she was several miles away. She pulled over onto a quiet residential street to take stock.

Her clothes were torn in multiple places from her escape through the shattered window. Various superficial cuts on her hands were seeping blood, but nothing worse. She gingerly touched her ribs producing a sharp pain.

"Son of a bitch," she winced. At least one rib was bruised and maybe cracked from her fall.

But nothing was broken or sliced or punctured.

She checked her gun. A handful of rounds remained after her defensive shooting back at the house.

She drew in a fortifying breath while replaying the chaos of the last hour on a loop in her head.

One second, she'd been calmly discussing Preston's case with that brutal hulk Benny. The next, all hell broke loose. Gunfire, bodies dropping, that mad scramble to escape through the damned window.

Scarlett slumped back against the headrest and took a deep breath.

Was Benny's reaction related to Preston at all? Or did she step into a brewing battle fueled by something else entirely?

There were too many unanswered questions. And regardless of who killed June Pentwater, what had really happened to Marilyn Baker four years before that?

When she pulled up to the office, Scarlett climbed out, clutching her ribs with a wince. Once at her desk, she put Gaspar on video conference.

"What the hell happened?" Gaspar said with genuine concern. "You look like you went toe-to-toe with a freight train."

She brushed off his worry. "You could say that. I'll explain everything later."

Gaspar's jaw clenched and he scrutinized her carefully as he followed up. "How can I be of service?"

Scarlett met his gaze steadily. "I think I may have just kicked the lid off a hornet's nest."

CHAPTER 17

Key West, Florida

DRAKE DROVE THE STILL soggy Jeep back to the
Pilatus to collect their bags. "Think Trawler will still be
waiting for us at the Southernmost point?"

Flint shook his head. "We're too late. He won't be there.
But we found him once. We can find him again."

"Okay. Where to?" Drake asked.

Then, following Flint's directions, Drake drove
toward Mallory Square and on to Truman Annex, a newer
development near the historic Truman White House.

"What is this place?" Drake asked as he rolled through
the high-end gated community on the waterfront.

"Originally built as a US Army installation," Flint
replied. "Later, it became a naval station through the end of
World War II."

"Why is it named after Harry Truman?" Drake continued carefully along the route as Flint pointed out each turn, dodging pedestrians, bike riders, roller bladers, and a variety of other conveyances that surely were not street legal.

Flint shrugged. "I guess Truman liked it here. Came down to stay at the former naval officer residence quite a bit while he was president. Called it the Little White House."

"So they tore the place down and built a bunch of condos when he left office?" Drake scowled. "Strange way to honor a former president."

"Truman wasn't the only president to use the place. And the building is still here. It's a museum now. You should take the tour sometime. It's interesting," Flint said as inclined his head. "Next driveway on the right up ahead. That's our place. Borrowed it from one of Scarlett's clients."

Drake parked the Jeep in the driveway beside a white clapboard building combining an impressive blend of historic and contemporary Key West architecture. The grounds were pleasantly landscaped with palm trees and colorful tropical plants.

"Not a bad place to spend a few months of the year, for sure," Drake said with his usual understated appreciation for all good things.

They retrieved their bags from the back of the Jeep and carried them up a flight of entrance stairs to a wide porch that surrounded the townhouse with a view of the Gulf of Mexico.

Flint punched a code into the lockbox, opened the front door, and entered. Drake followed.

As soon as they stepped inside, the open floor plan displayed the entire living area. Across from the front door was a wall of windows overlooking the azure waters beyond.

The rental agent had turned on the air conditioning, stocked the fridge and the bar. She'd also left a bottle of Macallan single malt Scotch whiskey on the table with a welcome note.

"Nice," Flint said as he picked up the bottle and found a couple of glasses. He poured them each a drink and they split up to get showered and changed.

When Flint returned to the main room twenty minutes later, Drake had his head in the refrigerator, pulling out meats and cheeses. "There's a selection of charcuterie in here."

"Good. I'm hungry," Flint said as he set up his laptop and a secure hot spot for a video call with Gaspar.

A few moments later, Gaspar's image popped onto the screen. "So you're in Key West, then. Nice work if you can get it."

Drake grinned as he put the charcuterie on the table and grabbed a couple of crackers to go with it. "Come on down. We've got room for one more."

"Can't. Unfortunately. I'm on dad duty. And I've got a real job," Gaspar smirked while raising a cup of the sweet Cuban coffee he mainlined during every waking hour.

"Find anything on that camera I asked about?" Flint asked, cutting through the nonsense.

Gaspar nodded, swallowed the coffee, and pushed a couple of buttons on the keyboard. The video footage from the camera filled the screen now. Gaspar's face moved to the bottom right of the screen.

"Took a while to find this. Fortunately, Key West is a prime target for terrorists, so Homeland Security's footage never gets deleted. They put it in archives. And usually forget about it," Gaspar said with a grin. "But that makes things easier to find. If you know how to search."

Flint didn't ask about Gaspar's methods. Hacking into Homeland Security had to be about a dozen felonies. Maybe more. He preferred to think Gaspar had official access of some kind. But this was another area where Flint applied his personal don't ask, don't tell policy. Often, it was better not to know.

Gaspar started the video. The events leading up to the submersible launch unfolded as they had on that day two years ago.

The video was crisp and vibrant in Key West's morning sunlight. The camera captured the scene from a vantage point high above the bustling dock. The submersible sat poised for launch, sleek and shiny against the backdrop of clear skies and tranquil waters.

The colorful and festive crowd was held at bay by orange and white construction barricades. A uniformed security team stood between the barricades and the staging area for *Galeane II*. The support crew was loading equipment and supplies while the five passengers checked their safety gear one final time.

Flint squinted, trying to catch any detail out of place, any clue that might have been overlooked.

"What are we looking for?" Drake asked.

"It's a 360 camera, so the viewing angle changes oddly. It's positioned high off the ground, which gives the images a distorted quality sometimes," Gaspar said.

Flint squinted to get a clearer view. "Looks like several hundred people out there at the launch site that day."

"Only authorized personnel were allowed to approach the submersible, according to the report you sent me," Gaspar replied. "Most of them are gathered behind those sawhorses at this point. They should have stayed there."

"Can you give us a better look at the dive team? Which one is Ward Lyman?" Drake asked, squinting at the laptop screen.

Gaspar replied as he leaned in to adjust his controls, "I can try."

"Hang on a second," Flint said, moving across the room toward a monstrously oversized television mounted on the wall. "I'd like to see everything on a bigger screen, even if we lose some image clarity. Let me get us connected."

A few seconds later, Gaspar had restarted the video and it projected from the eighty-five-inch screen.

Flint stared intently trying to catch details out of place that might have been overlooked.

"Here it comes. After they get the *Galeane II* fully loaded," Gaspar said, his gaze never leaving the screen.

The preparations concluded and the five passengers moved toward the submersible. That's when a surge of spectators broke through the barriers in a wave moving with determination toward *Galeane II.*

"Damn," Drake muttered with a mouth full of olives and spicy cashews. "What set them off?"

"Opportunity. One of the security guards was called away from his post. That gave them an opening," Gaspar pointed out as he talked. "They moved two of the barricades aside and spilled out of the safety zone."

The happy, celebrating spectators, mingling where they shouldn't have been, seemed caught up in a moment of uncontrolled excitement rather than aggression. Cheers and well-wishes filled the audio. The video showed the crew and passengers boarding the submersible amid the chaos, threading through the crowd, waving.

Gaspar leaned closer to his microphone and used a pointer to identify one member of the crowd. "Watch this guy in the blue shirt."

On the screen, the man wearing a bright blue shirt threaded the throng with purpose instead of aimless enthusiasm. He struggled through and finally reached the edge of the dock. He stared at the submersible wistfully, as if he'd like to be one of the crew.

He watched for a while and then he turned and disappeared into the rowdy crowd of spectators.

"Where did he go?" Flint asked, peering toward the screen.

"I don't know. I was searching video from other sources to try to pick him up somewhere else. So far, no luck," Gaspar replied. "Most of the footage we have is black and white, so looking for one guy in the crowd isn't as easy."

As the video played, the crowd started to disperse. Flint, Drake, and Gaspar watched as they moved away from the dock and returned to their vehicles or wandered toward Old Town.

But the man in the blue shirt had disappeared. Seemingly swallowed up by Key West as if he'd never been there.

Flint leaned back. "Let's see that part again."

Gaspar reached for the controls. Before he could replay the sequence, the image froze. Then, without warning, the video feed died, leaving them staring at a blank screen.

"What happened?" Drake's question was tight with frustration.

Gaspar said, "Cut off. Squelched at the source."

"Tell me you kept a copy," Flint said wearily.

The silence that followed his comment was broken by the sound of Flint's chair scraping back as he stood. "We need that footage back."

"I'm working on it," Gaspar said, preoccupied with his equipment. "But if we were discovered, they'll lock me out. I'll have to figure out another way to retrieve whatever we can get."

"Can you do that?" Drake asked.

"Possibly. The 360 camera caught the blue shirted man because it's a unique angle. The other fixed cameras around the launch site wouldn't have captured his image," Gaspar said, preoccupied. "I'll have to find another source."

"Let's get the best image we can. Run him through facial recognition. Maybe figure out who he is and whether he's got any intel we can use," Flint said wearily.

"Yeah. Okay," Gaspar replied. "I'll let you know when I have something to report."

"Thanks," Flint said just before Gaspar hung up.

Drake had finished his beer and more than half the charcuterie. "What about that dinner you promised me?"

"I need to check something first," Flint said, returning to his laptop. He searched the reports Spencer Lyman provided until he found the video he was looking for.

"What's that?" Drake asked.

"One of these videos might have captured our blue shirt guy. I just want to take a quick look before we go," Flint replied, already focused on the image frames sliding across his screen.

"Okay, but let's walk to dinner. I can use the exercise," Drake said from his position behind Flint where his gaze, too, was glued to the laptop screen.

CHAPTER 18

FLINT AND DRAKE MADE their way from Truman Annex to Duval Street. The storm had passed, leaving no trace of its fury aside from the still soggy upholstery in the Jeep. The buzz of Key West's nightlife was just beginning to pick up.

The cruise ships had departed before sunset leaving a mix of mostly locals and a few tourists wandering the streets. A gentle breeze cooled the heat, and a few high pink and orange clouds dotted the sky. A small crowd had begun to gather for the daily Mallory Square sunset celebration.

Walking south on Duval Street, Drake spotted a quaint Italian restaurant. A welcoming glow spilled out onto the sidewalk through the open windows. The aroma of garlic and fresh bread wafted through, drawing him in by his nose. A hand-painted sign above the door read, "Café Paradiso."

"Looks promising," Flint commented as if he'd been asked before following Drake inside.

The interior was cozy. Rustic wooden tables, worn marble floors, and walls adorned with vintage Italian posters invited them to sit and linger. Soft chatter, clinking glasses, and a classic Italian song provided the soundtrack.

A hostess greeted them with a warm smile. "Table for two?"

"Yes, please," Drake replied. She led them to a table near the window, offering a view of the street.

They scanned the menu. Flint realized he was famished. The charcuterie had served only to whet his appetite.

Moments later, a waiter approached. He wore a crisp white shirt and black apron, but there was an edge of urgency in his demeanor that felt out of place.

"Good evening, gentlemen. My name is Dino and I'll be your server tonight. Can I start you off with something to drink and an appetizer?" he asked pleasantly enough.

Flint glanced up to order when he noticed the waiter subtly shaking his head.

Dino leaned in closer, speaking quietly. "There's a guy outside waiting for you—doesn't seem friendly."

Flint continued to scan the menu. "What kind of guy?"

Dino glanced around as if to be sure no one was paying undue attention. "Didn't give his name. Said he was an old friend. But something about him felt off."

"Bring him inside. We'll buy him a drink."

Dino shook his head. "He wouldn't be welcome here. Not that kind of guy. If I brought him in and he starts any trouble, I'd get fired."

Flint exchanged a quick look with Drake. He shrugged. "Okay. Where is he?"

"The kitchen leads to a back alley. You can slip out unnoticed," the waiter replied, pointing subtly toward the rear of the restaurant. "I can hold your table until you get back."

"We'd appreciate it," Drake said, a tight smile on his face as he tossed his napkin on the table and pushed his chair back.

Dino nodded, adding before he turned to leave, "Be careful. He seemed...determined."

Flint tossed enough cash on the table to cover a generous tip and led the way toward the back. Drake followed Flint into the kitchen.

His stomach growled as the smells and sounds of cooking enveloped them. The staff was harried and too busy. No one gave them a second glance as they navigated through the bustle toward the back door.

Flint pushed the door open and stepped into the dimly lit alley. Duval Street's noises faded to a dull throb coming from the music club next door.

He swiveled his neck to look in all directions. The narrow alley was paved with crushed shells. A huge rat scurried under one of the two large dumpsters. They had been carefully placed because the alley was too narrow to accommodate the size of the truck that would be needed to empty them.

Aside from the rat and a couple of yowling cats, Flint saw no one lingering outside the restaurant or anywhere else in the alley.

Just as they were about to give up and go back inside, he glimpsed a sudden movement in the shadows. A man stepped out of the dark standing in the weak glow of the corner streetlight.

Flint peered in his direction until his features came into sharper focus.

It was Trawler, looking worse than he had earlier in the day. His clothes were rumpled, his hair disheveled, and there was a desperation in his eyes that hadn't been there before.

"Trawler?" Drake's voice was a mixture of surprise and suspicion. "What the hell are you doing here?"

"I had to find you," he gasped, "before they did."

Trawler's gaze darted between Flint and Drake, his chest heaving as if he had been running.

"Who's 'they'?" Flint asked. "And why are you lurking in this alley?"

"I thought they were just financing the scientific expedition, but there's more to it." Trawler took a step closer and lowered his voice to a frantic whisper. "They know you're here. They saw me with you before."

Flint said, "Come inside where we can talk."

"Ward Lyman was my friend." Trawler's voice cracked with urgency.

"Okay, well, that's great," Drake replied. "What's the problem?"

"I'm being threatened." He paused, swallowing hard. "Because I found something."

Trawler reached into his pocket. He pulled out a small flash drive and offered it to Flint. "This has everything I've found so far. Documents, videos, emails. It's all there."

"What are you talking about?" Drake said, losing patience.

Trawler gave them both a startled stare. "The *Galeane II's* real purpose that day. What happened to Ward Lyman. What they're planning next."

Flint reached out to take the drive before Trawler could change his mind and slid it into his pocket. "Why are you giving this to us?"

Trawler swallowed hard. "Because maybe they won't kill me if I'm not the only one who knows."

"Yeah. Or maybe they'll just kill all three of us," Drake said dryly.

Before Trawler could say more, sudden noises from both ends of the alley caught Flint's attention. Two SUVs slammed to a stop, engines idling, sealing the alley.

A large man climbed out of the SUV blocking the north end. His heavy work boots landed hard on the shells and the sound echoed off the narrow walls as he approached.

Trawler's face went pale. "He's one of them."

Drake instinctively stepped between Trawler and the man while Flint scanned the area for an escape route. There was no way out. With both ends blocked, the alley was a dead-end trap.

Another man stepped out of the other SUV, sealing the south end of the alley. He walked toward them, and a dim light glinted off the handgun he held at his side.

Which meant they were both armed.

"Take Trawler inside. I'll be there shortly," Flint said quietly.

Drake grabbed Trawler's arm and propelled him through the back door of the restaurant into the kitchen. "Wait here. We'll join you when we're done."

CHAPTER 19

FLINT'S EYES NARROWED AS he assessed the double approach. Drake's stance shifted ever so slightly, bracing for the onslaught. They had been in tight spots before. They knew what to do.

"Looks like they want to dance," Drake quipped, tension lining his voice.

"Party crashers." Flint's focus was laser-sharp on the two armed men. The one closest to Flint's position was coming in fast.

Flint lunged toward the thug as he emerged from the shadows. Closing the distance before the man could fully raise his weapon, Flint's arm shot out, striking the thug's wrist with a hard chop.

His pistol clattered to the ground and slid from view.

Utilizing the momentum he'd created, Flint followed through with a swift uppercut to the man's jaw, sending the thug staggering backward into the wall, dazed and grunting with pain.

Drake engaged the second adversary like a seasoned street fighter. He feinted to the left, drawing the thug's attention, before sweeping the man's legs with a calculated kick to the side of his right knee.

As the thug fell, Drake's fist connected with a solid right hook to the side of his head. He was stunned before he hit the ground. Drake bent to collect his sidearm and tucked it into his belt.

Flint ducked a wild swing from the bigger man and countered with a hard elbow to the ribs. He felt bones crunch beneath the impact. The thug wheezed, folding over. Flint slammed a knee to his face that sent him to the ground.

Drake's opponent, still dazed from the initial blow, struggled to stand. But Drake was relentless, driving forward with a series of strikes, leaving the thug reeling.

A final, powerful shove sent the man sprawling. Drake gave him a swift kick to the ass that caused his face to land hard on the crushed shell pavement and mashed his nose to a bloody pulp.

He didn't get up again.

While Drake collected the second gun, Flint knelt beside both men, rummaging through pockets until he found ID on both and confirmed the thugs were down and out.

The names were unfamiliar and likely fake, but he stuffed the IDs in his pocket anyway.

Drake took a few photos of the unconscious men with his phone. "Gaspar might be able to ID these guys with facial recognition. They look like they've probably been in prison at least once."

"Yeah. Let's not wait for round two," Flint said, scanning the alley's shadows as he dusted himself off. "We'll get Trawler and go."

Flint opened the back screen door of the restaurant and stepped inside. Drake followed. A quick glance was all Flint needed to confirm that Trawler wasn't standing near the exit.

"Where is he?" Flint asked and Drake shook his head with a shrug. "Check the men's room. I'll talk to our waiter. Meet you out front."

Drake headed to the men's room as Flint hustled in the opposite direction. He scanned the main dining room, noticing three things instantly.

The table they'd left was now occupied by a young couple.

The waiter was gone.

Trawler was nowhere in sight.

Flint left through the front door and waited on the sidewalk.

"Where's Trawler?" Drake asked when he emerged a couple of minutes later.

"It was a setup. The whole thing." Flint shrugged and set off. Drake fell into step beside him. "The waiter's disappeared. Trawler's in the wind."

"Trawler set us up? Why?" Drake asked, bewildered.

"Great question. When we find him, we'll ask," Flint replied.

"Damn. I'm still hungry, too. Anywhere we can get a burger around here?" Drake wanted to know.

Up ahead on the right Sloppy Joe's neon sign beckoned. They navigated around the rowdy crowds drinking beer on the sidewalk out front. The notorious tourist hangout, long known to have been Ernest Hemingway's favorite, was wall to wall with patrons.

"This is nuts. Let's try the place next door," Flint said, leading Drake inside the marginally less busy establishment and found a table near the bar.

They ordered burgers and beers. The waitress dropped off two long neck bottles and promised the burgers would be coming right up.

"They knew we'd be in that alley," Flint said, taking a long drink.

Drake nodded, wary now.

Before they could delve deeper into their theories, Trawler slid into the seat across from Drake, long neck bottle in hand. His expression showed both relief and urgency.

"I had to bolt from the restaurant," Trawler began, setting his beer down. "Saw those guys in the alley. Knew they were after me."

"So you ditched the whole scene," Drake's tone was icy.

Trawler held up a hand, palm out. "I sent the waiter to call police. Figured they'd get there quick."

"No way you could have known the police would arrive before those two guys beat the crap out of us. Or worse," Flint said.

Trawler grimaced but had no defense to offer. Concentrating intently, he found a loose corner of the label on his beer bottle and peeled it off.

Flint leaned in. "Start talking, Trawler. What's going on? Why are these guys after you?"

Trawler took a sip of his beer and gave Flint a level gaze. "It's about Ward Lyman."

Flint's interest perked up. "What about him?"

"I was there. I saw what happened." Trawler's response was haltingly deliberate. "It's all on the flash drive I gave you. Everything you need to know."

The promise hung between them while the waitress, oblivious to the tension, approached with a tray of burgers. She delivered the food, including a burger for Trawler, and left with a smile and a promise to return soon.

Flint's focus was solely on Trawler while Drake fell on the food like a ravaging wolf.

"We can't discuss this here. Eat. Then we'll take this conversation somewhere private." Flint said before he started on the burger. "You can show us what's on that flash drive and answer our questions."

Trawler's eyebrows shot up and his nostrils flared as if the very invitation was too frightening to contemplate. But he nodded and ate the burger and nursed his beer and didn't bolt, all of which Flint took as a good sign.

"You've ducked out on us twice before. It pisses me off. Don't think you'll succeed the third time," Drake said between bites, glaring fiercely.

Trawler nodded again and seemed to settle uneasily into the idea.

But Flint didn't relax. He didn't trust Trawler, either. Not even remotely.

CHAPTER 20

Houston, Texas

SCARLETT HAD SENT THE burned calendar pages
to be meticulously examined by three of the best experts
in forensic document analysis. She wanted to ensure there
was absolutely no doubt about their authenticity and origin
before moving forward.

But that wasn't the only reason she was dragging her feet.
If the calendars proved what Wagner and Taylor claimed,
Scarlett would need to tell Flint. Which was something she
knew he didn't want to hear.

The experts would take time. Time that she filled with
work and Maddie to avoid Flint. But her thoughts returned
to him and his biological mother repeatedly.

Scarlett had confirmed that Marilyn Baker was actually
Flint's biological mother via sophisticated DNA analysis
when her body was exhumed by the state to relocate the
cemetery recently.

Against Flint's expressed wishes, Scarlett had sent one of the small bones to be tested. He was still angry with her about that. But Flint had been angry with her a million times before. He'd get over it.

DNA didn't tell Baker's whole story, which they had begun to piece together.

Tearfully, Baker had left Flint at a school for orphans when he was two months old. The same school where Scarlett met him eight years later.

Flint and Scarlett grew up together on that ranch in dusty West Texas, raised by the school's owner, Bette Maxwell.

Bette did a damned good job of being a substitute mom as far as both Scarlett and Flint were concerned. They thrived under Bette's care and never looked back.

Scarlett went off to fight for Uncle Sam at eighteen and Flint followed two years later. In all those years, neither Flint nor Scarlett had known that Marilyn Baker existed. Nor were they the least bit curious about their biological families.

Flint never spent any time wondering where he came from, or what if this, and what about that. He lived in the moment. Always had. He liked it that way.

And Scarlett? Perhaps she'd been curious about Flint's origins. Perhaps she'd dumped that curiosity into the mix of all things Flint.

But Scarlett had her own life to figure out. And Flint had no desire to chase down the rabbit hole of his conception. So they let it go. Simple as that. Which had worked well enough until they had stumbled upon the truth.

Marilyn Baker never came back to the orphanage to collect her son because she was murdered when Flint was only two years old.

The murder was a cold case that remained buried more than thirty years.

Flint had no memory of Baker at all, he said. Still, Scarlett imagined learning one's birth mother had been violently killed would deeply affect anyone.

Even Flint.

Whether he wanted to admit as much or not.

Which was why she felt conflicted about this potential new evidence from Naomi Wagner. On one hand, if Preston could be definitively ruled out as Baker's killer, investigators might try again to discover who really killed her and why.

On the other hand, dredging up the details could wound Flint in ways that might never heal. Scarlett would never be the instrument of such pain.

When the first expert reports came back on the calendars, Scarlett had carefully examined every word.

The analysis confirmed that both calendars were old enough to be genuine. The expert found no indication that the pages had been tampered with. The paper, ink, vinyl cover, handwriting, and other forensic details were consistent with Taylor's story but inconclusive.

The entries that directly contradicted the prosecution's timeline against Preston for the Pentwater murder appeared genuine and valid.

The entries made during the time frame of Marilyn Baker's murder four years before also seemed legitimate.

Beyond that, the experts found no obvious signs of tampering. No reason to believe the calendars were fake, either.

But Scarlett felt no sense of triumph. Her stomach knotted with worry over what Flint's reaction would be. She hadn't mentioned anything to him yet because she still didn't know what to say.

She'd hoped the Preston calendars would prove to be a dead end. Which would have justified never discussing the matter with Flint at all.

Now that one expert had weighed in, even though she had two more lined up to confirm, she couldn't put Flint off any longer.

Before she gave the results of any kind to Wagner, and Wagner made a public spectacle of Marilyn Baker, Flint deserved a heads-up and a chance to make that decision himself.

She fortified her courage with strong black coffee, squared her shoulders, inhaled deeply, and made the call. The phone rang a dozen times and Flint's voicemail finally picked up.

He could be home. He could be screening his calls. Or he might be on the other side of the world. But usually, he let her know if he planned to be gone for a few days.

He might call right back.

Scarlett cleared her throat before leaving her message. "We need to meet. In person. It's important. Call me."

Scarlett hung up and waited, toe tapping on the carpet.

Wagner's podcast had the potential to upend everything surrounding the decades-old mystery of Marilyn Baker's death.

Mentally, Flint was harder than granite in every conceivable way. He was strong enough to handle whatever came.

But some stones should stay unturned, leaving the crawling creatures to hide under the rocks.

Naomi Wagner should know that by now.

So should Scarlett. What the hell was she thinking?

CHAPTER 21

Kansas City, Missouri

BOLDO STEPPED OUT OF the sleek black sedan onto the Lyman Estate's snow-white concrete driveway. His glossy leather shoes landed on the hard surface breaking the tranquil silence as he approached the house.

The air was crisp and cool, carrying with it the faint scent of wood smoke and the earthy aroma of the gardens. The sprawling grounds, bordered by dense woods, seemed too peaceful, too removed from the bustling world beyond its borders.

Which, of course, was exactly the effect Lyman's award-winning architects had intended to create.

Spencer Lyman stood waiting on the broad, sweeping porch. He stood tall and straight. The years had etched lines into his face and silvered his hair, but his posture reflected a man who had spent his lifetime commanding industries and influencing markets.

His sharp blue eyes, still bright and keen, watched Boldo's approach with a mixture of familiarity and wariness.

"Spencer," Boldo called out as he climbed the steps, his voice carrying a well-practiced warmth. "It's good to see you."

"Tony," the old man replied, voice neutral. "Seeing you is like watching your father, alive again."

They shook hands, grips firm and unyielding. Each man measured the other as experienced players in a game neither wanted to quit.

Boldo felt the strength in Lyman's grasp. Calluses on his palms reflected a life spent in the trenches of a rough business. Calluses Boldo did not now and never would have.

"Shall we?" Lyman gestured toward the open door, politely.

Boldo nodded, and the two men stepped into the grand foyer of the Lyman mansion.

The interior of the house was a testament to old wealth, the kind that whispered power and influence rather than shouting it. Boldo's nose appreciated the scent of polished wood, antique books, and the faint, lingering traces of expensive cigars.

They walked through the hall, footsteps loud on the designer's concrete floors, and entered Lyman's study, a room that seemed to breathe history from every corner.

The walls were lined with bookshelves that reached from floor to ceiling, filled with leather-bound volumes and precious first editions. A massive mahogany desk dominated one end of the room.

The desk was adorned with neatly stacked papers and a silver-framed photograph of a young man bearing a striking resemblance to Spencer Lyman. His missing grandson, Ward.

"Drink?" Spencer offered, moving to an antique cabinet that predated them both. The soft clink of crystal underscored his words.

"Bourbon, if you have it," Boldo replied, sinking into one of the plush leather armchairs that flanked the stone fireplace. The chair seemed to embrace him as the leather creaked and adjusted to his weight.

"This room looks exactly as I remember it when I was ten years old," Boldo said with a grin.

Lyman poured two generous measures of amber liquid into cut-crystal tumblers. He dropped a single ice cube into each glass with two loud clinks. He handed one to Boldo and settled into the chair across from him.

"That's probably the time you and my son broke in here without permission," Lyman replied without humor.

"And got a good thrashing for it, too," Boldo said with a smile. "I often wonder what kind of boss Jonathan would have been. He was what, twenty-seven when he died in that boating accident? Such a long time ago."

Lyman pursed his lips but made no reply.

Boldo took a moment to appreciate the aroma of the bourbon, the rich scent of charred oak and caramel teasing his nostrils. He swirled the liquid in the glass, watching as the firelight caught in its depths, before taking a slow, appreciative sip. The bourbon was smooth and full-bodied, with a subtle sweetness that gave way to a warm, lingering finish.

"I'll get straight to it," Boldo began, setting his glass down on the low table that separated them. "I'm here about your company, Spencer. You know the position you're in. I'd like to help."

Lyman's hand tightened almost imperceptibly around his glass, but his gaze remained steady, unwavering.

"I know what you and others think my position is," he said, his voice level. "But I assure you, Lyman Enterprises is as strong as ever."

Boldo leaned forward, elbows resting on his knees, hands clasped loosely. "It's not just what I think. It's the reality of the market. Without a clear line of succession, the sharks are circling. You need a plan."

"My plan," Lyman said, his tone firm and final, "is to find Ward. He inherits my stock position and total control, as you well know."

"That isn't going to happen." Boldo's controlled, measured words belied frustration barely held in check. "Ward's been gone for more than two years. He died with the others in that submersible implosion. He's not coming back. You should prepare for that."

Lyman set his glass down with a decisive clink, his jaw tightening. "I'll face that possibility when, and only when, I have a body to bury. Until then, my grandson is out there, and I intend to find him."

"Look, Spencer, you and my father were more than just colleagues. You were brothers in all but blood. I have a deep respect for what you've built here, for the legacy of the Lyman name. I don't want to see it dismantled by corporate vultures." Boldo spread his hands, a gesture of conciliation. "Let me help. Let me take over the reins, keep the company in the family, so to speak."

"It's a generous offer. I appreciate the sentiment. But Lyman Enterprises isn't just a business to me. It's a legacy, yes, but it's my legacy. My life's work." Lyman's eyes narrowed, a flash of steel behind the blue. "I'm not ready to let it go based on nothing but hypotheticals and what-ifs."

"This isn't about sentiment, Spencer. It's about survival." Boldo's expression hardened. "The business world hates uncertainty. If you won't sell, at least consider a partnership. Let me help steer the ship until Ward is found, one way or the other."

Lyman set his glass down and pushed himself to his feet. He walked to the large window that overlooked the grounds, his hands clasped behind his back.

Boldo joined him, glancing briefly at long shadows across the lawn and trees swaying gently in the evening breeze. When he owned Lyman Enterprises, maybe he'd move his wife and kids out here.

"A partnership with you means releasing control. Putting my trust, and every employee at Lyman Enterprises, in your hands. You know I can't do that." Lyman's tone left no room for argument.

Boldo tried again anyway. "What I know is that you need to protect what you've built. What your father built, and his father before him. I can help you do that. I want to do that. My father would want me to do that."

Lyman turned from the window, his gaze finding Boldo's. The weight of years, of a lifetime of decisions and responsibilities, seemed to settle on his shoulders.

"I appreciate what you're trying to do, Tony. Truly. But I'm protecting my legacy and my grandson's birthright by finding him." Lyman's tone hardened. "That's my final word on the matter."

Boldo held the old man's gaze for a long moment, a silent battle of wills playing out between them. Finally, he nodded, a slow, deliberate motion that conveyed understanding, not agreement.

"I hope you find him, Spencer. For your sake, and for the sake of everything you've built," Boldo said. "Because if you don't, Lyman Enterprises will die with you."

Lyman replied, "I'll see you out."

The two men walked back to the foyer in silence. At the door, they shook hands once more.

"Thank you for the drink," Boldo said, his voice subdued. "And for hearing me out. If you change your mind, you know where to find me."

"Safe travels back to the city," Lyman replied, his own voice heavy with the unspoken. "Give my regards to your family."

Boldo stepped out into the chilly evening. He paused on the top step, turning back to look at the old man, his face half in shadow.

"The wolves are at the door, Spencer. Let someone help you fight them off. Before it's too late."

With that, he descended the steps and climbed into the waiting car. The engine purred to life, and the sedan pulled away.

Boldo glanced in the side view mirror. Lyman stood on the porch, watching the car.

"Damned old fool," he muttered under his breath.

Lyman Enterprises was meant to die, along with every Lyman still alive. Boldo would make sure of that.

As the sedan wound its way back toward the city, Boldo found his thoughts drifting to the past.

Big Tony Boldo and Spencer Lyman had been fast friends once. Back when they were young men just starting to make their way in Kansas City. Two ambitious, driven boys who recognized a kindred spirit in each other. They'd been inseparable in those days, as had their fathers before them.

But then, as so often happens, a woman came between them.

Mae, with her quick wit, sharp mind, and bewitching smile, had captured the hearts of both men.

For a time, it seemed that their friendship would weather the test, that they would find a way to remain close despite their shared desire for Mae.

In the end, Mae chose Spencer, and the betrayal cut Big Tony to the core. He accused Spencer of stealing her away. No matter how much Spencer protested, no matter how much Mae insisted that her choice had been hers and hers alone, Big Tony could not, would not, forgive.

From that day forward, the two men were rivals. Their once-unbreakable bond was shattered. They went their separate ways, each building his own empire, each striving to outdo the other in wealth, influence, and power.

Years later, the sins of the fathers had come to rest on the shoulders of their children. Boldo had grown up in the shadow of Big Tony's bitterness and steeped in the stories of Spencer Lyman's treachery. Big Tony's resentment consumed him until there was nothing left but unfettered grudges.

When Big Tony died, Boldo inherited the grudge. He carried the weight of that old betrayal as if it were his own, nurturing it, feeding it, letting it grow and fester in the depths of his heart.

And Boldo was a patient man. His patience had paid off.

Finally, Spencer Lyman was vulnerable, and Lyman Enterprises hung in the balance.

Boldo had the chance to settle old scores and claim victory in a war that had begun before he was born.

This was personal. Making the Lymans pay for Spencer Lyman's sins and proving Boldo was the better man.

He would have Lyman Enterprises, one way or another. He would see Spencer Lyman brought to his knees, forced to confront the consequences of his actions.

Spencer Lyman thought he could protect his legacy by finding his wayward grandson.

But Boldo knew the only way to protect his legacy was to destroy anyone who dared to threaten it.

CHAPTER 22

Key West, Florida

THEY LEFT SLOPPY JOE'S and headed back toward the Truman Annex condos. Drake walked ahead, threading through the crowd and occasionally glancing back at Trawler with a mixture of suspicion and annoyance.

Flint followed, walking beside Trawler, keeping a watchful eye and ready for sudden movements or attempts to bolt.

Key West at night was wilder and crazier than it was in daylight, if that was possible. They passed a few bars, each with live music and drunks spilling onto the streets. A man dressed like Darth Vader playing a banjo and a pit bull wearing sunglasses were only two of the strange sights Flint noticed.

As they entered the residential area, Duval Street's rowdy crowds had thinned to small groups walking to and from the condos. When they reached their rental, Flint signaled Trawler to wait while he climbed the front steps to the entrance.

He unlocked the door, then cleared the hallway and the main living area. Drake followed Flint and Trawler inside, took a final look around to be sure they weren't followed, then closed and locked the door. Drake hustled up the stairs to clear the second floor while Flint and Trawler settled into the situation.

"Alright, Trawler, start talking," Flint said when Drake came back signaling all clear. Flint crossed his arms and pinned Trawler with a stern gaze. "What's on that flash drive you gave me and why are those thugs after you?"

Trawler fidgeted, running a hand through his tousled hair. "It's...it's about Ward Lyman. What really happened to him."

"We know what happened to him. He was on that submersible and when it imploded, he died. Along with the other passengers," Drake said, dismissing Trawler's claims.

Trawler shook his head. "That's what people think. But they found the other bodies and not Ward's. They looked for weeks and never found Ward, did they?"

Flint frowned toward Drake and leaned forward, his eyes narrowing. "We're listening."

Trawler took a deep breath and began. "I was there. That night at the docks. I witnessed the whole thing."

Flint gave him a curt nod. "Go on."

"Ward was meeting with some...unsavory characters. Men I recognized from my time working security details for some of the local bigwigs." Trawler paused, taking a sip of water. "They weren't happy with Ward. Accused him of skimming funds, of trying to cut them out of some big deal they'd cooked up."

"That's crazy. Ward Lyman is the last man on the planet who might need to steal cash. He's rich enough to buy his own country," Drake scoffed.

"Seems like that, but he was in trouble with those guys, and they're loan sharks," Trawler replied. "Makes sense their argument would be about money."

"How'd Lyman react?" Flint asked, to keep the story moving.

Trawler shook his head. "Not well. Things got heated. They argued, but I couldn't hear what they were saying. Then..." He trailed off and he swallowed like his mouth had dried up.

Flint said, "Then what, Trawler? What happened?"

"One of them pulled a gun. Ward tried to run, but he didn't make it far." Trawler's voice was barely above a whisper. "They shot him, right there on the docks. Left him to bleed out."

"You're saying Lyman never got on that submersible in the first place?" Drake flashed a surprised glance toward Flint. "Anybody who can confirm that? Because there are dozens of people who say they saw him go aboard."

"I...I recorded it all. On my phone." Trawler gulped, mouth opening and closing like a fish. "It's all there. On the flash drive I gave you. The confrontation, the shooting, everything."

Drake let out a low whistle.

Flint nodded. "And that's why you've been running. Because they were coming for you."

Trawler replied, his eyes wide with fear, "I didn't know what else to do. You've got the evidence now. Maybe they'll leave me alone."

Not likely. Trawler no longer possessed the flash drive, but if what he said was true, he'd witnessed a murder. He'd never be out of trouble until the killers were found and handled.

Flint opened his laptop and reached into his pocket for Trawler's flash drive. "Let's take a look at this. Then we'll figure out what to do."

Trawler's eyes widened. "You mean to protect me?"

Flint inserted the drive and pressed the play button.

The video started. Dimly lit footage showed the area across from the submersible launch site. A man who could be seen walking along the pier, meeting with a group of rough-looking men.

"That's them," Trawler murmured, gaze glued to the screen, pointed. "See the guy in the blue shirt? That's Ward Lyman."

"Who are the others?" Flint asked. At least the blue-shirted guy Gaspar saw on the hacked video was now identified. Seemed like Ward Lyman didn't board the submersible at all.

"Not sure," Trawler replied.

The conversation on the video quickly escalated. Lyman gestured frantically as the other men crowded in, voices raised.

Then one of the men pulled a gun and Lyman turned to run.

Trawler's breath turned quick and shallow as one of the men fired multiple shots. Lyman stumbled and fell, but the men quickly dragged his body away from the camera's view.

"They didn't leave him there," Drake murmured, his brow furrowed. "They took the body."

"To cover their tracks," Flint said grimly. "Where did they take him?"

Trawler's face was pale. He stumbled over his next words. "I didn't see. I still hear the gunshots in my nightmares."

"Yeah, that kind of thing hangs with you for a long time," Drake said. "But you'll get past it."

Trawler nodded shakily. "What do we do now?"

"There's an extra room upstairs," Flint replied, gesturing in that direction while ignoring Drake's astonished expression. "Go on up and get some sleep. We'll figure out the rest in the morning."

"Hang on," Drake said striding toward Trawler. "Gimme your phone and your weapons."

"I don't have any weapons. I'm a nerd, not a brawler." Trawler said as he reached into his pocket for his cell phone and handed it over.

Flint and Drake watched as Trawler climbed the stairs. When he was out of hearing range, Drake said, "You're sure he won't call half a dozen buddies to kill us in our sleep?"

"If we're lucky, he'll do exactly that. Which is why we're going to watch him," Flint grinned. "You've got the first shift. I'll send this off to Gaspar. Then I need to call Scarlett."

"What does she want?" Drake asked. He adored Scarlett and her daughter, but he'd had about enough of puppy sitting for a while.

Flint grinned again. "I'll tell her you're free this weekend."

Drake gave him a rude gesture and climbed the stairs to deal with Trawler.

Still grinning, Flint pressed the number one button on his speed dial. Scarlett had occupied that position on his cell phone forever. She was his family. The most constant relationship in his world since he was eight years old.

Always had been.

Probably always would be, given the state of his love life.

When she answered, he said, "Got your message. What's up?"

Instead of babbling about the weather or Whiskers or Maddy, she replied, "It's your mother. Marilyn Baker."

After a long, long pause Flint responded, his tone subdued. "I told you to let that go."

"I know. I heard you. I tried. But—"

"But you couldn't just leave it alone. You always think you know best. It's my history, Scarlett. Not yours." He knew his hard tone and harsh words cut through Scarlett like a hot sword. He'd have softened his approach if she were in the room, strictly for self-preservation. "I'll chase all that down when I'm good and damned ready."

She spent about a nanosecond feeling chastised, or whatever, and then she got her back up. "Yeah, well, maybe I should have just left your ass hanging out there for Naomi Wagner to destroy, then. Crazy me. I thought you'd want to get ahead of this thing and keep it quiet."

"Naomi Wagner? The true crime podcaster?" Flint replied, bewildered. "What's she got to do with anything?"

"You've heard of her? I hadn't," Scarlett replied, working up a good head of steam. "Not until she busted into Maddie's soccer game with this wild story."

Flint was wary now. "How does Wagner know Baker was my mother?"

"I don't think she does. In fact, I don't think she knows you exist." Scarlett replied, still miffed. "Lucky you."

Flint paused to take that in, shaking his head as if to clear enough space for Naomi Wagner. "Okay, then why does she want to find Marilyn Baker's killer?"

"Because it gets millions of views, or whatever podcasters care about," Scarlett said as she blew a frustrated breath through the air. "Wagner thinks James Preston didn't kill Baker. Or June Pentwater, for that matter. She's trying to exonerate him. Posthumously. For ratings, I guess. Or whatever motivates her."

Flint went quiet for a few seconds, letting it all sink in. "And, let me guess. You found something that will help her exonerate Preston?"

"Maybe," Scarlett hedged. "But we should discuss this face-to-face before Wagner finds out about it."

Another pause, longer this time. Finally, he swore and then said, "Okay. Come over when I get home. We'll figure it out. Can you wait that long?"

"When will you be back?"

"Not sure yet. Marilyn Baker's been dead for thirty-two years. She can wait a bit longer. I'll let you know when I get to Houston," Flint replied and finished off with "Give my love to Maddy."

"Don't wait too long. Naomi Wagner doesn't strike me as a woman with loads of patience," Scarlett said before she hung up.

The last thing Flint wanted or needed was to be the subject of any sort of exposé or crusade or whatever Wagner thought she was doing. Naomi Wagner was well known as a pit bull. Once she locked her sharp teeth into a story, she'd never back down.

And Scarlett. What was she thinking?

Probably that she could head off trouble if she could redirect Wagner. Which was probably true.

But this was Flint's personal business. He should be the one to handle it.

He was sure Scarlett would agree with that, actually. She had plenty of work to do already.

CHAPTER 23

FLINT HAD PUT SCARLETT'S call out of his mind and began to focus on the Lyman case again when Drake returned to the room. "Trawler's all set. What did Gaspar say?"

"Dunno. Calling him now," Flint replied and picked up the phone to place the call. Gaspar didn't pick up. Flint left a message. "He'll call back shortly. He always does."

Drake snagged a couple of beers from the fridge and brought them to the sofa. He handed one to Flint and they settled in to wait.

"Gaspar's quite a catch for Scarlett Investigations," Drake said after he swallowed the first mouthful. "She got lucky hiring him. He's one of a kind."

Flint nodded. "Yeah, you could say that. I wasn't sold on the idea when it first came up. But it's working out better than expected."

Drake cocked his head. "Why didn't you want her to hire Gaspar? He's got solid credentials, and he fills a big hole in her staff."

"Because when something, or someone, seems too good to be true, he usually is," Flint replied. "Gaspar could have stayed on the FBI payroll indefinitely. So why was he on the job market at all?"

Drake nodded. "I see your point. What's the answer?"

"He wasn't. On the market, that is. Scarlett hired him away from the FBI." Flint shrugged. Gaspar's all-purpose gesture. Could mean anything.

"Hard to believe," Drake said. "Guy like that seems like a lifer to me."

"Yeah. Me, too," Flint said as his cell phone rang and he picked up the call. "Hey, Gaspar. Thanks for calling me back."

"Sorry for the delay. I've got your new video pulled up here. Tell me what I'm looking at," Gaspar said, sounding preoccupied.

"We were hoping you could tell us. A witness says that video recorded Ward Lyman's murder in real time," Flint said, taking another sip of his beer.

"And you think otherwise?" Gaspar asked, clacking the keyboard.

"I've read hundreds of pages of reports and watched hours of video from a variety of sources. I never saw anything like this in the materials we gathered," Flint explained. "And it's not likely that Trawler was simply in the right place at the right time."

"Stranger things have happened," Drake replied.

"So the first question is whether it's legitimate," Gaspar said, still clacking the keys, working on something.

"Let's assume it is. For now. What can you do with it to improve the images? I'd really like to know whether that guy is Ward Lyman before I take this much further," Flint said.

"I tried to work with that footage. Tried improving the images, the sound, the lighting. No go. Too far away, too dark, too much interference," Gaspar said. "The best I can do is confirm the victim is a man. Average height and weight. Brown hair."

"All of which fits Ward Lyman, I guess," Flint agreed.

"And a million other guys," Drake replied dryly on his way to the fridge for a refill.

"Right. Which is why I've been looking for a better video showing that same location at the right time," Gaspar said, sounding pleased with himself. "I got lucky. I can show you on your television screen. Ready?"

The television seemed to come to life on its own. A few moments later, Gaspar's face was on the screen and his voice came through the speakers. "Hang up the phone to avoid feedback and sound distortion. That whole place is wired. I can hear you just fine."

Flint disconnected the cell and faced the television with a scowl. "What do you mean the whole place is wired? We're being watched?"

"You should always assume you're being watched. I've told you that before. Every inch of this country is under some kind of surveillance by someone every minute of every day," Gaspar said. "That's the good news and the bad news. Unless you know what you're looking for, finding a random event is worse than looking for a needle in a stack of needles."

Drake laughed. Flint didn't.

"Who is watching us?" Flint demanded to know.

"Did you miss your nap today?" Gaspar teased. "For a man of the world, you're very grumpy."

Drake laughed again, and Flint shrugged.

"Can you block the surveillance inside this condo, or do we need to find another home base?" Flint asked easily.

"Sure. If you want whoever is watching you to know you know, I can block it," Gaspar replied. "Be prepared. They might come looking for you if they can't watch from afar."

"Everybody can mind their own damned business," Flint said. "Can you run a constant loop showing nothing but the empty, silent condo. If they don't like being shut out, they can come here and tell me in person."

"Roger that." Gaspar chuckled as he flipped a couple of switches to make the adjustment. Then he displayed Trawler's video on the television screen. "Here we go. This is your witness's video. The picture quality won't be great. But it should be good enough."

Gaspar played the Trawler video first. Flint leaned forward as if being closer to the screen would make the images clearer. Drake, arms crossed, leaned against the wall, his jaw set tight, eyes fixed on the screen.

The grainy footage flickered with the shadows of the late evening. Pale streetlights illuminated the ground beneath them and not much else on the side of the inlet across from the docks where the submersible was undergoing final prep for launch.

The video was color, but it looked like black and gray.

Flint heard the celebrating spectators in the background. Some wag had queued up "Yellow Submarine," an old Beatles song, and turned the volume up loud enough to cover other sounds.

After the first run-through, Flint said, "Okay, take us through what we've got here."

"Copy that," Gaspar's voice crackled through the television speakers. "First off, this video from Trawler is not great, but it's the clearest shot of the murder scene. See here?"

The footage resumed. A man ran into the frame, panic evident in his stumbling gait. Two older, heavier men pursued him.

Gaspar paused the video on the face of a man who looked vaguely familiar, the one Trawler said was Ward Lyman.

Drake stepped forward, squinting at the screen. "That could be him. I've seen videos from Lyman's stint on the marathon running circuit while he was in college. His lanky style is distinctive."

"I'll check those old videos. See if I can definitely match it," Gaspar replied, as the video continued.

The scene unfolded with brutal swiftness. The runner was rapidly putting distance behind him.

One of the pursuers, a broad-shouldered brute with a bald head, stopped chasing, pulled out a gun, and fired. Flint saw the muzzle flash, even if the sound was muffled.

The runner fell instantly, crumpling onto the cold ground. He didn't move.

The two thugs holstered their weapons and hustled up to the body. Because of the angle, both men turned to face Trawler's camera.

"Pause it, Gaspar," Flint said, his voice low. The screen froze. "That's our money shot. Those two, we need names. Better headshots, too, if we can find them."

"It's likely they've got mug shots somewhere. I'm on it." The clacking keystrokes echoed through the speakers as Gaspar worked to start the facial recognition software. "Now, here's where it gets interesting. I pulled footage from two other cameras."

The screen switched to show a different angle. This time, they saw the submersible in the background, its hatch open, light spilling out onto the dock. The crew was boarding. Five men approached the vessel's entrance, all carrying gear, moving steadily forward.

"Count 'em. Five," Gaspar pointed out as they walked single file along the dock. "And if we enhance this right here..."

The image zoomed in on one of the men. Even with the grainy resolution, the man's general resemblance to Lyman was obvious. Medium height, medium build, wearing a Kansas City Royals baseball cap.

Drake whistled softly. "So, he gets on the submersible?"

"All five are wearing gray jumpsuits, so it's tough to make a positive ID from this distance," Flint said. "But Lyman Enterprises is big in Kansas City. Ward Lyman played baseball in high school and college. If that's not Lyman boarding with the others, someone definitely wanted spectators to believe it was."

"Looks that way," Gaspar agreed. "Which means the one who got on the submersible could have been a decoy and the guy they shot and dragged away in the first video could be Lyman. Or not."

"Have you matched either of these guys to the man wearing the blue shirt that you identified earlier?" Flint asked.

"Hard to say for sure, but I'd bet fifty bucks they're one and the same," Gaspar replied. "Position, silhouette, clothing are basically the same. I can't find anyone else hanging around that's a better match."

Flint nodded. "Can you display both videos side-by-side?"

"Yep. Hang on," Gaspar replied. A moment later, both videos played.

Flint's gaze darted between the two, trying to catch every detail.

On one side, the two thugs dragged the lifeless body out of frame. On the other, Lyman, or someone who looked very much like him, boarded the submersible with the four crew members.

"I'm still running facial recognition on the thugs now," Gaspar said. "We may get more than one hit. But it's taking longer than expected."

"Did you find any other video of the scene at the time the submersible was boarding? Could the blue-shirted man have blended into another crowd?" Flint asked as he stood to get a different view of the television screen.

"There's several CCTV cameras around the launch site. There were also spectator videos uploaded to the cloud," Gaspar replied. "I haven't had a chance to go through it all yet."

"And government satellites? There should be more than one with a clear view of that area," Flint suggested, standing to stretch. "I checked the official report and the earlier private investigator reports Spencer Lyman gave me. But no mention of government satellite footage."

"This is a mess," Drake muttered, rubbing his temples. "If that's not Lyman they killed, who is it? And why kill him? And who got onto the submersible if it wasn't Ward Lyman?"

Gaspar's voice broke through. "Our bald friend is one Mickey 'The Mallet' Malone. Known enforcer for the Corsaro family."

"And the other?" Flint asked.

"Still working on it," Gaspar replied. "But with The Mallet involved, this is mob stuff. No wonder Lyman was running away from those thugs."

The screen now showed detailed files on Malone, including a rap sheet that read like a menu of mayhem. Charges for extortion, armed robbery, assault, and murder had been dropped in more than one jurisdiction. Witnesses died or changed their testimony. Evidence disappeared.

"So Malone is an enforcer for the Corsaros, but he's never been tried or convicted?" Drake said, as if he were actually surprised.

"Okay, let's theorize," Flint said, walking to the sink to dump the now warm beer and grab a bottle of water from the fridge. "Lyman's involved in something shady enough to get the Corsaros' attention. He gets on that submersible because he thinks they can't reach him there, at least for a while."

"Or he tries to duck out." Drake said. "Could be he was forced. Or it's a setup. Maybe he wasn't running from them. Maybe he was running to them."

"That still doesn't explain who the guy on the submersible was, or why they wanted to kill either of the two." Flint paced now, considering possible scenarios.

"Witness? Mistaken identity?" Drake offered but shook his head as if he knew those ideas were weak.

Gaspar said over the speaker, "Got the other thug. Vincent 'Eyebrow' D'Abruzzo. Gave him the nickname because he's got one bushy eyebrow that goes straight across his face. Another Corsaro goon who's no stranger to law enforcement."

"All right," Flint said, taking a deep breath. "We've got names, we've got a possible motive. What we need now is to track down where that body went."

"And ask ourselves why Lyman would board the submersible if he knew what was waiting for him when he got back," Drake added. "I mean, when he returned and climbed out of that thing, it would be fairly simple for the Corsaros to snatch him up."

"True dat," Gaspar said. "And there's something else. The submersible's registered to a shell company, which eventually, if you know where to look, loops back to the Corsaros."

"So, the circle closes," Flint mused. "Lyman, the Corsaros, a murder, and a destroyed sub that killed Lyman. Or whoever impersonated him."

"But where does all that lead?" Drake asked, his brow furrowed in thought. "Is Ward Lyman dead or not? And if he's dead, where's his body?"

"The Corsaros have their fingers in all sorts of pies. One is concrete manufacturing and sales. They're Lyman Enterprises' competitors. Long time rivals," Flint said sourly. "Ward Lyman could be buried in any concrete foundation in the country."

CHAPTER 24

THE FIRST SHARP BLAST of a bullet shattering the wall of windows came like an abrupt clap of thunder in an otherwise silent night.

Instantaneously, Flint's heart jolted, and he dove behind the couch, feeling the spray of glass shards cascading over his back as more bullets peppered the room.

The cold floor beneath him seemed to pulsate with each gunshot, sending vibrations up his arms as he ducked his head for cover.

"Drake!" he shouted, but his voice barely rose over the racket of splintering wood and breaking glass.

"Here," came Drake's muffled grunt from somewhere behind the kitchen counter followed by the deep thud of another bullet embedding itself into the decorative plaster.

"Sniper," Flint hissed, inching toward the relative safety of a thick, structural column.

"Where is he?" Drake asked, sticking his head out briefly and ducking back when the shooter sent another round.

Flint risked a glance and saw the flutter of a dark curtain in a second-story window of the abandoned condo across the street. "Second floor, middle window. He's looking down on us."

Drake crawled across the floor, a shadow against the debris, to join Flint. His face was set, eyes sharp and calculating. "All these windows. We're sitting ducks here."

Flint said, "Can we get these lights off?"

As soon as he uttered the words, the lights extinguished inside the safe house as if a central circuit breaker had been flipped.

"What the hell?" Drake asked with genuine surprise.

"Thanks, Gaspar," Flint said into the darkness as he scanned the room, his gaze darting from one potential cover to another. Gaspar was worth his weight in gold, for sure.

Flint settled on the large mirror mounted on the wall adjacent to them. "I've got an idea, but it's risky."

"Riskier than staying here?" Drake retorted dryly, his gaze following Flint's to the mirror.

Quickly, Flint outlined his plan. "We use the mirror to draw his fire. While he's focused on that, one of us moves out the back door, circles around behind him."

"Makes sense," Drake nodded, his jaw tightening. "I'll draw the fire. You move."

"No, I'll do it. You're quieter and quicker on your feet." Flint's decision was firm as he pulled the mirror from the wall. The frame snapped with a harsh, grating sound, echoing ominously in the gunfire-punctuated silence.

"Got it," Drake replied without argument and checked his weapon as he positioned himself by the back door. "On your go."

Flint gripped the mirror, his palms sweating as he raised it slowly, using the dim light from the streetlamps to create a moving reflection that might mimic a person shifting position.

A shot exploded, shattering the mirror in Flint's grip.

He barked, "Now!"

Drake bolted, disappearing into the shadowy depths of lush foliage outside as another bullet whizzed past, burying itself with a thud in the door.

Left alone, Flint noticed the acrid smell of gunpowder and the faint, underlying odor of damp tropical earth that wafted in through the broken window. He crawled to the edge, peering out to keep tabs on the sniper's position.

The minutes stretched taut, every second a drawn-out heartbeat as Flint waited. The sporadic gunfire stopped as suddenly as it had erupted, plunging the night into a tense silence that was worse than the noise.

Flint's ears rang in the quiet, straining for any sound that might signal what was happening across the street.

His phone vibrated against his thigh, startling him. It was Gaspar. Flint's fingers fumbled to answer, pressing the phone against his ear. "Not a great time."

"I know, but you need to hear this," Gaspar insisted urgently. "That sniper. I can see him. It's Trawler."

A cold shiver ran down Flint's spine. "Trawler? Are you sure?"

"Positive," Gaspar confirmed. "He slipped out earlier when we thought you were protecting him from local muscle. You were right to be wary of him. He's been leading you into a trap."

"Makes no sense. He could have tried to kill us a dozen times already," Flint said. "And he didn't have a weapon on him. We checked."

"Which means he had to get to the weapon," Gaspar said. "How'd the rifle get there?"

Flint shrugged. "Trawler left it there. Or someone else did."

Another bullet slammed into the column near Flint's head. Splinters of wood and plaster peppered his face. He dropped the phone, cursing under his breath.

The shooter had shifted position. He was now firing from a window closer to the ground. Which gave him a better angle.

Flint couldn't wait for Drake. He had to move. Clutching his gun, he prepared to make a break for the back door. The sharp, lingering scent of his own sweat mixed with the dusty, earthy air of the besieged condo.

Before he had the chance to get out, Drake darted through the door. Blood was smeared across his brow, and he looked like he'd been fighting an entire battalion, but he was dragging a semi-conscious Trawler by the collar.

"Got him," Drake gasped, shoving Trawler onto the floor. "Caught him trying to start a car down the block. Had to double back when he slipped past me."

Flint nodded, relief momentarily washing over him before the gravity of their situation resettled in his gut. "Good work. We need to get out now. He's working with those guys who ambushed us in the alley. They'll come looking for him."

They quickly cuffed Trawler with a zip tie, dragging him toward the exit.

Flint glanced at Drake, tension etched deep in both their faces. "Get him into the Jeep. Stuff him into the back footwell to keep him out of sight if you can. Find a place to lay low until I call you."

Drake asked, "What are we going to do with him?"

"Take him with us," Flint replied. "He's not leaving our sight until we get the full story."

Drake stared at the condo. "What about this place? People will notice the damage at some point."

"I'll handle that, too. Hang on," Flint said on his way to the bedrooms to collect their gear. He returned and dumped the gear into the Jeep. "Get going before Trawler's backup arrives."

Drake shifted the Jeep into gear and headed out. Flint watched the taillights until Drake turned the first corner.

Then he pulled the new burner phone he'd removed from his bag. He punched in a number he'd memorized long ago while he walked deeper into Truman Annex. He slid into a stand of trees for cover from visual surveillance.

When his contact picked up, he said, "Sorry about your safe house. It wasn't quite as safe as you thought."

The man on the other end chuckled. "I'd take a look, but you blocked my security system."

"Yeah. In retrospect, that might not have been a smart move," Flint grinned. "Anyway, the neighbors will notice the damage as soon as day breaks."

"No problem. I'll send over a termite tenting company. They'll get the tents up before dawn. We'll repair the damage. It'll be good as new," the man said pleasantly. "And we'll send you the bill."

"That's fair. My client will pay it," Flint replied just as easily.

"Clients with deep pockets have got to be the second-best thing to government work," the man said. "I've got to get the tenters moving, though. What else can I do for you right now?"

"I need some old video footage."

"How old?"

"Two years, give or take."

"Okay. Where and what are you looking for?" his contact asked, preoccupied with locating the tenting crew.

"Remember that submersible that launched in Key West? Went down somewhere in the Gulf. Imploded a few hours later with five crew members on board?"

"Yeah. I remember. Weirdest damn thing. But there's gotta be tons of video footage on that situation. Didn't the FBI and the Coast Guard and several private investigators run that down sixty ways to Sunday?" he said.

"That's right. But there was a murder the night of the launch. At the same marina. I need video of that incident. Two killers and a victim. Went down not long before the submersible launched. Across the marina in the shadows," Flint explained as succinctly as possible.

A couple holding hands and laughing were stumbling toward his location. He stepped farther into the shadows, but if they looked over, they might see him.

He gave the time, date, and approximate address to his contact. "Call me back on this number when you find the video. But send it to my secure server. You have the number."

"Will do. That it?" the man was impatient now, ready to get to work.

The couple stopped to make out a little. It was Flint's chance to nonchalantly move away.

"Yeah. Thanks," Flint said and disconnected the call. He shoved the phone into his jeans and walked through the shadows to the other side of the street. The couple never came up for air. He passed them on the opposite sidewalk and ducked around a corner.

He turned up the collar on his jacket and strode toward Duval Street. The nightlife was still going strong. He stepped around a few drunks passed out on the sidewalk as he made his way back to the bar.

CHAPTER 25

FLINT PUSHED THROUGH THE swinging doors of the place next door to Sloppy Joe's Bar. The familiar combination of spilled booze and salt air hit him like a wall of stench. He scanned the room, making a quick threat assessment.

The place buzzed with raucous chatter, loud music, and more than a few arguments. The band was playing Jimmy Buffet songs in the corner. Drunks joined in for the chorus.

Four men were playing darts. Two women were watching. A small crowd had gathered, cheering on their favorites. It was a harmless situation. For the moment.

In short, it was a normal night in every bar on Duval Street. So far, so good.

Flint scanned the room for the waitress who had served them earlier. His gut told him she was somehow a part of whatever Trawler was involved in.

Which meant she might have known Ward, too. Possibly had intel on what happened to him.

It was a long shot. But before he left Key West, he wanted to close the open question. If he could find her.

Flint threaded the crowd to approach the bar where patrons were standing three deep waiting to be served. He shuffled along the sticky floor and a couple of minutes later, he moved closer and stopped short to avoid the sloppy, sticky, polished wood bar top.

The bartender, a tall man with a tattooed forearm and a no-nonsense look, slid over to him.

"What can I get you?" he asked, wiping his hands on a cloth. The plastic name tag on his shirt said he was Ralph from Ohio.

"I'm looking for Lydia. She was serving here earlier," Flint said, trying to sound casual.

"She's gone home for the night. Can I help?" he offered, raising an eyebrow.

Flint pulled out his phone, showing the bartender a photo of Trawler. "I'm looking for this guy. Have you seen him around tonight?"

Ralph took the phone and spent a few seconds studying the picture. "Trawler. Yeah, he wanders in occasionally. Not here at the moment, though. I keep a pretty close eye on the customers, you know. Why you lookin' for him?"

Before Flint could answer, the same two thugs from the earlier alley fight moved in, scanning the room with cold, hard eyes.

Both locked on Flint immediately.

The energy shifted as if a silent switch had been flipped.

The band played on, but patrons sensed the brewing storm and quieted down. Some backed away, their drinks forgotten on the damp tables. Others seemed to perk up to the promised excitement.

"Looks like this conversation will have to wait," Flint muttered to Ralph, slipping the phone into his pocket.

He turned to face the approaching trouble. He wouldn't start a fight. But he wouldn't back down from one, either.

The bigger of the two thugs, a hulking brute with a scar across his cheek, sneered. "You got a way of popping up where you ain't wanted, friend."

Flint sized them up, noting the way they spread out slightly, trying to flank him. They were gym rats, which was okay. Flint had already subdued these guys once tonight. He could do it again.

But they were also armed, which would be a problem if they started shooting in these crowds.

"I'm not your friend," Flint retorted coolly, positioning himself so his back was to the bar, giving him a clear view of both men.

The thug smirked, cracking his knuckles. "Let's see if you bleed as much as you talk."

The first punch came fast, a right hook aimed at Flint's head. He ducked under the swing, feeling the breeze of it brush his face.

Swiftly, before the guy could throw another punch, Flint countered with a sharp jab to his gut. The man grunted, doubling over just as his sidekick lunged forward.

Flint spun away, but the stool beside him caught the second thug's thigh, throwing him off-balance. Flint seized the opportunity to deliver a solid kick to the side of the guy's knee.

A sickeningly loud pop echoed over the murmurs of the crowd, and the thug collapsed, writhing in pain. The knee would never be the same, but he'd still walk. If he found a good orthopedic surgeon soon enough.

The first thug had recovered. The damage to his pal fueled the rage contorting his features.

He pulled a knife from his pocket.

With one press of a button, a nasty blade glinted in the bar's dim light.

Flint's heartbeat thundered in his ears as he eyed the sharp edge. The guy waved the knife around a little, threatening, as if Flint couldn't see the blade well enough already.

Flint watched him closely, waiting for the right opportunity.

The dart game produced something amazing, and the spectators offered up a big cheer.

The abrupt noise threw off the big thug's concentration for a moment.

Flint took the chance.

Swiftly, he grabbed a long neck bottle from the bar, smashing it against the thick, polished edge as he turned. Flint moved in fast and swung the jagged edge in a quick, hard, wide, downward arc.

The blow connected with the thug's wrist, cutting through a vein. Blood pulsed from the cut and spewed out before he felt the pain.

A moment later, blood pulsing out with every heartbeat, he howled and dropped the knife.

The blade clattered to the floor, skidding under a table.

He grabbed his bleeding wrist with his opposite hand, intently focused on attempting to stop the gushing blood.

Flint used the distraction to drive the broken bottle into his side.

The thug howled, stumbling back, still clutching his wrist and trying to cover the second bleeding gash in his side with his forearm.

Flint lunged, grabbed the knife from the floor, spinning to face the other thug who was trying to get up on his damaged knee.

He saw the knife in Flint's hand.

Rage flashed in his eyes.

He shifted his weight to his good knee and lunged, fisted arms ready to pummel.

Flint waited patiently until he was close enough.

In one fluid motion, using the man's momentum against him, Flint plunged the knife into his belly.

He fell forward shouting angry curses.

Flint stepped out of the path of his falling body as it thudded to the ground, knocking people and furniture aside.

But the thug was smarter than he looked. He made no effort to get up.

The band's song had ended and the dart players' cheers from across the room echoed strangely in the suddenly silent bar.

Flint straightened up, scanning the room, panting slightly as he regained his equilibrium.

The patrons stared, some in shock, others with their phones out, likely calling the cops or filming the bloody scene.

"Police are on their way," Ralph said to Flint as he hung up and backed away.

The sirens were already wailing in the distance, coming closer fast. It was a small island. They'd arrive shortly.

Flint didn't have time to explain and wait around for the Key West PD to sort things out afterward. Time to go.

He strode out the back while pulling his phone from his pocket and punching Drake's number as he hustled.

"Meet me at the Pilatus, now," Flint said when Drake picked up. He was jogging now, dodging through the alleys and leaping over a low fence.

"Got it," Drake replied. "Where we going?"

"Houston."

"Everything okay?"

"It will be when we get in the air," Flint said ending the call.

The airport was on the other side of the island. Less than a mile to run from here.

CHAPTER 26

THE SIRENS WERE GROWING ever louder as the flashing lights painted the night in bursts of red and blue behind him.

He put on some extra speed as he neared the plane.

The hangar loomed ahead. The Pilatus was visible under the harsh white lights. Drake was already there, engines whirring, ready for a quick departure.

Flint rushed aboard and closed and locked the door.

"Let's go," he said, strapping in as Drake began the roll to the runway. Shortly after that, they were in the air.

As the jet ascended, Flint looked down at the shrinking lights of Key West. He could see Duval Street and the police vehicles in the front and back of the bar.

With luck, the thugs would get arrested and taken to the hospital, in that order. When they were identified and booked by police, identity would be a matter of public record. Which would make them easy to find again, if he needed to.

"Where's Trawler?"

Drake tilted his head toward the back of the plane. "Taking a nap."

Flint turned to see for himself. Trawler's chin was on his chest, and he was snoring quietly. He grinned. "Nice work."

"Yeah, well, about that," Drake said. "He was agitated. Couldn't have him flying like that. And he got chatty after we left you."

"About what?"

"Ward Lyman, mostly. He doesn't have a lot of warm fuzzies for the guy."

"Did he say why?"

"It was more like a rant, but yeah." Drake flipped on the auto pilot and settled more comfortably in his seat. "He said Lyman was a spoiled rich kid who didn't deserve or appreciate what he'd been born into. He was really incensed about it."

"I thought they were friends?"

"Which, he said, didn't stop him from being objective," Drake grinned. "But the biggest nugget was when he let it slip that since Ward Lyman expected to die before he was thirty, speeding up the timetable wasn't such a big deal. No harm, no foul, he said."

As the Pilatus cut through the dark sky, Flint turned back to Drake, who was focusing intently on the controls.

"Is Trawler suggesting that Ward promised them a chunk of the Lyman fortune to stage his death on the submersible and things just got out of hand?" Flint asked, skeptically. "That's convenient."

"Yep," Drake responded, his voice steady despite the tension. "Seems Ward claimed to believe deeply in that family curse. Thought faking his own death was his best shot at dodging it. Trawler figures if Ward was already dead, how could the curse kill him a second time?"

"Or something like that." Flint shook his head, pondering the depraved audacity of the plan. "And what? Trawler and his buddies bought into the whole thing just for the money?"

"Greedy or desperate, take your pick." Drake shrugged. "People do crazier things."

The conversation was interrupted by a subtle change in the engine's hum. Flint's ears picked up the faint, yet distinct, stutter in its rhythm.

"You hear that?" he asked, leaning forward slightly.

"Yeah, I feel it. Been there since we leveled out." Drake's hand went to the throttle, his expression turning serious. "Something's off."

The steady drone of the engine carried an uneven tremor, an unsettling syncopation that grew more pronounced. Drake's eyes flicked to the instrument panel, scanning the gauges.

"Fuel pressure's dropping," he announced, calm but firm. "We're losing fuel faster than we should. Could be a leak. Maybe a faulty gauge."

Flint's gaze hardened. "Can we make it to Houston?"

"Doubtful. We could go back to Key West. Possibly."

Flint shook his head. "Not really an option."

"We passed the Dry Tortugas. But looking at the charts, there's an abandoned airstrip on a tiny island ahead. We'll

divert there. On the ground, we can figure out what to do."
Drake swiftly began to adjust course.

"You gonna be able to find a tiny, uninhabited island in the dark? It's black as pitch out here," Flint said, scanning the miles of dark water below. "Good thing we can swim."

"We won't see this one from high altitude unless there's a light. Which is not likely," Drake replied. "Let's hope the coordinates are accurate."

"You've landed in the dark before. You can do it again," Flint said.

Drake kept his concentration on the instruments and didn't respond.

As the island came into view, it was nothing more than a speck against the endless Gulf of Mexico. The Pilatus circled once, allowing them to view the area. From the air, it looked like lush, dense foliage and not much else.

Flint spied decrepit small buildings and two old boats. The island was a long way from everywhere. Which wasn't unusual. The old airstrip wasn't unusual, either. If one owned an island in the middle of nowhere, the best way to get there was by air.

"Looks abandoned, doesn't it?" Drake said.

"Can't really tell from here. A few years ago, real estate agents were selling private islands to the rich and famous. But this is not that," Flint replied. "You'd need to be a real Robinson Crusoe to live here. Strong survival skills, too."

Within minutes, a weak light from near the rural airstrip appeared, a lonely beacon amid the vast darkness. Drake's hands moved expertly. The Pilatus began its descent, which Flint felt in his gut as the ground approached.

"Brace for landing," Drake warned, as he guided the struggling aircraft toward the short, rough runway that was little more than a flat patch of grass.

The Pilatus shuddered as it contacted the ground. Metal screeched. The cabin vibrated harshly as the tires bounced on the earth.

But they'd landed in one piece.

Once the jet rolled to a stop, Drake killed the engines. An oppressive silence enveloped them for a couple of seconds.

Flint was the first to disembark. Salty air hit him with a gust that carried the distinct smell of seaweed and brine. The island was silent except for the sound of waves crashing against the shore and the distant calls of seabirds.

The airstrip was deserted, surrounded by dark fields and sparse trees and the Gulf of Mexico. Stark, eerie quietness set him on edge.

"Stay here. Keep an eye on Trawler," Flint instructed Drake, who was already checking the fuel line at the wing.

Nodding, Drake stayed focused on the plane while Flint scanned their surroundings, his senses heightened, every shadow a potential threat.

Suddenly, the distant sound of an engine sliced through the silence, followed by crunching shell gravel. Flint tensed, his hand instinctively going for his gun as a pair of headlights turned from a side trail onto the airstrip, illuminating the Pilatus in a harsh, white glare.

CHAPTER 27

Kansas City, Missouri

ON THE OTHER SIDE of the city, Boldo's mansion stood like an old sentinel. A gala to benefit one of his wife's many charities was unfolding. Guests adorned in the finery that only money and taste could buy mingled like old friends. The gardens were filled with laughter, the clink of glasses, and the soft strains of a string quartet nestled beneath a canopy of stars.

Boldo moved among his guests, his face set in a smile that belied his annoyance. He had no time for galas and gladhanding, but his wife had spent an entire year organizing this event. Boldo's attendance was mandatory.

He moved among the guests, shook hands, clinked glasses, exchanged pleasantries. But his gaze swept the scene with a hawk's vigilance, taking in every face, every movement. A crowd like this could be a dangerous thing. He'd tasked his security team with keeping things civil.

Boldo eventually made his way to where his personal assistant stood, her own eyes scanning the crowd as if her interest were mere casual observation.

"Everything in place?" he asked with a false grin, leaning in as if sharing a jest.

"All set. Cameras, checkpoints, the works. If he tries to get within a mile of here, we'll know," she replied, her voice low, matching his casual demeanor.

"Good." Boldo nodded, sipping his champagne. "And the rest?"

"Monitoring all routes. No sightings yet. He's out there. And he'll surface."

They parted with a smile and a nod, Boldo returning to his role as the genial billionaire host. The night air was cool, the stars sharp above, the music a gentle swell of violins and cellos.

As the evening wore on, Boldo slipped away from the throng to the quieter confines of his study. The room was dark, save for the light from a single lamp on his desk. He approached the desk, pressing a sequence on the side of the lamp that clicked softly.

A panel on the wall slid open, revealing a bank of monitors.

The screens showed various angles of the estate, the roads leading up to it, the dense tree lines that bordered the property. Each was manned by security.

He picked up a radio from the desk. "Report."

"Nothing to report, sir. All clear," came the crackling response.

Boldo set the radio down, his finger tapping a steady rhythm on the desk. He pulled out his phone to dial a number memorized long ago.

"Status?" he asked when the call connected.

"Still on the move. We don't think he's here," said the voice on the other end.

"Keep on him. Don't lose him this time," Boldo instructed, his tone firm.

"Yes, sir."

He ended the call and sat back, the chair creaking under his weight. He raced through scenarios, plans, contingencies. He could not afford to lose him now. Not when he was so close.

The sound of footsteps drew Boldo's attention. He looked up to see his assistant standing at the doorway.

"Trouble?" he asked, noting the urgency in her step.

She walked in, closing the door behind her. "Emily Royce is here. Spencer Lyman was invited and sent her instead, apparently."

Boldo felt a surge of adrenaline. "Here? At the gala?"

She nodded. "Just arrived."

"Why was Lyman invited?"

She shrugged. "It's a fundraiser. He's got money."

Boldo stood, his plan suddenly shifting, adapting. "Where is she now?"

"Main hall. Mingling."

"Okay. Thanks for the heads-up."

His assistant nodded, turning to leave.

"And," Boldo called after her. She paused, looking back. "Make sure she doesn't suspect. We can't afford to tip our hand."

She nodded again and disappeared, leaving Boldo alone in the room. He stared at the screens, each flickering with images of the party continuing outside.

He turned off the monitors, plunging the room into darkness. The distant music of the quartet filtered through the walls, notes lingering in the air like a promise.

Boldo left the study, stepping back into the gala. The faces of his guests were masks of gaiety and ignorance. He moved through, each step measured, each smile calculated.

As Boldo re-entered the grand hall, his gaze swept over the crowd, feeling the pulse of the party beneath the surface calm. The murmur of refined voices and the musicians' delicate harmony blended into a pleasing soundtrack. Everyone seemed engrossed in the revelry of the night, unaware of the undercurrents Boldo felt keenly.

His focus was drawn to a sudden commotion near the main entrance. Two guests, likely fueled by too much drink and unchecked grievances, had begun to grapple with each other. Voices were raised in heated anger. The argument quickly escalated from shouts to shoves, drawing a circle of startled onlookers.

Boldo watched as the crowd backed away from the two brawling men. He signaled to his security personnel, who were already moving swiftly toward the scuffle.

Not fast enough. Two others joined in. Boldo recognized the four. Security for two of the big donors. Boldo's wife would not be pleased.

The brawl drew an audience. Some guests attempted to break up the fight.

Boldo, attempting to reach the epicenter to exert control, was inadvertently caught in the expanding brawl.

A sharp elbow caught him square in the chest, knocking the wind out of him and stopping him short. He regained his breath, grabbed the man who had hit him and pulled the guy back with a forceful jerk.

"Enough!" he shouted to no effect.

The four fighters were out of control. A hard punch connected with Boldo's jaw, spun him around, and sent a jolt of pain searing through his skull.

The room seemed to spin as the music and lights and the noise blurred into a disorienting jumble. Boldo had participated in many fights over the years. He'd won more than he'd lost. But it had been a long time since he'd taken a hard punch like that.

Gritting his loose teeth, Boldo shook off the pain and turned to face the crowd. His usual composure cracked. Rage flashed, reddening his face and flaring his nostrils.

"Get them out!" he barked at his security team, who were now pulling them apart and dispursing the crowd with increased vigor.

Boldo grabbed the man who had hit him and shoved him toward the nearest exit, hard. The man stumbled and fell. Boldo reached down and jerked him to his feet.

"Get the hell out. And don't come back," he growled as the man hurried away.

Boldo's security team pushed the brawlers toward the doors and out into the cool night. Guests who had kept their distance murmured among themselves at the spectacle. Boldo's wife would be horrified, but what more could he do?

As the last of the miscreants were escorted out, Boldo straightened his jacket, ignoring the pain in his jaw. He'd have a dandy bruise there tomorrow.

He scanned the room, meeting the eyes of his guests with fierce determination and forced calm.

"Please, return to the party," he said. "The matter is resolved."

His assistant joined him, scanning the crowd for further signs of trouble. "Are you alright?"

"I'm fine," he muttered, though the pain in his jaw suggested otherwise. "Stay alert. This night isn't over yet."

As the music resumed and the guests cautiously returned to their conversations and dances, Boldo took a moment. The unexpected punch had rattled him, not just physically but mentally. It was a reminder of how quickly things could spiral out of control.

The fragile order he tried so meticulously to maintain at home could be destroyed in an instant. A point he'd be well served to remember.

A few guests still buzzed with shocked whispers and nervous glances after the luxurious evening turned briefly to chaos.

"Please, everyone, return to your enjoyment," Boldo said as he offered them more champagne and canapes. Calm and commanding while restoring order. "Let us remember the purpose of our gathering. Charity depends on all of us."

When the party resumed, Boldo took a moment to survey the room. Guests were slowly settling into the rhythm of the party again. The quartet continued their soft serenade.

Yet, the brief outbreak had shifted something in the atmosphere. Boldo could feel the eyes on him.

No one in the room who had lived more than thirty years was unaware of Boldo's criminal connections. Because of his stature in the community, they pretended he was one of them. Gentile, refined, cultured.

But he wasn't.

The brawl underscored Boldo's violent world. A world neither his guests nor his wife wanted to acknowledge, even as they were all too well aware.

Boldo walked to the bar and ordered a drink while watching the crowd. Each face seemed to mask its own secrets, each gesture now a potential problem.

With a glass in hand, he moved to a quieter corner of the garden. He stood in the shadows, thinking about Lyman Enterprises and his plan to acquire the company.

Spencer Lyman had made it clear he would not step aside.

Which meant Boldo needed to take the company by force and that was fine by him.

The rustle of leaves nearby caught his attention, and he turned sharply. She stepped from the shadows and stopped a few feet away. Her features were obscured by the darkness yet unmistakably familiar.

Boldo set down his glass, his voice low and steady. "What are you doing here?"

"I came to learn what progress you've made on our project," she replied.

CHAPTER 28

Unknown Island in the Gulf of Mexico

AN OLD PICKUP TRUCK, engine rumbling in the quiet night, pulled up and stopped. The driver's side door opened, and a man stepped out. He raised his hands, palms out, when he spotted Flint's weapon.

"Everything alright here?" he called out, his voice carrying across the short distance. "Heard you comin' in. Saw your landing. Looked like you might be in trouble."

Flint kept his gun trained on the newcomer, not dropping his guard. "We had a fuel issue," he replied cautiously. "Who are you?"

"Name's Harlan. Just checking to see if you need help," he explained, his tone was friendly but cautiously respectful of Flint's weapon.

"We might need some assistance," Flint conceded, lowering his gun slightly. "Need to check the damage and refuel."

Harlan nodded, walking over. "I can help with that. Let's take a look."

Inside the cone of light from the Pilatus, Harlan looked older than he'd sounded. Late sixties, maybe. Early seventies more likely. He had a full head of white hair and a matching beard that covered most of his face.

"Thanks," Drake said. "Can we get some lights over here?"

Harlan said, shaking his head, "I've never seen one of these birds before. Heard it can operate from grass, wet earth, dry sand, gravel, and even snow. That true?"

Drake replied, "Yeah. Made sense to get one we could use everywhere."

"Lucky you did. Lotta planes couldn't land here at all, let alone in the dark," Harlan said. "She's a beauty."

"What about the lights?" Drake asked again.

Harlan shook his head. "Sorry."

"Anybody else we can get some floodlights from?"

"Nobody lives here except me since Fred died a while back," Harlan replied. "Best you can do is wait for daylight in a few hours."

Harlan's eyes flicked to the Pilatus, then back to Flint. "You guys got a place to sleep until daylight? The plane should be fine here, and I've got food and coffee if you're hungry."

Harlan's expression was relaxed but watchful. He was a quiet man with a gray beard and a limp that suggested a hard life. Despite his easy demeanor, his eyes were sharp and his stance both casual and ready for anything.

Flint wasn't sure if staying overnight was a good idea, but it was the only idea. The plane had landed on this strip by necessity, and they couldn't work on it in the dark. They had no food or coffee on board. And the Pilatus wasn't really set up for three tall men to stretch out for sleep.

He glanced at Trawler, who was awake but drowsy, still feeling the effects of the drug Drake had used to keep him docile during the flight.

Drake was on high alert, watching for any signs of trouble as was his habit.

"Follow me," Harlan said, gesturing to his truck.

The vehicle was old and beat-up, with rust patches along the sides, but it was functional. Flint and Drake helped Trawler into the backseat, making sure the zip tie around his wrist was secure. Harlan watched but made no comment.

The ride to Harlan's compound was short and bumpy. The truck jolted over holes and uneven ground, making Flint's teeth clench with every bounce. The scent of pine and salt filled the air, mingling with the earthy smell of the truck's worn upholstery.

Flint hadn't spent much time in such complete darkness. Most places boasted ambient light of one kind or another. Not here. Only the faint glow of the truck's headlights and Harlan's expertise guided the way.

A short time later, Harlan stopped the truck and turned off the ignition.

The compound was a collection of small buildings, each constructed from rough lumber. A fire pit sat at the center, the last embers of a fire casting a dim glow across everything within its circumference.

The sound of waves crashing in the distance and the rustling of leaves were the only noises. Flint felt an oppressive sense of isolation, the kind that could swallow a man whole.

"Welcome to my palace," Harlan said with a grin, leading them inside the largest building.

The air was warmer in here, thanks to a wood stove burning in the corner of the simple but comfortable room. A table with mismatched chairs stood in the middle, surrounded by bookshelves and a couple of faded photographs hanging on the walls.

Flint sat down, feeling the wood creak beneath him. The chair was rough but sturdy, much like everything else. Drake took a seat across from him, keeping a close eye on Trawler, who was slumped in his chair, still cuffed but coherent.

Harlan made coffee, the smell strong and invigorating. Flint accepted a cup. He took a sip. "Whoa. Now that will put hair on your chest."

Harlan smiled. "Glad you like it. Buy it from Uncle Sam. The army's got the best coffee, hands down."

"You got any food?" Drake asked, eyeing Harlan.

"Yeah," Harlan replied, pulling out a box of MREs from a cabinet. "It's not gourmet, but it'll fill you up."

Flint accepted an MRE, tearing it open and eating in silence. The food wasn't great, but it was better than nothing. "So what's your story, Harlan? Why are you living out here on the edge of the world all alone?"

Harlan's rough voice told the kind of story that comes from a life lived on the edge. Flint had heard similar stories many times over the years. Usually from men like Harlan who had walked away.

"I was a POW in Vietnam," Harlan said, his gaze distant, lost in the memory. "Came back, tried to fit in, but it didn't work out. Too much noise, too much chaos. Found this place peaceful enough and decided to stay."

"You said Fred was living here with you, though?" Flint asked.

Harlan grinned. "Yeah, Fred was the last in a long line of best friends. He was sixteen when he died. That's old for a dog like Fred. I do miss him, though."

"You own this place?" Drake asked, glancing around at what little there was to see.

"Nah. I'm squatting. No clue who owns it. Uncle Sam, maybe." Harlan said with a cackle that might have been just a shade too close to madness. "Could be he figures I'd been through enough and since I'm not asking for any handouts, he's leaving me alone, you know?"

"What do you do with your time?" Drake wanted to know.

"Mostly, I swim. Catch a fish for dinner some days. There are a couple of wild fruits growing here. Avocado. Mango."

"I see you've got some books over there," Drake nodded toward the rough board shelf near the fireplace where two lines of about fifty well-thumbed paperbacks rested in a neat row. "You a Jack Reacher fan?"

"Read all of those a dozen times. Kim Otto, too. Figure she'll catch Reacher one of these days. I don't know what she'll do after that, but hope I live long enough to find out. She's a sharp cookie and I enjoy the ride," Harlan said with a shrug as he drained the last of his coffee. He held up the empty cup in a gesture that offered a refill to the group. "Reading's a luxury for me. Always loved it. POW camps didn't have good books. And after I came home, I had no time, you know?"

"I give you a lot of credit, Harlan," Drake said, offering his cup for a refill. "I don't know if I could live like this. I see the appeal, though. Peace. Quiet. Safety. I think I'd like to have a float plane or a helo. Have to go see my mother occasionally or she'd skin me alive."

Harlan threw back his head and laughed. "My mother died years back. But I know exactly what you mean."

Flint nodded, understanding Harlan's need for isolation while agreeing with Drake that this place might be too much of a good thing.

Yet, Harlan's home was quiet, peaceful in its own way. The lifestyle could be appealing to a person who had the right set of assets, both personal and financial. Maybe he should buy an island while he had the money and figure out how to live on it over time. No reason why he couldn't bring Scarlett and Katie for a couple of weeks. Other friends, too.

The thought flashed into his head, swooped in and settled quickly.

A private island was exactly the kind of place where someone like Ward Lyman could hide for years.

Ward had the resources to stage his own death, as Trawler claimed. He could easily have set up a sanctuary. He was wealthy enough to deck it out a lot better, though. Add regular supply delivery, maybe a couple of employees to handle the dirty work. Yeah, with enough money, anything could be done.

Flint turned to Trawler. The sedative Drake gave him in Key West had worn off a while ago. He stared at his coffee cup like it held the answers to all his problems.

"Tell me more about what happened to Ward Lyman," Flint said. "Minute-by-minute details. We've got nothing but time here. Might as well make the most of it."

Trawler looked up, his eyes narrowing. "Why should I? I got nothing to gain."

"You're not seeing the big picture," Flint replied. "If you don't tell me, you're going to prison for sure. And that's only half your problem. Not to mention Lyman's grandfather would squish you like a bug, given half a chance."

"Yeah, I'm not an idiot. Why'd ya think I've stayed quiet all this time?" Trawler said with a scowl. "What are you offerin'?"

"If you tell me what I need to know, maybe we can work something out," Flint replied, promising only the sleeves of his vest.

CHAPTER 29

TRAWLER HESITATED WHILE FLINT'S question lingered between them and then gave up with a defeated sigh. "Ward said he was setting up a new life. Got a private place. He promised us a cut of the family fortune if we helped him disappear."

"Where's the place?" Flint asked, pressing for more details.

"Near Mexico," Trawler replied, his voice low. "Totally private. A few buildings. He said he'd be impossible to find once he got there."

"Was it a private island?" Flint asked.

Trawler shrugged. "Could be. He didn't say. Makes sense, though."

Flint nodded, taking in the information. It was a lead, but a vague one.

The Gulf of Mexico was vast, and private islands were scattered around its expanse. If Trawler was telling the truth,

Ward planned this escape in advance. He would have been very careful about it, considering he believed the stakes were his own life and death.

"Tell me exactly what happened." Flint leaned in resting his forearms on his thighs and holding the hot coffee cup between his palms.

"You saw the important part. Two guys shoot Ward in the back and carry his body off just before the submersible is launching. People were distracted. Nobody noticed," Trawler said. "An hour before, he gave up his seat on the submersible to the alternate explorer who'd been shut out when Ward agreed to go. I don't know the guy's name. He sorta resembled Ward's build so he could wear Ward's suit."

"What about the Kansas City baseball cap?" Drake asked.

"He wore it as a favor to Ward. In exchange for Ward letting him go on the expedition. The point was for observers to believe he was Ward as he got on the thing," Trawler smiled. "Ward knew his grandfather would leave no stone unturned when Ward didn't come back. That's why the submersible had to be destroyed."

"You're saying Ward Lyman killed five men just so he could escape some ridiculous curse?" Flint's tone was hard.

The suggestion was appalling. Yes, the extremely rich were very, very different. But killing five people underwater and blowing the bodies across the seabed was more depraved than normal men could stomach.

More to the point, none of Flint's sources had suggested Ward Lyman was a sociopath.

Trawler shrugged. "I'm not sure Ward understood exactly who he'd climbed into bed with. He was terrified that he'd be dead before he was thirty. I mean, seriously terrified. He was already twenty-three He was running out of time. When the invitation to join the expedition came up, he just …"

"Just what?" Flint pressed. "Decided to kill five people and stage his own death and hide out forever in some private luxury playground?"

"Sounded different when Ward described it," Trawler shrugged again and shuffled back out of Flint's reach, just in case. With a furtive glance toward Harlan, he finally said, "Doesn't matter now, does it? I told you what happened before they took him. I figure he's dead now, anyway."

Flint couldn't argue with that, so he said nothing.

The rest of the night passed slowly, with the wood stove crackling in the background. Harlan told stories about his life out here, the few animals he'd seen which were mostly birds and fish, the dogs he'd shared his home with, the storms he'd survived.

It had been a peaceful life, but it also felt fragile, as if one wrong move could upset the balance.

Flint tried to rest. Ward was out there, somewhere, and they needed to find him before someone else did and he vanished forever, another victim of the curse after all.

As the first light of dawn filtered through the windows, Flint felt a sense of urgency. They needed to get the plane fixed and in the air.

He stood, stretching his legs, feeling the stiffness from the long day. The air smelled of wood smoke and pine, both comforting and unsettling. He looked around the compound. A chill settled over him.

This place was too quiet, too isolated. It was a perfect place to hide from the world, but also a reminder that Harlan was far from help if things went wrong. Had Ward Lyman made that same mistake?

Drake was already outside, checking the plane. Flint joined him feeling the crisp morning air against his skin. Harlan was there, too. They were talking like two old friends by now.

When Flint walked up, he heard Drake ask, "So those books on your shelf. Some of them seem pretty new. Your buddy bring them out to you as they're published?"

"Yeah. Maybe I get a new Reacher once a year and a new Otto twice a year, if I'm lucky," Harlan replied. "Which is okay. I like rereading. It's like spending time with old friends, you know?"

Flint said, "When is your friend coming back again?"

Harlan shrugged. "He shows up when it's convenient for him to stay a couple days. Every month or so, usually. Brings MREs. Water. Coffee. He can still get on base and shop."

"Tell me his contact details and I'll send you some stuff. We really appreciate what you've done for us," Flint said.

"No need. Enjoyed it myself. I don't have many folks to talk to since Fred died." Harlan shook his head, but he gave Flint the information he asked for and Flint put it into his phone.

"We need to get out of here," Flint said to Drake as he watched the sun rise over the horizon. "Can I help?"

Drake stood up and wiped his hands on a shop rag. "I'm done."

"What was wrong?"

"Not sure. Nothing too serious. Probably a bit of bad fuel. When we have a chance, I'll get a real wrench monkey to figure it out. But for now we should be good to go," Drake replied. "Where's Trawler?"

Flint turned to shake hands with Harlan and thank him for his hospitality. "Can we leave Trawler here with you? We'll come back for him when we can. Or let your friend take him back to the mainland next time he comes over."

"That's a big ask," Harlan said, moving a toothpick around with his mouth as he talked, thinking about it. "You had him cuffed when he got here. And he looks a bit beat up. What's he done?"

"Honestly, I don't have a full file on him yet. He's not trustworthy, I can say that." Flint glanced down a moment and then raised his gaze to Harlan's craggy old face. "He and a couple of buddies tried to mess us up. The reason we had him cuffed was to keep him controlled in the plane."

"Is he crazy? Crazy dudes are too exhausting. I'm not up for that."

"I hear you. He's got all of his mental faculties."

"I guess he must know he'd be a fool to kill me before I get him out of here," Harlan grinned and chuckled slightly. "He'd never survive here alone."

Flint grinned back and clapped Harlan on the shoulder. "Something tells me he'd be a fool to try."

Harlan nodded and moved the toothpick around. "More fools in the world than we'd like to think."

CHAPTER 30

Miami, Florida

FLINT SETTLED INTO THE leather seat in the Pilatus as the plane lifted off from Harlan's island. The engine droned as it should, and the sparkling Gulf waters stretched out below. Drake piloted the aircraft expertly, gaze flicking from the instruments to the horizon ahead, his moves practiced and expert.

"When we touch down in Miami, you deal with the plane. I'll head over to meet with Gaspar. Get him going on the new intel," Flint said.

"Works for me," Drake replied. "Engine's working fine now. Could have been something passing through the fuel line and now it's gone."

"Let's find out for sure. Get another plane if we need to."

"Copy that," Drake said. "You think Trawler was straight with us? Ward Lyman orchestrated the shooting on the docks so he could disappear?"

Flint shrugged, watching the horizon, "He might be playing us, but both stories can't be true. Ward's dead or he's not. And we've been hired to find him either way."

"Would Ward Lyman fake his own death? Seems extreme, doesn't it?" Drake asked a few minutes later, still focused flying the plane. "The way Trawler described Ward as young and naive sounded like he was protecting him."

"Trawler's not the type to cover for Ward without a very good reason. Even then he'd only do it as long as it suited him." Flint rubbed the stubble on his face. He could use a shower and a shave. And a decent steak. "Gaspar should have more intel by now."

The flight to Miami took about an hour. Drake landed the Pilatus at the executive airstrip on the outskirts of Miami.

They deplaned into warm and humid air that enveloped them like a hot, wet blanket. The traffic and crowds were especially jarring after Harlan's secluded island, and it took a couple of seconds to shake it off.

Drake headed to the hangar to find the mechanic while Flint called his usual car service for a lift to Gaspar's place.

Carlos Gaspar lived in a modest house in the quiet Cuban neighborhood where he grew up. The place looked normal and unassuming from the street. His wife and five kids were off somewhere, as usual.

Flint had been here before. Gaspar's office was in the back and packed with high-tech gear. But the rest of the home oozed welcoming ambiance. All of which gave Flint hives. Living in such a small space with six other people seemed like a nightmare of constant chaos, even though Gaspar and his family thrived in it all.

Flint entered through the front door and was greeted by the aroma of steamed coffee. He followed his nose to the kitchen.

"Hey, Flint." Gaspar was leaning against the counter, ankles crossed.

He tilted his head toward the woman standing out of Flint's sight line to his right. "You know Kim Otto."

Flint gave her a grin. "Good to see you again, Agent Otto. What brings the FBI to our powwow?"

"Honestly, I was just leaving. You guys have business to discuss, and I've got a plane to catch. We'll swap stories another time," Otto replied with a good-natured smile. "If you see my boss, I was never here."

She put her cup in the sink and patted Gaspar's shoulder on her way out.

"Got anything to report?" Flint asked after she'd gone.

"Yeah. Come on back with me."

Flint stepped into Gaspar's dimly lit office bathed in the blue glow of multiple computer monitors.

Before Gaspar launched into his results, Flint said, "I've got new information about why Ward Lyman disappeared."

Gaspar swiveled in his chair, eyebrows raised and deadpanned, "Can't wait to hear it."

"According to Trawler, this whole thing was engineered by Lyman himself," Flint explained. "Because of this crazy Lyman Family Curse. Trawler says Ward is absolutely convinced he'll die before he turns thirty. Says he's terrified about it."

Gaspar scoffed. "The guy faked his own death because of some superstitious nonsense?"

"That's what Trawler claims," Flint confirmed grimly. "Ward thinks he'll beat the curse if he survives past the age of thirty. He's twenty-five now. Which means he's got five more years to stay dead."

Gaspar shook his head. "That's one of the nuttiest things I've heard in a while. Guy stands to inherit billions, so he kills himself, figuratively speaking? What kind of idiot would do that?"

Pacing the room, Flint ran a hand over his face. "It makes a twisted sort of sense, if you buy into the curse garbage. Kill himself on his own terms to avoid whatever fate the universe has in store. Especially when he knows he won't really die."

"So he thinks he can cheat fate. Orchestrated this whole bizarre scheme..." Gaspar shook his head in disbelief. "Gotta hand it to the kid, he's got a flare for drama at least."

"Or he's so self-involved that he believes he can play God and to hell with the consequences to everyone else," Flint replied. "I didn't have the impression he was like that from talking to the grandfather, but if we can believe Trawler, it seems to be working out that way."

"That's a fair point, though. Wasn't Trawler trying to kill you yesterday? Why do you believe him now?" Gaspar asked.

"I didn't say I believed him. It's the only lead we have, so we're chasing it down," Flint replied.

Gaspar pursed his lips as if he were thinking about it. "What about the submersible? Did Lyman orchestrate that, too? Killing five people like that is definitely not a tariff most people would pay just to maybe stay alive themselves. Changes how I view Ward Lyman, for sure."

"Trawler claims Ward might not have known about that part. Which is hard to believe. Or maybe someone really is trying to kill him, and the submersible would have been his coffin if he'd boarded instead of sending the other guy." Flint's jaw tightened.

"Regardless, he's put a lot of people through hell," Gaspar said. "Doesn't sound like such a model citizen to me."

"Not to mention all of the Mexican and Central American cartels would kidnap him for ransom in a hot second. He's worth too much money to let an opportunity like that slide."

"Cartels aren't the only risk. Kidnap for ransom is a thriving worldwide business. Hell, the Mexican government might even arrest him to wring concessions out of the US government," Gaspar agreed, all business again.

"So we've got to find out where exactly he's hiding and extract him before this all goes beyond sideways and more people die," Flint said grimly.

Ward Lyman's motives might have been rooted in delusional thinking, but that didn't change the status quo.

"Assuming he didn't die when they shot him in the back, any thoughts on how we can locate our would-be tragic hero?" Flint asked cynically.

"I'll try the usual channels like money trails, communications intercepts. But we're not likely to find anything." Gaspar stretched out, ankles crossed, hands resting across his flat belly. "Crazy scheme like this, he'd think it through and cover his tracks pretty damned well before he ended his whole life."

"Maybe not well enough," Flint said thoughtfully. "Trawler mentioned Lyman has expensive tastes. Chances are he's living it up in an environment exactly to his liking."

Gaspar grinned slowly. "You're a crafty son of a bitch, Flint."

"I try."

"I'll run some searches, see if I can pinpoint any luxury purchases or bookings worth taking a closer look. Are we sure he's in Mexico?" Gaspar asked.

"No. It makes sense that he landed in Mexico when he fled. That was two years ago. He might have moved on since then. But we can start there," Flint replied.

"Got it," Gaspar murmured. "Smug little bastard can't be as clever as he thinks."

"They never are," Flint replied. "Let's find the foolish young heir and drag his reckless ass back to safety, whether he likes it or not. We can sort out the blame when we've got him."

Gaspar frowned. "If Ward Lyman wants to thwart fate, that's his business, isn't it?"

"His grandfather is our client, and he doesn't see it that way." Flint shook his head and grabbed his coffee cup for a refill. "And then there's the five dead explorers on that submersible. If we discover Ward was involved in those deaths, he's at least a witness and he could be a fugitive."

"Wonder if Grandpa would want you to find him if he knew Ward might be sent to prison for murder," Gaspar mused as he turned his attention to his keyboards.

"You think I should ask him that question," Flint said flatly.

"Only if you're not interested in having a happy client willing to pay your outrageous fees at the end of all this."

"And your outrageous fees, don't forget."

Gaspar grinned. "My kids do like to eat."

CHAPTER 31

Odessa, Texas

WHILE FLINT WAS OCCUPIED on the Lyman case, Scarlett focused on what she called The Wagner Problem. One way to keep Naomi Wagner satisfied and block her from asking too many questions about Flint's mother was to redirect her attention.

The June Pentwater case investigation was the obvious shiny object to wave in front of Wagner's greedy eyes.

Since the entries in the calendars appeared to be genuine, proving or disproving Preston's alibi was the obvious place to start.

She might have asked Gaspar to assist, but he'd ask too many questions. Flint would never forgive her if she spilled the beans about his mother. Which meant this had to stay a solo operation.

Scarlett took a flight to Odessa, picked up a rental and drove south through miles of undeveloped land toward Sand County. She followed the navigation system in the rental and parked near the entrance of the now quiet and deserted fairgrounds.

A sign on one corner of the first building suggested the business offices were inside. Scarlett waited until the dust her tires had kicked up resettled. Then she picked up her phone and stepped out into the heat.

She scanned the sprawling expanse where throngs of people gathered for the annual county fair. She'd been to events just like that many times growing up in West Texas. She visualized the crowds, noise, and oppressive heat. She remembered the tired and cranky kids along with drunken adults as the evening wore on.

She imagined the buzz of activity, the laughter, the music that filled the air. Her boots kicked up dust as she crossed the empty space, each step stirring echoes of the past.

One man like James Preston, wandering alone among the chaos, could easily have been overlooked by every person at the fair the night June Pentwater was murdered.

Standing there, Scarlett realized that Preston's alibi might be true.

The anonymity of crowds encouraged all sorts of anti-social behavior.

Her college psychology and sociology professors had taught her that. But she didn't need to be a PhD to know that people behaved very differently in small groups than they did in large ones.

The fairgrounds seemed unchanged, save for the wear of time on the wooden booths and the faded paint on the signage. She headed toward a large, weathered barn that now served as a makeshift stable and workshop.

Inside, she found an older man adjusting the straps on a saddle. The comforting scent of hay and horses filled the air.

"Excuse me, sir?" Scarlett called out as she approached.

The man looked up, squinting slightly. "Yeah?"

She put a friendly smile in her voice. "I'm Katheryn Scarlett. I'm investigating an event that might have happened here about thirty years ago. Were you working here then?"

"Harry Redford." He wiped his hands on a rag, nodding. "That's a long while back, but yeah, I've lived here all my life. So sure, ask away."

Scarlett pulled out the old driver's license photo of James Preston and showed it to the man. "Ever seen this man around here? Might've been around the time of the fair back then."

Harry took the photo, studying it with a furrowed brow. "Can't say that I recall him. He looks like a regular guy. Nothing unusual about him. Lot of faces pass through during fair season and we've had a lot of fairs since then."

"Here's a more recent photo." She showed him the one recently circulated in the news.

His expression changed subtly. "Isn't that the guy who was executed a few months back for murdering that young woman over in Thompson County?"

"Yes, that's him," Scarlett confirmed, watching the man's reaction closely.

"I heard some talk. I was just a kid, in high school, you know?" Harry said as if he were giving the matter serious consideration. "I remember the girls chattering about a handsome dude hanging around the fair. No one knew him. But he was good-looking, they thought. And a handsome stranger in town was enough to gin up the gossip."

Scarlett returned her phone to her pocket. "Do you remember who these girls were? Anyone who might still be around that I could talk to?"

"Well, maybe. Let's see..." He closed his eyes to think. "There was Jenny Colter, she was a year ahead of me. I was kinda sweet on her at the time. And then the Miller twins, Kathy and Karen. They were real social, knew everyone and everything going on. They might know more."

"Do you have any idea where they might be now?" Scarlett asked.

"Jenny married a guy from out of state and moved away, not sure where to. The Millers, they still live around here. Kathy runs the floral shop in town, and Karen, she's a teacher over at the middle school."

"Thank you, that's very helpful," Scarlett said with a slow nod. "Appreciate your time."

"No problem. Good luck with your searching," Harry said, turning back to his work.

Scarlett drove into town past the quaint buildings to the floral shop run by Kathy Miller. The bell jingled cheerfully as she entered. The shop was a riot of colors and scents, from roses to daisies, pleasingly displayed.

Kathy, a woman in her forties with a friendly face framed by light curls, looked up from arranging a bouquet. "Can I help you?"

"Yes, I hope so," Scarlett replied, introducing herself and explaining her purpose. "I was told you might have been at the county fair about thirty years ago. I know it's a long shot. But do you remember anything about a man that none of the locals recognized?"

"The county fair is always a buzz of activity. Tons of people from all over. Friends and strangers, too. But yes, you're right, a stranger among us would have stood out." A frown creased her brow as she searched her memory as she continued her work. "That was a long time ago, but I do remember a handsome man, alone, didn't seem to know anyone. My sister Karen and I thought he was quite mysterious."

"Something must have happened to cause you to remember him," Scarlett probed gently.

Kathy set down her clippers, her expression turning somber. "Well, nothing we saw directly. But later, rumors flew around about him being a bit too forward with one of the local girls. It was just talk. You know how teenage girls are. And nothing seemed to come of it. We didn't see him again after that."

"Do you remember who the girl was?"

Kathy shook her head. "I'm sorry, I don't. It was just one of those things young girls whisper about and then forget. You know how it is in small towns."

"I do. Grew up in a small place, myself." Scarlett handed her a card. "If you remember anything else, please give me a call. It could be important."

Kathy took the card and slipped it into the cash register. "What could be so important about something trivial that happened thirty years ago?"

"Thanks again," Scarlett said on her way out.

She walked three blocks down and took a side street to the middle school. She found Karen Miller in a classroom, tidying up after the day's lessons.

Karen was more reserved than her sister. Her demeanor was cautious but polite.

After the initial introductions, Karen invited Scarlett to sit. "Kathy called and mentioned you stopped by the shop. What exactly is this about?"

Scarlett explained again, this time showing the two photos of James Preston. Karen studied them intently before handing them back.

"Yes, I remember him," Karen said slowly, handing the phone back.

"Tell me what you remember."

"He wasn't local, and he didn't fit in. Kind of stuck out, actually," She frowned. "There was talk about him and a girl. It was all hushed up pretty quickly. I think her family wanted to avoid a scandal."

"Any idea who the family was?"

Karen hesitated as if she didn't want to gossip, then sighed. "It might have been the Daltons. I don't remember the daughter's name. They didn't live here very long, and the girl was shy. Kept to herself, mostly. I barely knew her. They moved away not long after that. I haven't heard anything about them since."

Scarlett thanked Karen and left her card with a request to call if she remembered anything else.

As she walked back to her car, she made a call to Brad Webb, the detective she'd contacted at the local police department. He'd agreed to look through old records to find anything pertaining to Preston. If such records existed.

"I've got a name we need to check," she said when he picked up. "The family's name was Dalton. They had a daughter in high school at the time James Preston might have been in town for the fair."

"We've got a list of residents from back then. Let me check," Detective Webb said. "The Dalton family, right? The girl's name was Eliza. Parents Joe and Vivian. I found a forwarding address for them in Austin. It seems they moved there about six months after the fair."

"Any complaints or other police activity while they were living in the area?" Scarlett asked.

"I don't see any, but these old records aren't computerized. Honestly, they're not even filed very well. So I suppose they could have called something in, and it just got lost," he said apologetically. "I'm sorry I just don't have the time to go through thirty years of paperwork for you."

"If they had reported a physical attack on their underage daughter, would you have stored that report somewhere else? Somewhere we might be able to find it?" Scarlett said.

"Maybe. I suppose it's possible. Same problem, though. If no charges were ever brought, then…" his voice drifted off into the hot, heavy air. "You're welcome to come over to our storage facility and look for yourself if you want."

"I'll go at this another way. But if I don't find what I'm looking for, I might take you up on that." Scarlett thanked him and rang off.

She hadn't planned to be away from Houston overnight. With both Flint and Drake out of town, there was no one to stay with Maddy and Whiskers. So she headed back to Odessa to catch a flight home.

Austin would have to wait.

CHAPTER 32

Miami, Florida

"LET'S FIGURE OUT WHETHER Trawler's intel is reliable first. Then, I'll figure out a way to tell Spencer Lyman that his only remaining heir could be a killer," Flint replied.

"You say that like you think he'll be surprised," Gaspar said. "My dad always says the apple doesn't fall far from the tree."

"And then there's that." Flint deadpanned as he savored the Cuban coffee. "Spencer Lyman comes from organized crime. He claims he went legit a long time ago. But he's not going to disinherit the kid for being a member of the family, as it were."

"Did he, though? Abandon the criminal life, I mean?" Gaspar mused while focused on his screens. "That's the public story, sure. But how many times does it actually happen that they leave the mafia and live to a ripe old age planting tomatoes?"

"Looks like we'll need to broaden our search. Just because the curse is nonsense doesn't mean Ward Lyman's life was not in danger." Flint shook his head and drained the last sip of coffee. "Something else could have pushed him to fake his death. Something a lot more lethal than a curse."

Gaspar nodded. "Which would also give him a good reason to stay out of sight as long as he can."

"Let's hope he succeeds. It's a lot easier to find a stationary target than a fleeing one," Flint said as he pulled his vibrating cell phone from his pocket. "One way or another, this twisted game is over."

A text from Drake. The Pilatus was ready.

Flint sent a thumbs-up in response and sat down in a creaky chair, his eyes scanning the screens. "Drake's good to go. What have you found?"

Gaspar pulled up the grainy video Trawler had shown them which he said was Ward being killed on the docks.

"I've been analyzing this." Gaspar paused the video at the critical moment. "I've bumped the resolution as far as I can, and the original images still aren't clear. I've pieced this sequence together with video from several sources. Watch the two thugs who shoot Ward."

Gaspar played the video and Flint leaned in, his eyes narrowing as the footage advanced.

The thugs dragged Ward into the trees and loaded him into the back of a van.

The camera angle changed, and the images became more distinct as Gaspar moved to footage from one set of cameras to another.

The van drove through city streets, passing now familiar landmarks Flint had seen several times in Key West.

Gaspar pointed to the screen where the van pulled into a private hangar at the airport. "They loaded Ward's still limp body onto a private jet, jumped aboard, and took off. The flight plan was filed for the Bahamas, but it never arrived there."

Flint watched the video twice more, noting the time stamps and the landmarks in the background.

Something didn't feel right. Ward was either an amazing actor or they'd done something to make him appear dead.

"Where did the jet actually go?" he asked, trying to focus on the details.

"That's the tricky part," Gaspar replied, tapping on the keyboard. "The plane seems to have disappeared after crossing into international airspace. It could have gone anywhere."

"It *seems* to have disappeared?"

"Well, we know it didn't get beamed to Mars, right?" Gaspar grinned. "So if the jet *seems* to have disappeared, to alter the video feeds of several government satellites is a damned tricky hacking job."

"Is that feasible?" Flint asked, simply to confirm.

"I could do it, if that's what you're asking. So sure. With the right resources and a bit of time, it could be done," Gaspar said. "If there's one thing Ward Lyman has, it's access to plenty of resources."

"Which means this was all pre-planned." Flint mused. "And that jet was headed to a specific location."

"And a destination they intended to hide."

Flint looked at the route on the screen, tracing the trajectory with his finger. The jet had deviated from its expected course, heading southwest instead of east toward the Bahamas.

He pointed to the shift in the jet's path. "It's heading toward Mexico. Look at the angle."

Gaspar leaned in, enlarging and studying the screen and applying a bit of math to project the route. "Toward the general direction of La Pesca, Mexico, at that point."

"Small town. People would notice strangers," Flint said, thinking aloud. "Which suggests he might have bought one of those islands off the coast. Living on an island would be safer and he could control who comes and goes as well as what intel gets out."

Gaspar nodded. "I'll check land records for the past five years. Ward Lyman probably wasn't planning all this that far back. So I should be able to find it, if it was a legitimate sale."

"Could have been a private sale. Could have used a shell company or a straw man buyer," Flint mused. "This is where the luxury goods idea could come in. See if there were unexplained deliveries or construction happening within the right time frame."

"And whatever else I can think of." Gaspar turned his attention to the screen again. "I'll also unmask the jet. Whatever they did to alter the video can be undone. We just need to find satellites that were recording and not compromised by Ward's hacker."

While Gaspar was occupied, Flint located La Pesca, Mexico, on the map and enlarged the view of the coastal area looking for options.

Flint stood, feeling the tension in his shoulders. The hum of the servers and the smell of coffee filled the room. "After a shower, a meal, and a few hours' sleep, looks like Drake and I are heading to Mexico."

"With luck, I should find the right island, if there is one, before you finish dinner," Gaspar replied with his gaze focused on the screen already preoccupied with the task. "You don't need to waste time on a trip to La Pesca if Ward Lyman isn't there."

"Amen to that," Flint said as he texted his car service and walked outside to wait. Thick humidity and noisy traffic seemed to engulf him. He called Drake. "All set?"

"No damage to the plane during that bumpy landing. The fuel's been drained and topped up. We're in good shape. Should be fine," Drake replied.

Flint ignored the nagging unease about the plane and said, "I need a shower and a meal that doesn't come in a bag. And maybe some shuteye. You interested?"

"It's been a long time since I've been forced to subsist on MREs and sleep on dirt floors," Drake said. "And that roar you're hearing? Not the ocean. It's my stomach."

Flint laughed and climbed into the car waiting at the curb. "I'll see you at the Hilton. Bring the bags and meet in the lobby."

"Copy that," Drake replied.

CHAPTER 33

FLINT STEPPED OUT OF the sleek hotel, squinting against the brilliant Miami sunlight. Drake fell into step beside him.

"You're sure about this lead?" Drake asked, one hand shielding his eyes as he scanned the crowded plaza. "La Pesca is a hell of a place to go chasing after Lyman unless we're sure he's there."

"It's our best shot, given what we know. Intel points to Lyman probably holing up on one of the smaller private islands down there." Flint gave a curt nod. "You go ahead. I need to make a call."

"Copy that." Drake shrugged his broad shoulders. He cut across the plaza toward a waiting taxi that would take him to the Pilatus.

Flint watched him go for a moment before his gaze landed on a nearby newsstand. He bought a local paper and a cheap burner phone, then made his way over to a quiet cafe across the street. Sliding into a shaded booth, he quickly scanned the headlines before tossing the paper aside and powering on the burner.

A few coded texts later and he was connected to a contact who always seemed to have her ear to the ground in Mexico.

The minutes ticked by in tense silence as Flint nursed the strong black coffee, eyes focused on the encrypted messages flickering across the burner's screen. Finally, his contact came through with promising coordinates in La Pesca.

Flint left a generous tip and slid out of the booth.

As he crossed the plaza toward the taxi stand, Flint set his mouth in a grim line. Ward Lyman was close. He'd find the missing heir, drag him back from whatever hideaway he'd chosen, and put this whole case in the closed file.

The Lyman family could sort out their curse nonsense on their own time.

Drake was waiting in the cockpit running through his preflight checks. He looked up as Flint climbed aboard, pulled in the jet stairs and closed the door.

He settled into the copilot's seat, fastened his harness, and adjusted his headset.

"Gaspar pinged locations we can start with down in La Pesca." Flint held up the burner phone with a tight smile. "I found a few more coordinates to add to that list."

Drake's eyes returned the smile, all business. "Yes sir. Next stop, Mexico."

The Pilatus jet lifted easily from the tarmac and cut smoothly through the warm Caribbean air, leaving Miami and the Florida coastline behind. Flint stared out the window as the brilliant blue waters stretched out endlessly below.

After they'd been in the air for a while, Drake spoke through the headset. "You want to go over the plan one more time?"

Giving himself a small shake, Flint pulled his focus back to the matter at hand. "Once we hit local airspace, be on full alert. Lyman should have eyes and ears everywhere if he's embedded on one of these islands trying not to be found."

Drake nodded, eyes flicking between his instrument panels. "Understood."

"We can't assume he's alone down there either. He should have hired muscle standing guard."

Flint pulled out the burner phone, reviewing the grid of coordinates they'd compiled from Gaspar's intel and his own source. Half a dozen potential locations, all small private islands dotting the coastline and nearby waters.

"Once we're on the ground, we split up and start doing recon sweeps of each location," Flint continued, committing the coordinates to memory. "Stay on comms at all times. If we get a lead on Lyman's whereabouts, we formulate an extraction plan."

Drake nodded again, releasing a slow breath as he banked the jet into a gentle turn. Ahead of them, the rugged coastline of mainland Mexico was already coming into view.

"This is gonna get hairy, isn't it?" he mused, more statement than question.

A grim smile played across Flint's lips. "When doesn't it with this kind of gig? But we've been in tighter spots before."

"Truth." Drake chuckled lowly. "Just saying, I wouldn't mind a little more backup on this one."

Arching an eyebrow, Flint gave him an appraising look. "You know anyone who can lend a hand?"

Drake was quiet for a long moment, muscles shifting in his tanned forearms as he gripped the controls. "Might have a couple names worth calling in..."

"Let's take a look first. See what we're dealing with."

The jet banked again, lining up with their descent vector into La Pesca. Flint gazed outward as the glittering waters ahead came closer.

The jet's engines whined as they began their drop toward the coastline below. Flint's senses were hyper-focused. Somewhere out there amid those islands, Ward Lyman could be waiting.

Flint was more than ready. It was time to show this kid just how overmatched he was. With any luck, he wouldn't put up a fight. Flint preferred to return his quarry undamaged.

The Pilatus sliced low over the azure waters off the coast of La Pesca. Flint scanned the small islands searching for any hint of unusual activity.

"Anything more from Gaspar or your backup contacts yet?" Drake asked.

"Not yet." Flint shook his head. "Lyman likely has hired guns watching over his hideout. Mercenaries, probably."

"Makes sense," Drake replied. "This would be easier if we knew which one of these islands has been sold lately."

Flint flashed a grin. "If this job were easy, anyone could do it."

"Yeah, yeah." Drake deadpanned. "But we need to narrow this down somehow. We can't just go blasting onto private property."

Craning his neck, Flint watched as a small sandy cay slid into view off the jet's wing. Dense palms swayed in the ocean breeze, encircling what looked like a few modest structures. Not exactly a lavish resort for the spoiled heir to the Lyman fortune, but it was a damned site better than Harlan's island.

"Too humble for our boy," he remarked with a shake of his head. "But run your scans anyway. I want this locked down tight."

The jet banked in a wide arc as Drake brought them around the island's perimeter. Flint searched the shoreline for any signs of human activity and flipped on the thermal imaging system.

The screens lit up with detailed scans of the buildings and surrounding area.

"Looks abandoned," Drake reported.

Flint leaned forward. "Faint heat signatures near that bigger structure. Could be some kind of basic security system or early warning measures."

"Sounds promising. Lyman wouldn't leave his hideout completely defenseless," Drake said.

"Then again, given the world we live in, just about anybody would want basic security regardless," Flint said. "Let's take a look at the other islands and then we'll narrow it down to the best options."

"You're the boss," Drake said cheekily.

"Damned straight," Flint replied with a grin.

After a full pass along the coastline, they eliminated the larger islands with more than a dozen people wandering around. They also eliminated the smallest ones that appeared uninhabited.

Which left four possible targets.

"Alright, here's what we'll do..." Flint drummed his fingers against his knee as he began, mentally mapping out an infiltration strategy.

Flint outlined his rapid-fire thoughts and Drake listened intently while guiding the jet into a slow holding pattern.

Drake offered a curt nod. "Solid plan. Let's just hope the kid only has a few warm bodies for security."

"Guess we'll find out," Flint said, checking his sidearm one last time.

The jet banked again, slipping past the first island to begin running preliminary sweeps of the next potential target area. Flint drew a slow breath, savoring the familiar thrill of imminent action thrumming through his veins.

Part of him had to admit Scarlett was right. He lived for this stuff.S

CHAPTER 34

La Pesca, Mexico

AS THE SUN BEGAN to set over the tranquil waters of the Gulf of Mexico, Flint and Drake touched down on an abandoned gravel road just north of the coastal town of La Pesca. The Pilatus rolled to a stop. Drake shut down and they disembarked.

While Drake was securing the plane, Flint pulled out a fresh encrypted satellite burner phone and dialed Gaspar. The connection was unstable, but the call rang through to Miami.

"We've landed," he said when Gaspar picked up. "Got any intel on those islands?"

"There's four options, but only two might fit," Gaspar's voice crackled across the miles.

"Why?"

"Two of the islands have been owned by Mexican nationals for several decades. Nothing unusual going on there other than tourism," Gaspar replied.

"If Trawler's intel is right, it's not likely Ward would try to hide out in a tourist trap," Flint said. "What about the other two?"

"Isla Verde looks like your standard tropical getaway. Vacation homes, a couple of small resorts, nothing out of the ordinary."

"And the second one?"

"Isla Paraíso. That's a different story," Gaspar said. "Farther from the coastline and mostly abandoned. Too hard to develop or something. Until it was bought through a series of shell companies five years back."

"Sounds promising."

"The whole place was redone," Gaspar said. "Serious money spent on the project. Lots of construction, deliveries, workers ferried back and forth, you name it."

"So Isla Paraíso could be what we're looking for." Flint frowned as he considered the options. "Any idea who owns the place?"

"The trail gets pretty murky, but it could lead back to Lyman Enterprises, one way or another," Gaspar replied. "Or not. Whoever put the deal together knew his way around. It would take a team of forensic document examiners to sort out."

"Okay, thanks. We'll head to Isla Paraíso tonight after dark. See what we can learn."

"Call if you need anything else." Gaspar added, "Oh, and Scarlett's looking for you. She wants you to call."

"Did she say what it's about?"

"Course not. You know Scarlett." Gaspar chuckled before he disconnected.

Flint slid the phone into his pocket and turned to Drake. "Gear up. We're heading out to sea as soon as its dark enough."

"We've got some time to kill. How about a taco?" Drake said.

They walked a couple of miles south into town in search of food, intel, and a small boat to ferry them across the water.

Hours later, having learned only that the locals claimed to know nothing about the inhabitants of Isla Paraíso, a couple mentioned Lucky Jones. They said he lived on Isla Paraíso, came into town occasionally, but no one had seen him around lately.

They talked about all the improvements the new owners had made a few years ago. Two men in the bar said they'd worked on the villa. They seemed impressed with the amenities, which included a helipad.

Flint texted Gaspar with Lucky Jones's name and asked for background intel. After snooping around in the shadows, they found a small fishing boat tied up at one of the docks.

There was gas in the tank and keys in the ignition.

"We'll borrow this one," Flint said quietly as he untied the line and they stepped aboard.

Under the cover of darkness, Drake at the tiller, the boat cut through the calm waters surrounding Isla Paraíso. They didn't talk in the boat because sound carries across the water. The motor was making enough noise as it was.

As they approached the Isla Paraíso shoreline, Flint could make out the silhouettes of several buildings nestled among the palm trees. The largest of these, a sprawling villa, was perched on a rise overlooking the ocean.

Drake found a secluded cove around the back of the island. He beached the boat, and they quickly secured it, gathered their equipment, and moved carefully along the narrow path leading into the heart of the island.

As they drew closer to the compound, an eerie stillness hung over the area. Tropical sounds like night chirping insects and rustling leaves in the warm breeze, were muted and replaced by an unsettling quiet.

The compound was an inviting open space. A freshwater swimming pool with a few loungers around its edges. A hot tub nearby. Tennis courts across on the other side.

All were unoccupied. Flint saw no people at all.

They approached the main villa cautiously, hugging the shadows.

Up close, the building was impressive. A minimalist structure constructed of hurricane-proof glass and steel, designed to blend with the natural surroundings. Floor-to-ceiling windows offered broad views of the ocean.

Flint glimpsed sleek, contemporary furnishings through the transparent walls.

The villa appeared to be deserted. No lights glowed from within. He detected no movement at all in the area. Not even a nocturnal animal.

Flint and Drake moved to the villa's entrance. The door was unlocked. They slipped inside, weapons ready.

The interior of the villa was just as luxurious as the exterior suggested. An open-plan living area featured plush couches, a state-of-the-art entertainment system, and an expansive kitchen equipped with top-of-the-line appliances. Artwork from renowned contemporary artists adorned the walls, while sculptural light fixtures cast a soft glow over the space.

Flint and Drake moved through the rooms methodically, checking for any signs of Ward Lyman or clues to his whereabouts.

Flint found a bedroom that appeared to have been recently occupied, the bed unmade and personal items scattered about. Men's casual but expensive clothes filled the drawers and closets. The sizes and the price tags suggested they could belong to Ward Lyman. Not many locals would or could pay those prices.

But Ward Lyman was not there.

They expanded their search to the other buildings on the compound. A smaller guest house and a pool house. They discovered a private cinema off to one side.

Each was as lavishly appointed as the main villa, bearing all the hallmarks of Lyman's expensive tastes. But like the villa, they stood empty, with no indication of where he might have gone. Or why everyone else seemed to have left, too.

When they regrouped outside, Drake's frustration was evident. "He was here. I'd bet on that. But where the hell did he go?"

Flint shook his head, equally perplexed. "It doesn't make sense. Why pour all this money into the place, then just abandon it?"

A man emerging from a smaller outbuilding caught Flint's eye. He was dressed in a simple uniform suggesting he was an employee. He sauntered toward the villa.

In an instant, Flint was moving. Drake followed close behind.

CHAPTER 35

Isla Paraíso Island, Mexico

FLINT CLOSED THE DISTANCE between them quickly. The man didn't notice them approach until it was too late. He turned to run, but Flint was faster.

He tackled the man to the ground. He struggled to break free, but Flint pinned him tight to the sand. Eventually, he succumbed to the inevitable and stopped trying.

"What's your name?" Flint demanded while pressing the side of the man's face into the sand.

"Pedro."

"Where's Ward Lyman, Pedro?" Flint demanded, his voice low and intense. "We know he was here. Now he's not. Where is he?"

Pedro struggled briefly, but Flint pressed him harder to the ground and he gave up again.

"He's gone," Pedro gasped. "Left a couple of weeks ago."

Flint's grip tightened. "What do you mean, gone? Where did he go?"

The guy shook his head, sweat beading on his brow despite the cool night air. "I don't know. He just took off one night. Took a boat from the dock. We didn't know he was gone until it was too late. We couldn't find him."

Flint gave him another push. "How hard did you try?"

Pedro's eyes widened, darting between Drake and Flint. "He disabled the tracking systems on the boat. And we're not equipped for a manhunt out here. We maintain the property. That's all."

Flint exchanged a frustrated look with Drake.

Flint lifted the man off the ground and fixed him with a penetrating stare. "Why was Lyman here in the first place? What was he doing on this island?"

Pedro hesitated as if he were weighing his options. He quickly realized he had none.

"He was recovering," Pedro said. "When he first arrived, he was in bad shape. Injured, exhausted, malnourished. He said he needed a place to lay low. Heal up without anyone knowing where he was."

Flint's brow furrowed. "Recovering from what?"

Pedro shrugged. "I don't know the details. We were just told to make sure he had everything he needed, and to keep his presence here a secret."

"And after he recovered?" Drake prompted. "Why did he stay?"

"Why would he go? Look around," Pedro said. "He had everything he could want here. Privacy, luxury, no one bothering him. He spent his days lounging by the pool, reading, watching movies in the cinema. He seemed happy enough. We were shocked when he left."

Flint nodded slowly, processing the information. It fit with what they knew of Lyman's state of mind. The young heir had become increasingly paranoid, convinced that some curse or conspiracy was out to get him. A secluded sanctuary that offered everything he might want or need would have seemed like the perfect answer to his anxiety.

"But then something changed," Pedro continued. "A couple of weeks ago, he started getting restless, agitated. He was on the phone a lot, arguing with someone. And then, just like that, he was gone."

Flint leaned in closer, his voice dropping to a low, dangerous register. "I need you to think very carefully. Did Lyman say anything, anything at all, about where he might be going? Even the smallest detail could be important."

Pedro closed his eyes and scrunched his face in concentration. "I don't know. He didn't tell us his plans. But I did overhear him on the phone once. He seemed worried. He was talking about needing to go somewhere else, somewhere no one would think to look for him."

Which meant there was at least one person who knew about this island and knew Lyman was hiding out here. Flint was sure his grandfather didn't know where Ward was. So who was that person?

"Where did he go?" Flint asked again with an extra push with his knee in Pedro's back.

"I don't know," he repeated, desperation creeping into his voice. "But he mentioned something about going back to the beginning."

"The beginning of what?"

Pedro didn't reply.

Flint released his grip. Pedro stood and brushed himself off.

"'Back to the beginning,'" Drake murmured. "What the hell does that mean?"

Flint shook his head. He extended his hand and pulled Pedro to his feet. "Take me to Lucky Jones. I'll ask him my questions."

Pedro shrugged. "Mr. Jones is gone, too. Left a few days ago. I don't know when he'll come back."

"Where did Jones go?" Drake demanded.

"Mr. Jones doesn't confide in me," he said.

"Who would know where Jones went?" Flint asked. "His wife? Someone else here?"

He shook his head again and shrugged.

Drake gave Flint a quizzical glance and Flint nodded. They'd done all they could do here.

Drake moved quickly. He approached the man from behind and held him in a choke hold until he passed out. Drake lowered him to the ground.

"That'll keep him quiet long enough for us to get out of here," Drake said, retrieving a plastic zip tie from his pocket and securing Pedro's wrists behind his back.

"He doesn't know anything. And we've already tossed Ward Lyman's room. There's nothing more to find here." Flint replied and they hurried back to the boat they'd hidden to return to the mainland.

CHAPTER 36

Kansas City, Missouri

IN A NONDESCRIPT OFFICE laden with monitors and hastily assembled surveillance equipment, Boldo slammed his fist on the metal table, causing a small quake through the array of papers and electronic devices.

The screens flickered under the brunt of his frustration. Michael Flint had somehow located the island where Ward Lyman had been sequestered for two years. Lesser men had searched and failed. Boldo had thought they were in the clear.

Until Flint showed up.

Turned out to be a good thing for Boldo that Lyman had already escaped.

Now, Flint and Drake had left the island, and Ward Lyman was out there. He'd slipped through Boldo's grasp twice since his escape. Now, with competition on Lyman's tail, the stakes were even higher.

If Flint found Ward Lyman first, Boldo's entire plan would crash and burn. He wouldn't let that happen. No way in hell.

"Marino," Boldo barked, summoning his top operative who stood by the door. Marino stepped forward, tense but focused.

"They breached the island searching for Lyman. Flint and his muscle, Drake," Boldo growled, his voice thick with anger. "They know he's alive and out. We need to find Lyman before they even get a scent."

Marino raised an eyebrow. "Do we have any leads? Any idea where Lyman might have headed since Romeo and Paulie lost him a few days ago?"

"Not yet," Boldo admitted, grinding his teeth. "But we are going to change that. Get Romeo and Paulie on video."

Marino set up the feed and Boldo took over.

"You found Ward Lyman yet?" Boldo demanded. He saw the answer by the blank looks on their faces. "Start with his known associates, places he'd likely use for hideouts. Shake them down if you have to. I want results."

The two soldiers, Romeo and his sidekick Paulie, nodded sharply. "Understood, boss. And what about those two guys? Flint and Drake our man on the island said their names were."

Boldo's eyes narrowed into slits. "I want eyes on them as well, Marino. Tell our team to hang back, see what they learn. If they find him first or become any kind of obstacle, remove them. Instantly. No questions asked. Clear?"

"Crystal," Marino confirmed, his voice a low rumble.

"Good. Now move out!" Boldo commanded, waving a dismissive hand toward the video.

Romeo and Paulie hurried away. What had happened to Lucky Jones was still fresh in their minds, no doubt. Good.

Boldo punched the off button on the video call and turned to the bank of monitors. Each screen displayed different parts of the island and several other locations Lyman might hide, all currently quiet.

Marino placed a call. "Increase surveillance on all transport routes. If Lyman or anyone else tries to move in or out, notify me immediately."

"Where are we looking?" Boldo asked after Marino hung up the phone.

"We've got a list of Lyman's contacts and movements before we imploded the submersible. We'll start there, but he's not likely to backtrack," Marino answered.

Boldo nodded approval. "We need to find Lyman before Flint does. What do we know about him?"

"Not as much as we will in a few hours," Marino replied. "Flint's former military. Worked covert operations for a while. Now runs a high-end investigations service for people like Lyman. By all accounts, he's both competent and clever."

"And Drake?"

"They were military buddies. Drake is no dummy. But he's mostly extra muscle for Flint," Marino said. "They have a casual relationship with a larger outfit called Scarlett

Investigations. Run by a woman. Kathryn Scarlett. Also based in Houston."

Marino paused and Boldo gave him a stern glare. "Out with it."

"Flint is surprisingly good at this work. His reputation and success rate are well above the norm for these sorts of guys," Marino said. "Scarlett, too. Both have a pretty good track record for getting the job done, by all accounts."

"Which means we have a significant advantage," Boldo growled in reply. "Flint's a law-abiding citizen and I'm not."

Marino, wisely, said nothing.

Boldo paced the confines of his nondescript office in Kansas City, focused on Ward Lyman. He had slipped through Boldo's grasp and now, with Flint and his associates also on the trail, locating Ward Lyman and securing him again was Boldo's top priority.

The phone on his desk buzzed, and Boldo snatched it up. "What?" he barked.

"Boss, it's Romeo," came the reply, tinged with excitement. "We've got him. Ward Lyman. We're holding him in a safe house just outside Juarez."

Boldo's pulse quickened, but he tempered his reaction. He'd been down this road before, only to be disappointed. "You're sure it's him?"

"Positive," Romeo confirmed, his voice unwavering. "Matches the description and intel perfectly. Paulie and I have him secured. What do you want us to do with him?"

Boldo glanced at Marino, who had been listening to the call on speaker. Marino nodded.

"Bring him to Kansas City," Marino said, his tone leaving no room for argument. "We've got a secure location set up here. I'll text you the address."

"Understood," Romeo said. "We'll be there by morning."

"Don't take any chances. Keep him sedated for the transport."

"Understood," Romeo said again.

As the call ended, Boldo allowed himself a moment of satisfaction. Finally, Ward Lyman was within his grasp.

"This could be it, boss," Marino said, a rare smile tugging at his lips.

Boldo nodded, but doubt and previous failures nagged at him. Things had been under control until that idiot Lucky Jones allowed Lyman to escape.

Boldo and Marino relocated to the warehouse on the outskirts of the city. The building was hidden among the industrial landscape, but it had been outfitted with everything they needed.

Time was of the essence, so Marino had hired a private jet to collect Romeo, Paulie, and Lyman. They should arrive at any minute.

Marino pushed the button and the overhead door rolled up outside. The nondescript van pulled into the warehouse. The door rolled down again. The van's back doors opened from the inside.

Boldo and Marino watched as Romeo and Paulie emerged, dragging a hooded, zip-tied figure between them.

"He gave us some trouble," Paulie grunted as they hauled the prisoner to Boldo, his voice strained with exertion. "Had to knock him around to subdue him and then kept him sedated pretty heavy."

Boldo waved a dismissive hand, focused entirely on the hooded man. "As long as he's alive."

They secured the prisoner to a chair with a single metal handcuff on his wrist and the other clinking against the chair's frame. Boldo stepped forward, reached out and yanked the hood off, eager to look Ward Lyman in the eye.

But the face that stared back at him was not Lyman.

A complete stranger, eyes wide with fear, his face bruised and swollen.

"Who the hell is this?" Boldo roared, whirling on Romeo and Paulie, voice echoing off the warehouse walls.

The two men paled, confidence evaporating under Boldo's fury.

"Boss, we were sure..." Romeo started, his hands raised in a placating gesture.

Boldo had heard enough. Red rage clouded his vision and boiled over.

Without a moment's hesitation, he drew his gun and put a bullet in Romeo's forehead.

Romeo's head exploded. Blood and brains splattered. He crumpled onto the concrete where blood pooled beneath his head.

Paulie barely had time to cry out before Boldo's second shot cut off his scream. He joined Romeo on the floor.

Boldo stood over the bodies, chest heaving with rage, the gun still hot in his hand.

Flint was out there, and Lyman seemed to be slipping further away with each passing moment.

He turned to the terrified man tied to the chair, eyes wild, and pointed the gun at his head. "Where is Ward Lyman?"

The man shook his head frantically, tears streaming down his face. "I don't know, I swear! Those guys just grabbed me off the street, I don't know anything."

Boldo silenced him with a vicious backhand, knocking the chair to the floor and the man's head against the concrete. He was out cold.

"Clean this up," Boldo ordered, gesturing to the bodies on the floor.

"What about him?" Marino nodded, pulling out his phone.

Boldo cast a cold stare at the unconscious man. "Get rid of him. He's a liability we don't need."

As Marino set about his tasks, Boldo stalked out of the warehouse.

He climbed into his car and pulled out onto the street, jaw clenched, knuckles white on the steering wheel.

CHAPTER 37

Mexico

FLINT LEANED BACK IN his chair across from Drake in the small, dimly lit dining room.

"Let's recap what we know," he said, low and serious. "Ward Lyman is alive and on the run. There's a good chance he's being targeted. All those narrow escapes from his past could have been a killer's failures."

Drake nodded as he considered each point. "The Lyman Family Curse has already claimed four heirs. Ward is the last heir still alive. If Ward dies, who inherits?"

"Good question. I'll check that with the old man. Some charity, I'd imagine," Flint replied before moving on to the next point. "Lyman Enterprises stock prices are falling. The company is on the brink of a hostile takeover. Unless something changes soon, there will be no business to inherit. Given the state of the situation, that could happen long before

Spencer Lyman dies. Which means the heirs, whoever they are, would get nothing but a pile of debts."

"Then there's the Lyman family's mafia ties in Kansas City," Drake added, his eyes narrowing. "That's a whole other can of worms."

Flint ran a hand through his hair and moved on. "Lucky Jones. He was on that island with Ward. Now, also missing."

"Do you think they're together?" Drake asked, leaning forward.

"Possibly. Although it sounded like Ward left and then Jones went after him," Flint replied. "We don't know what the relationship was there. Whether Jones was Ward's security, an enabler, or the warden."

They ordered more coffee while each considered the facts. Flint rolled things around in his head, twisting them this way and that, until the waiter departed.

"So, what's our play?" Drake asked when Flint didn't restart the conversation.

"We need a fresh approach," he said at last. "If we can track Jones down, he could lead us to Ward."

Drake frowned. "But how do we find Jones? We have no idea where to start looking."

"Ward said to go back to the beginning," Flint replied, echoing Pablo's words. "He could have meant Kansas City. Lyman Enterprises began there."

"The family's old mafia business?" Drake asked, surprised.

"Makes sense." Flint leaned forward. "Ward might be looking for protection. Old mafia ties could provide that. And Kansas City is a connection to his family's past, a place that holds meaning for him."

Drake nodded slowly. "So, we head to Kansas City, dig into the Lyman family's mafia connections, and hope it leads us to Lucky Jones and Ward Lyman?"

"Unless we come up with a better plan. Stay flexible," Flint said. "Let's get some sleep. We'll leave before dawn."

"Copy that," Drake replied. He signed the check, picked up the receipt for his expense account, and followed Flint.

They trudged to the lobby and climbed to the top of the stairs. Drake said good night and went to his room, which was two doors down from Flint's and on the opposite side of the corridor.

Flint stepped into his room, closed and locked the door, and opened the windows. Warm night air brushed against his skin. After the day's physical exertions and tonight's warm food, the breeze made him sleepy.

Before he quit for the night, he pulled out his encrypted satellite phone and dialed a familiar number.

After a few rings, a gruff voice answered. "Flint. Been a while."

"Too long, for sure," Flint greeted his source, who was also an old friend. "I need some information."

"Of course you do," he chuckled. "What do you need?"

Flint took a deep breath. "The Lyman family. I need to know about their ties to organized crime in Kansas City."

There was a pause on the other end of the line. "As in Lyman Enterprises? That's a question I haven't heard in a while. They're totally legit these days. Or so they want the world to believe. They were big players in the Kansas City mafia back in the day, especially the patriarch, Joe Lyman."

"How so?" Flint prompted.

"Joe Lyman was Spencer's father and Ward's grandfather. Born in Italy. Immigrated here during the mafia's heyday. He was a boss in the crime family. Contemporary of Anthony 'Big Tony' Boldo. Those two, they had a history."

"What kind of history?"

"The kind that involves friends and a woman. Joe and Big Tony, they were both in love with the same girl," his source chuckled. "Joe Lyman married her, and Big Tony? Well, he never got over it. Held a grudge for years. Probably till the day he died and maybe even beyond the grave."

Flint absorbed the information. "What about a guy they call Lucky Jones? What do you know about him?"

"Never heard that one. Lucky Jones?" he repeated as if he were scanning a long list. "Here it is. Real name's Nathan Jones. A soldier in the Boldo family. Nasty piece of work."

"I need to find him. Do you know where he lives, works, anything?"

"I'd have to dig around a bit," he said. "Give me an hour, I'll see what I can turn up."

"Thanks. Call me back when you have something on Jones."

"Will do. And Flint? Be careful. You're stirring up some old ghosts. The kind that don't like to be disturbed," he warned before he ended the call.

Flint stretched out on the bed to wait, keeping the phone in his hand. An hour later, as promised, his source called back.

"Flint," his voice was tight. "I got that info you wanted on Lucky Jones. Got something to write with?"

Flint grabbed a pen and pad from the nightstand. "Go ahead."

"He's got a place in Kansas City. An old neighborhood. 1542 Elm Street. Used to moonlight as a bouncer at one of Boldo's clubs downtown, a place called The Red Room. Not sure if he still does."

Flint jotted down the details. "Thanks, Buddy. I owe you one."

"Watch yourself. Jones is not a guy to mess with. And if he's mixed up with the Lymans and Boldos, you're wading into some deep waters."

"I'll keep that in mind. One more thing," Flint said. "Jones's wife. I heard she testified against the Boldo family on a double homicide case a few years back."

He let out a low whistle. "Yeah, that was a mess. She's the ex-Mrs. Lucky Jones, by the way. Nasty divorce, which fed into her willingness to testify. Got witness protection for her trouble. Caused a lot of bad blood."

"Do you know where she is now?"

"I can find out."

"Thanks. Let me know," Flint said and disconnected.

Drake would be starting the Pilatus in a couple of hours. Flint needed shuteye before then. He fell back into bed and instantly to sleep. A habit he'd learned in the Marines. Sleep when you can.

It seemed like five minutes later when Drake rapped twice on the door on his way out. Flint got up, stuck his head under a cold shower, jumped into his clothes, and followed.

"You look like hell, man," Drake said when they met up in the lobby.

"Thanks," Flint replied dryly as they left the hotel and hustled to the Pilatus.

They boarded quickly, and soon the jet was in the air. When they reached cruising altitude flying toward Kansas City, Flint brought Drake up to date.

"According to my source, Joe Lyman and Big Tony Boldo had a major falling out back in the day. They were both in love with the same woman, and Lyman ended up marrying her. Boldo never got over it, held a grudge forever."

Drake whistled softly. "Sounds like a solid motive for revenge. Too bad Big Tony's been dead since before Ward Lyman was a twinkle in his old man's eye."

"Yeah, but Boldo's son isn't dead. He's running the family now," Flint replied. "My source also had some info on Lucky Jones. Turns out his real name is Nathan Jones, and he's a soldier in Boldo's crime family."

"A soldier?" Drake asked, his eyebrows raised. "Meaning he's an enforcer, a guy who does the dirty work."

"But here's where it gets interesting," Flint continued. "Jones had a nasty divorce from his wife, Anna. She testified against a lesser member of the Boldo family in a murder trial, and in return, she got witness protection."

Drake let out a low whistle. "So Jones has ties to the Boldo crime family. You think Boldo sent Jones to kill Ward Lyman?"

"It's possible." Flint stood up, pacing the room. "But if Ward is running from something, if he's afraid for his life, he might have turned to Jones for help. Jones has the connections, the know-how to keep him alive."

"But why would Jones help him?" Drake asked, playing devil's advocate. "If he's loyal to Boldo, wouldn't he just turn Ward over? Or worse?"

"Maybe Jones has his own agenda. Maybe he sees helping Ward as a way to get back at Boldo, to settle some old scores or something," Flint said. "Or maybe Jones was supposed to keep Ward Lyman on that island. Which would mean that Jones either helped Ward escape or took off in hot pursuit."

"In either case, that pits us against both Ward and Jones. And they've got a two-week head start." Drake nodded slowly, the pieces starting to fall into place. "So, what's our next move?"

"We've got two angles. Lucky Jones and Ward Lyman. We'll follow up on both."

"And if we find Jones and he isn't willing to talk?" Drake asked, already knowing the answer.

Flint's expression hardened. "Then we use our powers of persuasion."

Drake grinned. "Scarlett always says you can sell ice cubes to Eskimos."

"Guess we'll see." Flint replied.

Drake said, "Then let's go pay Mr. Jones a visit. Where do we start?"

"We're likely to make more progress with his ex-wife. We'll start with Anna Jones."

Drake gave him a quick glance across the cockpit. "How will we find her?"

"Leave that to me," Flint replied.

CHAPTER 38

New Haven, Colorado

MICHAEL FLINT PARKED HIS rental discreetly a block away from the community center in New Haven, a suburb of Denver. The information he'd received from his source placed Lucky Jones's ex-wife deep under cover somewhere in this town.

The first challenge was to find her. He left the SUV parked at the curb and strolled the sidewalks around the downtown, eyes sharp.

His source had provided photos of Anna Jones taken five years before along with other intel. They reflected a thirty-five-year-old woman with mousy brown hair, dulled facial expressions, and fingernails chewed until they'd bled. During her testimony, she'd been timid and afraid, often hiding her face from the camera and refusing to comment when questioned.

Anna had been treated for clinical anxiety since she was a child, long before she put her life on the line to convict Boldo's soldiers and send them to death row.

Such fundamental traits were not likely to have changed with Anna's new name and new life, even if she felt safe and secure. Which Flint would bet she did not. Wisely so. If Boldo found her, he'd kill her for sure.

Flint's seemingly easy stroll and intense focus on local women was interrupted by the sound of laughter and conversation from a community event happening nearby. Public events allowed people to let their guards down and behave kindly toward strangers. He'd had good luck with the technique before.

He strolled toward the event, blending in with the crowd. Behind his Aviator sunglasses, his gaze moved from face to face, searching for Anna Jones. He spotted a woman standing alone at the edge of the gathering, eyes darting around the crowd.

Flint approached casually, grabbing a coffee from a nearby vendor before making his way to her.

"Beautiful day for an outdoor party, isn't it?" he commented as he stopped a respectful distance away. Now that he was closer, he was certain it was her.

"Yes, it is quite nice," she replied cautiously. She gave him a brief, somewhat forced smile.

"I'm Michael," he introduced himself, offering a hand. "I'm new here. Still getting to know the place."

"Beth," the former Anna Jones said, offering her new name and shaking his hand tentatively.

Flint nodded, keeping the conversation flowing naturally while observing her reactions. "I'm actually here looking for someone. Maybe you can help me. It's important. She might be in danger."

Anna tensed, her eyes narrowing slightly, "Who are you looking for?"

"A friend who might be in trouble because of past associations. I heard through the grapevine that New Haven could be his sanctuary," Flint said carefully while watching her closely.

Her demeanor shifted, a flicker of recognition passing through her eyes before she masked it again. She started to back away.

"You should ask someone else. I don't think I can help you."

"Please, I just need to know if he's safe. You don't have to tell me anything else. His name is Ward. I'm very worried about him." He paused, giving her time to get comfortable.

"This isn't the place to talk," Anna finally murmured, her expression softening. "Meet me at the old mill on the edge of town. In an hour."

"That would be great." Flint replied and they parted ways. He spent the next hour wandering around, making sure he wasn't followed.

He'd already found Anna Jones. He might stumble across Ward Lyman in the same way. Stranger things had happened.

But he didn't find Ward or anyone else he recognized. By the time he reached the old mill, Anna was already waiting, hands stuffed in her coat pockets and gnawing her lower lip.

Briefly, he wondered if she had a weapon in one of those pockets.

"You're not with them, are you?" she asked as soon as he approached.

"I'm here to help Ward, and possibly you too, if you need it," Flint said quietly, as if he were gentling a wild animal.

Anna looked around nervously before nodding slowly. Now that they were talking, she seemed more afraid than before.

"It started a few years ago," she began, her voice low. "Lucky wanted out, but Boldo wouldn't let him. They sent him on a job. Three of Boldo's men were killed. Lucky was totally freaked out because Boldo blamed him for the failure. Ultimately, that's what caused our divorce. I testified against the others to keep Lucky out of prison forever."

"Which worked, didn't it? The two killers were sent away and Lucky wasn't."

"But Boldo was furious when he saw my name on the witness list. He tried to kill me. Twice. That's when they offered me witness protection if I testified. So I did. I'd be dead now if I hadn't." Her voice dropped off as she chewed her lip like it was coated with chocolate.

"How long have you been living here in New Haven?" Flint asked, trying a less threatening topic to get her to relax.

"Two years. This is my third placement. Boldo found me in the first two," she whispered, her voice vibrating as if she were shivering with cold. She stuffed her hands deeper into her pockets. "He'll find me here, too. I'm like a dog in the road. It's only a matter of time."

Flint would have tried to reassure her, but she was right. Which meant she was better off being hypervigilant than relaxing her guard. She'd survive longer if she kept her wits about her.

"I need help finding Ward Lyman," he said, changing the subject to his reason for his interest.

"Ward?" she said, eyes widening. "I heard he died a couple of years ago. He was a nice kid. Lucky liked him. I was upset when I heard about Ward. They said it was an accident, but I'd bet Boldo got him."

"Boldo? Why did Boldo want to harm Ward Lyman?" Flint cocked his head.

"It's a long story," she said wearily, as if she were lost in memories. "Goes back years and years. Boldo's a man who can hold a grudge forever. Just like his old man."

"Does this have anything to do with the Lyman Family Curse?" Flint prodded when she stopped talking.

"Ah, yes. The famous curse." Anna smiled for the first time since they'd met.

The amused smile reached her eyes, revealing a lively sparkle for a brief moment. Flint saw that she might have been happy once, even if the years and her life choices had not been kind to her.

"You're a smart man, Mr. Flint. You know there's no such thing as a curse," Anna said without prompting. "It's a hit list, and Ward was an obvious target. I'm surprised he lived to be as old as he did. Boldo must be getting soft."

Before Flint could follow up, a sudden noise caught his attention. Anna looked behind him and screamed.

Flint turned to see two men emerging quickly from the shadows brandishing pistols.

"Come on." Flint grabbed Anna's arm.

Her feet seemed nailed to the floor. He gave her a hard yank and pulled her along. She stumbled ten feet to an alcove behind a rusted old apple press.

"Stay down until I give you the all-clear. Understood?"

She nodded rapidly, wringing her hands, teeth chattering. He had no confidence that she'd do as she was told. Nothing more he could do about that at the moment, either.

Flint drew his Glock and ducked for cover, waiting as the two men advanced quickly, loud footsteps pounding the concrete floor.

One of the men demanded, "We know you're here, Anna. We've got some unfinished business with you."

Flint peered around the edge of the apple press to assess the situation. Both men were twenty feet away from Anna, coming in fast.

He grabbed a piece of busted concrete from the old floor and hurled it toward a cluster of empty oil drums on the other side of the room. The concrete hit the drums with a loud clang, and both men turned toward the noise. One fired twice, hitting two drums. The liquid that had been stored inside gushed out.

Flint ducked out from behind the apple press and fired two quick shots. The first bullet hit one of the men square in the chest, sending him tumbling to the ground. The second man managed to return fire, but it went wide and ricocheted off a nearby steel beam.

Flint ducked back. He could hear the second man cursing as he moved closer.

"You're dead, you hear me?" he shouted in Flint's general direction. "Dead!"

Flint held his fire, waiting for his shot. When the second man was clear, Flint darted out again, firing as he moved.

The second man went down, dropping his gun to clutch his fractured, bleeding leg.

Flint moved quickly. He kicked the man's gun away and pressed his weapon to the man's forehead until he stopped writhing on the floor.

"Who sent you?" Flint demanded, his voice cold and hard.

The man spat at him. "Go to hell."

Flint pressed the gun harder against the man's skin. "Two seconds before you join your friend in Hell yourself. Who sent you?"

The man's resolve seemed to waver, but before he spoke sirens filled the air. Someone must have heard the gunshots and called the police.

Flint gave the man a swift kick that put him out cold.

He turned to Anna, still crouched behind the apple press, eyes wide with fear.

"We have to go. Now. Come on."

Anna nodded, scrambling to her feet. He took her hand and together, they raced toward Flint's SUV. He put Anna in the passenger seat and ran around to slip behind the steering wheel. The sirens were coming closer.

He started the engine and accelerated to the first corner, taking a sharp right. Two blocks later, he zigged left. After three more turns, he couldn't hear the sirens anymore.

Flint punched the navigation system button for a local map. A blinking red dot showed his location. A four-lane county road was two miles ahead.

"Where are we going?" Anna asked, once she controlled her shaking well enough to get the words out.

"You can't go back there. Those guys found you and someone else will, too," Flint replied. "You have a handler, right?"

"Yes."

"Call him. Tell him what happened. Ask for a safe house. I'll take you there and wait with you until he comes," Flint said, watching the rearview mirror and following the navigation route. He turned onto the county road heading toward Denver.

CHAPTER 39

Denver

ANNA'S HANDLER CAME THROUGH with a safe house tucked deep within the rain-soaked woods west of Denver. The house had no fixed address, which made it harder to locate. The navigation system was useless, which, if they were lucky, could thwart even seasoned hunters.

Flint drove more than an hour through a raging thunderstorm barely able to see, even with the windshield wipers swiping fast. As night fell, the SUV's headlights were barely up to the task, illuminating only a short distance ahead.

When they reached the narrow rural roads, Flint slowed until he'd located the place.

He parked around back, out of view of the road, and they hurried inside. Soaked to the skin and freezing, Flint flipped the lights on and went looking for the heat.

He found a fireplace with a wood fire already laid and a propane starter on the mantel. He pulled a couple of chairs closer to the fire. He searched until he found towels they could use to dry themselves.

Within a few minutes, the room had warmed enough to take the chill off.

Anna was almost catatonic. She pulled her knees close to her chest and doubled over in the chair, staring into the fire as if she were mesmerized. Her breathing was rapid and shallow. She had said nothing since they left the main road almost an hour ago.

Flint had tended broken people before. In his experience, there was only so much emotional trauma one human could take before breaking down completely. He hoped Anna hadn't reached that point because admitting her to a hospital or clinic was out of the question. Boldo would find her and kill her before she had a chance to breathe.

While the storm was raging outside, he left Anna again to rummage through the kitchen. He found coffee and a coffee pot. A few moments later, the aroma of fresh brew filled the air.

The refrigerator and the pantry were well stocked with provisions, including cream and sugar. He poured a big mug of coffee heavily laced with sugar and cream for Anna. Black for him.

He carried the coffee to Anna, who hadn't moved since he'd left her. "Take this coffee and drink it. It'll help."

She didn't look up. He reached for her hands, placed the cup between them, and held her palms against the warm porcelain until she seemed to realize it was there. She glanced up, her eyes filled with tears.

"Thank you," she said quietly before she took the first sip.

Flint secured the doors and checked the two bedrooms in the cabin. Both were as sparsely furnished as the main living area. But they were dry, warm, and well provisioned. Flint had stayed in worse places. Anna surely had, too.

When he returned to the fire, the color had returned to Anna's face, and she'd stopped shaking. Flint took both as positive signs. Time to persuade her to talk.

"Now, tell me everything. Start from why Ward Lyman is a target," Flint said, his voice carrying the weight of the situation.

Anna nodded and began to piece together the story. "It's about Lyman Enterprises. Boldo wants it. The company's value and influence are immense. Much bigger than anything Boldo owns now or could build in two lifetimes. He can't own Lyman Enterprises as long as the Lyman heirs exist. He had to get rid of them."

Flint stretched his legs, feet closer to the fire. "And the curse?"

"It's a tool. A terrifying fantasy used to cover up the systematic elimination of the Lyman heirs. With each heir that dies, the story of the curse grows stronger, keeping the others frightened," Anna explained, her eyes haunted by the things she'd witnessed. "They're right to be afraid. The threat is real. But there's nothing supernatural about it."

"Ward is the last heir," Flint pressed to keep her talking now that she'd started.

"If Ward dies, there's no one left to claim leadership of Lyman Enterprises after old man Spencer goes. He'll go soon, one way or another. Then Boldo steps in, takes over, and all of this," she gestured vaguely, encompassing the storm, the dark woods, the massive influence over Anna's life, "was to clear the way for that to happen."

"Lyman Enterprises is publicly traded. But the Lyman family owns the controlling interest," Flint mused aloud. "So whoever holds the family shares effectively owns the empire."

"Exactly," Anna nodded, draining the last of the sweet coffee and practically licking her lips. "Is there more of this?"

"Yeah. And food, too. Are you hungry?"

"I'll see if I can find us something to eat," she replied and headed toward the kitchen, which Flint took as another good sign.

She was up and moving and looking for food. Big improvement.

Two hours ago, she was practically catatonic. Now she was hungry and willing to cook. She was a remarkable woman.

He heard her opening and closing doors and rattling cutlery for about half an hour. She came back with two plates, two forks, and two omelets on a tray along with two cups of coffee.

She put the tray on the table between them. Flint hadn't realized how ravenous he was until he'd tasted the omelet. Anna ate heartily, too.

When they finished, he settled into his chair with the coffee again. He was warm, dry, and well fed. Three things he hadn't expected to happen tonight.

After a while, Anna restarted the conversation. "You said Lucky was with Ward. Are you sure Ward's alive?"

"I'm sure he didn't die in that submersible implosion. I'm sure he was alive two weeks ago. Right now, I can't say. But I hope he's still alive," Flint replied. "I need you to help me find him before Boldo does."

"Me? I haven't seen Ward Lyman in years, and then I only saw him in passing. We didn't travel in the same circles, if you know what I mean," Anna said, greedily drinking another cup of the sweet coffee. "What I can say is Boldo's men are everywhere. And they're like ghosts. Shadows that you don't see until it's too late."

"I need to find Ward. Can you help me with that at all?" Flint asked.

Sorrowfully, she said, "I would if I could."

"Okay, then help me find Lucky. We suspect your ex was Ward's security detail for the past two years. If they're not together now, Lucky will be closer to finding him than I am."

Anna said nothing while she stared into the fire sipping the sweetened coffee.

"Level the playing field for me," Flint coaxed. "Tell me something I can use to unravel this mess before Ward does get killed and Boldo moves on to his grandfather."

"If Lucky was watching Ward for Boldo and Ward escaped, Lucky's either dead already or he's a dead man walking," Anna said flatly. "Boldo has zero tolerance for screwups, and this will be Lucky's last chance."

Before Flint could reply, a loud crash echoed through the cabin when the front door burst inward under a violent kick.

Flint drew his weapon instantly and pulled Anna to the floor behind the chairs they'd been sitting in.

"Boldo," Anna said in a terrified whisper.

The intruders entered quickly through the broken doorway like a well-trained swat team. The raging storm shoved wind and rain inside immediately behind them.

Flint raised his head for a quick look, counting three armed men moving with tactical precision.

The leader, a broad-shouldered brute with a scar across his left cheek, sneered when he spotted Flint's flimsy barricade.

"We have no beef with you, man. But you can't protect her forever. Let her go and we'll let you go," he shouted over the roar of the storm.

Flint glanced at Anna.

"Stay down and keep quiet." Then he called out in response, "No thanks. We're good here."

Gunfire erupted and a volley of bullets splintered the wood around their shelter. Flint assumed they'd been ordered not to kill Anna. Otherwise, she'd be dead now.

Finally, some good news.

Their desire to take Anna alive could be leveraged for escape.

Flint waited for a pause in the shooting and then returned fire to push the intruders back.

The exchange was quick and fierce. Flint was outmatched. He needed an exit strategy and fast.

He grabbed Anna's hand. "We're going out the back. Move!"

They dashed toward the kitchen at the rear of the cabin. There was no back exit. But a small window offered a potential escape route.

Flint broke the glass with the butt of his gun, clearing the way. "Climb through. I'm right behind you."

He gave Anna a little push and she scrambled through the window. Flint followed, just as another barrage of bullets tore through the walls behind them.

They emerged into the storm. Rain as thick as Niagara Falls fell in sheets all around them, limiting visibility and movement.

They escaped deeper into the woods, running blind through the cascading water, slipping on the muddy forest floor.

Behind them, the shouts of their pursuers faded into the howl of the wind.

But they weren't safe yet.

CHAPTER 40

FLINT AND ANNA RAN through the dark forest and relentless rain. The thick canopy overhead offered little protection from the storm's fury. The ground beneath their feet had turned to a treacherous quagmire. Mud sucked their shoes deeper with every step.

Anna's foot caught on a gnarled root and she stumbled, nearly falling face-first into the mud. Flint's strong hand gripped her arm, hauling her back to her feet before she hit the ground.

"Keep going," he urged, his voice barely audible over the roar of the storm. "We can't stop now."

They pressed on, lungs burning with each labored breath. Pursuers crashing through the underbrush behind them spurred them forward.

Another flash of lightning illuminated the forest ahead. Flint spied the entrance to a small cave a few yards to his right.

"There," Flint shouted, pointing toward the natural shelter.

Anna changed course and ran toward the cave. Flint followed close behind.

They stumbled inside where the storm's roar was muffled by the cave's rock walls.

Flint stood at the edge of the cave, pulled out his satellite phone and pressed a preset number. The connection was unstable, but he heard the ring tones on the other end.

"This is Flint," he barked into the phone when his contact picked up. "I need an extraction."

"Copy that." His contact's voice on the other end crackled with static. "I've got a bead on your location. We can't get a helo to you there in those woods."

"I have a female civilian with me," Flint's jaw clenched. "What are the options?"

"I'm seeing a clearing fifty yards east of your position," he said. "The storm's letting up. Rain and wind should be slowing enough shortly. If you can get there, we can pick you up in fifteen."

"Understood." Flint ended the call and ducked deeper into the cave to join Anna. "We've got to move. There's a clearing nearby. A helo's on the way."

"How did they find us?" Anna was trembling with fear and cold.

Good question.

"We'll figure that out later." Flint extended a hand.

"Okay." She lifted her chin and grabbed his hand. "Let's go."

Before they could step out of the cave, the sound of footsteps and muffled voices reached Flint's ears. He held up a hand, signaling Anna to stay silent and peered into the darkness.

Two armed men were approaching his position.

He stepped into the shadows and Anna did the same.

A moment later the men entered the cave, weapons drawn.

Flint lunged first. His fist connected with the man's jaw in a sickening crunch, knocking him to the rocks at the base of the cave wall. His temple hit hard enough to knock him out. Maybe even kill him. He was unconscious and that's all Flint had time to check.

The second man had grabbed Anna and wrapped his arm around her throat. Her eyes were wide and terrified, but she didn't try to break away.

"Drop your weapon," the thug demanded, "or I'll snap her neck."

Flint hesitated, locked his gaze on Anna's horrified face with a silent order to stay both still and quiet.

No response.

She seemed catatonic.

With a sudden burst of speed, Flint dove forward, tackling the man and sending all three of them tumbling out of the cave and into the rain-soaked forest.

The man instinctively released his grip.

Anna seized the chance to scramble aside.

Flint grappled with the thug, wrestling on the muddy ground as they traded blows.

His hands closed around the man's throat. He squeezed until the struggling attacker went limp.

Flint staggered to his feet as Anna stood watching nearby.

"Run," he urged breathlessly.

She took off into the forest, heading for the clearing.

Flint followed, watching for the rest of Boldo's squad.

The ground was treacherous. Mud sucked at their feet with every step. It was slow going.

Anna stumbled again, landing on hands and knees in the muck.

Flint hauled her back to her feet again.

"Keep going," he said with a little push. "We're almost there."

Behind them, more men crashed through the underbrush, closing in.

All of a sudden, the storm let up. The wind gusts had blown themselves out. The rain slowed and then stopped.

The clearing was just ahead. He heard the approaching helicopter whapping closer.

Flint and Anna burst into the clearing just as the helo descended from the stormy sky. Rotors whipped the raindrops resting on the leaves into a frenzied dance.

The pilot set the bird down expertly on the wet leafy carpet.

Flint pushed Anna toward the waiting bird.

"Go," he shouted over the roar of the rotors. "I'll cover you."

Anna hesitated, eyes wide with fear.

"Go!" he repeated with a stronger push.

Anna ran for the helicopter as Flint turned to face Boldo's men.

Three burly thugs emerged from the tree line, weapons blazing. Flint took cover and returned fire.

Two lifeless bodies hit the muddy ground with heavy thuds, like felled giants.

But the leader charged forward, a wicked combat knife clutched in his hand.

Flint met him head-on, blocking the blade with his forearm.

The knife slashed again, catching Flint across the ribs. He grunted in pain and twisted away from the blade.

The leader pressed his attack, driving Flint backward while the helo's rotor wash created a chaotic maelstrom.

Flint ducked under a wild knife swing and then surged forward and slammed his shoulder into the thug's chest. They crashed to the ground and the knife slid deep into the mud.

Flint scrambled for the blade, his fingers closing around the hilt just as the thug lunged for him.

With a final, desperate effort, Flint brought the knife up and plunged it into the side of his attacker's thickly muscled neck.

Blood spewed and the thug's eyes went wide with shock. He clutched at his throat. His mouth opened and closed soundlessly while his blood pulsed out between his fingers.

Half a moment later he fell, and his body went still.

Flint staggered to his feet, chest heaving with exertion. He stumbled toward the helicopter, leaping aboard just before it lifted off.

Anna pulled him in, hands shaking, and Flint fell into his seat.

As the helo rose into the stormy sky, Flint looked down at the clearing.

"It's not over," he said, barely audible over the roar of the rotors. "If these were Boldo's men, he won't stop until you're dead, too."

"Unless someone stops him first," Anna replied, her pleading gaze fixed on Flint.

CHAPTER 41

Denver

THE HELICOPTER ASCENDED THROUGH the rain-soaked sky, the rhythmic thump of its rotors echoing off the glistening trees that pierced the low-hanging clouds. During the short flight to Denver, Flint made another call on his satellite phone to a contact at the US Marshals Service.

Flint and Anna leaped from the helo as soon as it touched down. Spinning blades whipped the air as they ducked beneath the decelerating rotor.

The acrid scent of exhaust fumes mixed with recent rainfall created a pungent cocktail that stung his nostrils as he ushered Anna toward the waiting SUV.

"Agent Riley," Flint said as he nodded to the waiting man as he settled Anna inside the vehicle and closed the door.

"What's this about, Flint?" Riley asked once Anna was sequestered.

"She's in witness protection. Her real name is Anna Jones. She's not safe. You'll need to move her," Flint said and then described the two thwarted attempts on Anna's life.

Riley nodded solemnly. "You're sure it was her they were after and not you?"

"Fair point," Flint replied. "But I'd rather not make a mistake on this. What worries me is her handler. He sent her to that safe house in the woods. Those guys found us there. Not too many ways that could have happened. He told them or they had eyes and ears on him."

"Or her. Or you." Riley seemed unpersuaded.

"I appreciate your loyalty to her handler. But do you want to be the one who makes a mistake on this, Riley?" Flint asked.

Riley considered the question seriously. "Okay. Get in. Tell her what's happening so she'll trust me. I'll take her into the office and get this sorted out."

"Thanks. She's been through a lot. She deserves to stay alive," Flint said.

"Yeah, don't we all," Riley deadpanned, and Flint agreed.

As the SUV merged into the early morning traffic, muffled sounds of the city seeped into the cabin. A distant siren, an impatient driver mashing the horn, a rumbling delivery truck.

Flint's muscles ached with exhaustion. The adrenaline that had fueled the fight slowly dissipated, leaving a bone-deep weariness.

"Where are we going?" Anna asked.

"Honestly, I'm worried. We need to know that you're still safe living here under your current identity," Flint explained. "I know Riley. I've worked with him before. You can absolutely trust him. He'll get this sorted out for you."

"You've saved my life twice already," Anna said quietly. "What choice do I have?"

Flint closed his eyes and leaned his head against the seat for a moment's rest.

Anna said, "There's something else you should know. It's Emily Royce. The Lyman Enterprises CFO."

"What's that?"

"Lucky told me that Emily Royce has been pushing Spencer Lyman to step down as CEO. She says it's long past time for him to retire. She wants the top job for herself."

"I see," Flint replied, still resting his eyes. "So, you think she's using Boldo and this old vendetta to create chaos within the company. Hoping to force Spencer out and take control. That about it?"

Anna sighed as if she carried the heavy weight of suspicion on her shoulders. "It's a ruthless power play. Lucky and Ward and I and who knows how many others are pawns in their game."

Agent Riley glanced back at them from the front seat, his voice reassuring. "You're not a pawn, Anna. Your safety is our top priority. We'll make sure you're protected."

"I don't mean to sound ungrateful, Agent Riley," Anna replied quietly, as if she were resigned to her fate. "But I've heard that before. And we see how it's worked out today."

The car slowed to a stop outside an office building. Agent Riley parked, exited the vehicle and opened Anna's door.

His voice was calm, professional, reassuring. "Anna, let's get you inside."

She hesitated, turning to Flint one last time. "If you find Lucky, will you let Agent Riley know? I'm worried about him."

Flint met her gaze. "I'll make sure Agent Riley is informed. He'll know how to get a message to you."

Anna nodded and offered a small smile. She stepped out of the SUV and Riley guided her toward the building.

Flint watched until she disappeared inside, and the glass doors slid firmly shut behind them. Anna was as safe as he could manage. Nothing more he could do here.

He fished out his cell phone and pressed the speed dial.

Gaspar opened with, "What have you gotten yourself into this time?"

Flint smirked. "Oh, you know, the usual. Corporate intrigue, dangerous liaisons, and a power-hungry executive with her eye on the throne."

"Sounds like a typical workday for you," Gaspar quipped in reply. "So, what do you need from me?"

"A deep dive background check on Emily Royce, the CEO of Lyman Enterprises. I've got a witness who says she could be in cahoots with Anthony Boldo and is pushing him to go after Spencer Lyman because she wants the top job."

Gaspar let out a low whistle. "You think she's sleeping with a mob boss to climb the corporate ladder? That's cold."

"I don't know what the connection is, but that's a solid guess. Or it could be just a business deal. Either way, it's cold," Flint agreed seriously.

"Who's the witness?"

"The former Anna Jones. Wife of Nathan "Lucky" Jones."

After a long pause, Gaspar said, "You believe the story? I mean, Anna Jones was married to a Boldo soldier and testified against Boldo. Could be she's carrying a grudge, and she wants you to put an end to Boldo."

"Totally possible. But it didn't come across that way," Flint replied.

"Okay. I'll check out Emily Royce. History, connections, any skeletons in her closet. The usual," Gaspar said. "End of the day soon enough for you?"

"Thanks, Gaspar. I owe you one."

Gaspar warned, "Several good agents have died already trying to bring Boldo down."

Flint glanced up at the towering skyscrapers. "I'll be in touch."

He slipped the phone into his pocket. The rain had ended, and clouds began to break apart and reveal patches of blue sky. Crisp damp air filled his lungs and cleared his head.

He had a lot of ground to cover.

Flint stepped off the curb, flagging down a passing taxi.

"Airport," he said as he slid into the backseat and made another call.

The line rang twice before Drake answered. "Where the hell have you been? I've been trying to reach you for hours."

"You worry too much," Flint grinned, his tone confident and self-assured. "Sorry about the radio silence. It's been a wild ride out here in Denver. But I've got a lead."

"Denver? What the hell are you doing out there?"

"I'll tell you all about it when I see you," Flint replied, glancing out the window as the taxi navigated the city streets. "I'm headed to Kansas City to have a chat with Spencer Lyman."

"What do you need from me?"

"Fly up in the jet and bring some hardware. I'll need to ship mine. Arrange a set of wheels. I'll meet you at the airport."

"Copy that," Drake replied. "I'll see you in Kansas City."

Flint ended the call and leaned back in his seat until the taxi pulled up to the departures terminal. The driver turned to look at Flint expectantly. He paid the fare with cash and stepped out onto the curb.

He watched the taxi leave the terminal before he flagged a second cab and gave the driver the address for a nearby shipping store.

Attempting to fly while in possession of a firearm could get him in the kind of serious trouble he didn't have time for today.

He carefully packaged his gun, filling out the necessary paperwork to have it sent to a secure drop box in Houston. He'd pick it up later.

When he returned to the airport, Flint approached the ticket counter, flashing his most charming smile at the attendant.

"I need a seat on the next flight to Kansas City," he said pleasantly.

The attendant, a young woman with a bright smile, nodded and began clacking computer keys. "You're in luck, sir. There's a flight leaving in just under an hour. I can get you a seat in first class."

"Perfect. Let's make it happen." Flint nodded, handing over his credit card.

Flint made his way through security and toward his gate. By the time he arrived, the flight was boarding.

He followed the line of passengers to the first-class cabin, found his seat, and closed his eyes to sleep until they reached Kansas City.

When the plane landed, he checked his phone where he found two texts from Gaspar about Emily Royce, both marked urgent.

CHAPTER 42

Austin, Texas

AFTER MADDIE AND WHISKERS went to bed, Scarlett had spent a restless night flipping through her notes and re-reading the witness statements she had gathered so far. She'd also searched a few public databases until she'd found Eliza Dalton Hammond.

Now in her forties, married, with two kids of her own, Scarlett had to hope Eliza would do the right thing.

She planned to approach Eliza first thing tomorrow. A cold call at night might spook her but giving her any kind of advance warning meant she could flee before Scarlett had a chance to question her.

During the short flight to Austin, Scarlett's thoughts were on the young woman who might hold the key to confirming or destroying Preston's alibi for the time of June Pentwater's murder.

She hoped that Eliza Dalton could shed some light on the case. She was a minor at the time, and her parents had tried to shield her. But she was an adult now and Preston was already dead. All of which might mean Eliza would tell the truth.

Scarlett deplaned, found her rental, and turned on the navigation system. She punched in the address and rolled into traffic headed northwest to West Lake Hills, a small but posh suburb of Austin.

She found the address easily. She drove around the block and past the house a couple of times to get a feel for the neighborhood. West Lake Hills was originally built in the 1970s and 1980s, and the homes seemed of the era. Ranch style, mostly. Large lots and modest buildings.

The Hammond residence was a well-kept ranch style home that fit in well with the others in this quiet, older neighborhood. Scarlett parked on the street out front, walked up the sidewalk to the porch and rang the bell.

A woman in her late forties answered, her expression wary but polite. "Can I help you?" she asked from behind the closed and locked screen door.

"Mrs. Hammond? Eliza Dalton Hammond?"

The woman nodded. "Yes, that's me."

"My name is Kathryn Scarlett. I'm investigating a case from many years ago and believe you might be able to help me." Scarlett held out her card and waited.

After a bit, Eliza unlocked the screen and reached out to take the card. She stepped back inside and latched the screen again. Then she studied the card for a few moments. Examined both sides. Felt it with her fingers.

"May I come in? It's about something that happened at a county fair in Pleasant Farms years ago when you were a young girl," Scarlett explained patiently. When Eliza continued to hesitate, Scarlett said, "It would really help a lot if you'd let me come in."

Eliza's face clouded with a mixture of recognition and discomfort.

"I remember that time," she said slowly, opening the door wider. "My husband will be home soon. Can we do this quickly?"

"Yes, of course." Scarlett followed her into the living room and sat down on the sofa across from the chair Eliza chose for herself.

Eliza's hands were tightly clasped in her lap, signaling her anxiety, probably about dredging up the past.

Scarlett took control of the conversation before Eliza had a chance to change her mind. She opened the photo of young James Preston she had on her phone. "I'm trying to find out about this man. His name is James Preston."

Eliza took the phone and studied the old driver's license photo. Her eyes opened wider, and her hands shook a little. She acted as if she were trying to recall the man, but she'd recognized him instantly. Scarlett could tell.

"Did you ever see this man before?" Scarlett asked. "Maybe at the county fair when you were in high school?"

Scarlett could see the hesitation on Eliza's face as the encounter from years ago flashed into her head. Emotional memories often surfaced like that, even when they were long forgotten.

The air in the room felt heavy, laden with the weight of unspoken details and years of silence.

"Eliza, can you tell me more about that night? Anything you remember could be important," Scarlett encouraged softly when it seemed she had withdrawn completely.

"It was a warm night, lots of people around, but it felt like we were in our own little world at first. He was charming, called himself Jimmy." Eliza sighed, her gaze distant as she traveled back in time. "He seemed interested in me, in my life... it was flattering, you know? I was fifteen. No man had ever paid attention to me before. No boys, either, for that matter. I didn't have many friends. I was kind of plain and my parents were strict. I had no experience at all in dealing with a man like Jimmy."

"I see. Of course," Scarlett muttered at the pauses to avoid breaking whatever spell Eliza had put herself under and keep her talking.

"We talked about the usual things—where we were from, what we liked to do. He was a smooth talker. Easy. Nice." Eliza paused, swallowing hard.

"Um hum," Scarlett nodded to gentle her through the obviously difficult story.

"But then, Jimmy wanted to go somewhere quiet," Eliza murmured. "I thought it was to talk more privately, but once we were away from the crowds, he changed. He became more demanding, forceful. I didn't expect that. It scared me."

"What happened then, Eliza?" Scarlett asked softly, noticing the tremble in Eliza's voice.

"We... we walked behind one of the barns to talk where it was quieter, no people. It was dark, and I said I thought we should go back, but he didn't listen." Eliza's voice cracked a bit. "I guess I was naive. I-I just didn't expect..."

She cleared her throat and clasped her hands tightly. "He pushed me against the barn and held my wrists so I couldn't move. He kissed me and rubbed up against me some. He didn't hurt me—not really. I squirmed out of his grip before it could go any further and rushed back to the fair. Later, I thought he wanted to hurt someone, but I was lucky. Just got a few bruises."

Scarlett noted every word, aware of the courage it took to speak them. "How did you get away from him, Eliza?"

"I just pushed him as hard as I could. He stumbled backward and I twisted free. I ran until I was back among the lights and the people." Eliza paused to wipe a single tear from the corner of her eye. "I never saw him again after that night. Far as I know, he never came back."

"You didn't tell your parents? Or your girlfriends?"

Eliza shook her head. "I never told anyone. Who would believe a small-town girl like me over a charming stranger like Jimmy?"

"But your parents were worried, weren't they? And the other girls suspected something, even if you didn't tell them what Jimmy did."

Eliza's chin quivered and glassy tears filled her eyes. She nodded without speaking and took a couple of moments to get herself under control.

"Later, when I heard he was called James and he was arrested for killing another woman," she whispered softly and Scarlett had to lean in to hear, "I couldn't connect that man to Jimmy. But it was him. I saw his picture on the news and in the papers."

"I'm sorry. It must be hard to remember those moments," Scarlett said, offering a compassionate smile. "Your experience is incredibly important. Thank you for telling me."

Eliza managed a small, sad smile. "It's been a long time, but it feels like it was just yesterday. I was just a kid. Very sheltered. No one had ever hurt me like that before. All I could think at the time was that I'd caused it somehow. That it was my fault."

"It absolutely was not your fault. Don't think that for a minute," Scarlett said firmly. "You were a child. What Preston did to you was a crime. He should have been prosecuted for it."

Eliza swiped her tears with the back of her hand. "I hope this helps somehow, to make things right."

"It does, Eliza. More than you know," Scarlett reassured her. "It helps in seeking the truth about what really happened to James Preston, and to June Pentwater."

Eliza nodded, eyes lowered, hands together.

"Did you see him again after you ran from behind the barn?" Scarlett prodded.

Eliza shook her head. "I just went home. Never saw him again. When I heard he was executed for murder, I thought I'd feel safer, somehow."

"Eliza, did you ever write down what happened, or tell someone later on?" Scarlett asked. Documentation or corroboration could be crucial.

"I wrote it in my diary a couple of days later. Thought it might make me feel better," Eliza admitted. "I've kept all my old diaries in a box in the attic. I haven't looked at them in years. But it should still be there."

Scarlett's pulse quickened. "Would it be possible to look at that diary?"

Eliza hesitated for a moment, then stood with a deep sigh. "Okay, let me get it."

She returned a few minutes later with a dusty box and together they rummaged through and found the old diary.

Scarlett turned the fragile old paper to the date of the fair and advanced a few pages until she found Eliza's detailed account of her encounter with James Preston. She read through the childish cursive quickly.

The story was a bit more vivid than Eliza's oral version, but young girls were much more emotional than adult women.

The pages also supported Preston's alibi, which could prove his innocence in the murder of June Pentwater.

The implications weighed heavily. Scarlett didn't take the time to sort her feelings about that. Nor did she dwell on the questions this evidence would inevitably raise. Not yet. There would be time for all of that later.

"Eliza, this could be incredibly important. With your permission, I'd like to take a copy of these pages to include in my investigation," Scarlett said, looking up at Eliza with a hopeful expression.

Eliza nodded. "If it can help in some way, please do."

Scarlett used her phone to take photos of the pages, the diary, and Eliza. There were a lot of scribblings. It was likely young Eliza had referenced the trauma several times.

Scarlett said, "Can I take this diary with me? I'll see that you get it back."

Eliza shrugged. Scarlett pulled an evidence bag from her pocket and slid the pink diary inside. She pressed the self-stick tape to the bag and shoved it into her jacket pocket before Eliza could change her mind.

"Will we be much longer? My husband is due home soon," Eliza said again, as if she didn't want him asking questions when he arrived.

"Thank you again." Scarlett stood to leave. "You have my card. Call me if you need anything, okay? And I'll be in touch."

Eliza didn't reply and Scarlett let herself out.

In the SUV on the way back to the airport, she wrestled with the facts she'd uncovered.

James Preston was tried, convicted, and, after several appeals, executed for murdering June Pentwater.

He'd had a dozen lawyers over the years. He'd claimed innocence from the moment he was arrested until he died.

How likely was it that he never mentioned that he had an alibi for the murder? Or that, once mentioned, his lawyers failed to investigate?

Not likely at all.

So why didn't his alibi rescue him from prison and death?

Scarlett wracked her brain for an answer but came up empty. She changed tracks.

What did this all mean for solving the Marilyn Baker murder? If Preston didn't kill June Pentwater, did that prove he didn't kill Baker, either?

If Preston didn't kill both women, then who did?

Back at the Austin airport, she dropped off the rental and hurried to the gate to catch an earlier flight to Houston, going home with too many unanswered questions.

She could use some help on this. Where the hell was Flint?

CHAPTER 43

Kansas City, Missouri

BOLDO'S PHONE VIBRATED ON the desk. He picked up. "Yeah."

"We've got a line on the kid." The voice was distorted, a digital mask for security. "He's been careful, but we picked up a trace in Mexico. We think he's using an alias, staying at small inns, moving often."

"We need a positive ID," Boldo replied. "Keep on him. I want daily updates. If he so much as buys a postcard, I want to know."

"Understood."

"Damn Lucky Jones," he muttered when he ended the call with a click and leaned back in his chair.

Ward Lyman was the wildcard. Unpredictable and uncontrollable. Lucky Jones had one job. Keep Lyman on that island. If Jones had been halfway competent, Boldo wouldn't be in this mess now.

No way to rewind the clock on all of this. Jones had paid the price for his failures. Boldo had to let his anger go. There was nothing more he could do to Jones at this point.

He paced the room, floorboards creaking under his weight, and paused by the window, gazing out at the city sprawling below. His phone buzzed again. He snatched it up, expecting another update.

"It's me," said the digitally masked voice, a different one this time, urgent but controlled. "We lost him in Guadalajara. He might have sensed something."

Boldo's grip tightened. "How?"

"Not sure. He was at a market, then gone. Vanished like smoke."

"You're certain it's him? You have a positive ID?"

"Not yet."

"Get more men on it. He can't have gone far." Boldo's voice was terse, a command more than a suggestion.

"Already done. We're spreading out, checking buses, taxis."

"Keep me posted. Minute by minute."

The line went dead and Boldo set the phone down. He walked over to a large map pinned across the wall, staring at the web of notes and markers. He traced a line from the north to the south stopping his finger at Guadalajara.

He turned as the door behind him opened. Emily walked in, her face drawn and tired.

"Any news?" she asked.

"He's slipping through. Might have made us in Guadalajara."

She frowned, leaning against the desk. "And Flint?"

Boldo shook his head. "No word yet. But he'll be too close for comfort."

Emily scowled. "Flint can't get to him first."

"No, he can't." Boldo picked up a glass from the desk, poured whiskey from a decanter. He offered her one, but she declined with a wave of her hand.

"What's our next move?"

"Pressure. On all fronts. We shake the tree, see what falls out. Someone's helping him, hiding him, feeding him cash," Boldo said. "We find who, we find him."

Emily nodded and made suggestions. "See what your contacts in the local police can do. Grease some palms, tighten some screws."

"We've done this before. We know what we're doing." Boldo took a sip, the liquor burning down his throat.

She nodded as if she were unconvinced.

Boldo set his glass down, considering scenarios, each move and countermove flashing through his mind like scenes from a film. "We'll keep on it. You, too. Ward Lyman cannot resurface before we're done. We'll take him out if necessary."

Emily nodded before she walked to the door. She stopped, looking back. "Tony, be careful. We're playing with fire here."

Boldo gave a half-smile, more grimace than grin. "I'm not planning on getting burned."

She left and the room fell silent. The old clock on the wall seemed unnecessarily loud. Boldo returned to the window.

Ward Lyman was proving to be a cunning opponent. Much more resourceful than Boldo had expected.

His phone buzzed again. The screen showed a number he didn't recognize. "Yes?"

"He's not alone. He's with a woman."

Boldo straightened. "Who? Do we know her?"

"Working on it. But she's shielding him."

"I want everything. Background, connections."

"Will do."

The call ended. Boldo stared at the phone. A woman. An unexpected variable. Where did Lyman connect with her? What did he promise her in return for her help?

His gaze shifted back to the map and traced a route south toward the coast. Maybe they'd try for the water. Easier to disappear on a boat.

He grabbed his coat. Time to move.

The door clicked shut behind him as he stepped into the elevator.

He walked swiftly to his SUV, which his driver always had waiting in the shadow of the building.

"Airport," he said simply.

As the car rolled off, weaving through the late traffic, Boldo felt the old thrill, the chase. But beneath that, unease.

This was a race now.

And races had losers as well as winners.

CHAPTER 44

AFTER FLINT DEPLANED IN Kansas City, he used the encrypted cell phone to return Gaspar's call as he walked toward the airport exit.

Gaspar picked up and launched directly into the reason for his call. "I'm still digging into Emily Royce's background, but I've found a few interesting things."

"I'm all ears," Flint said as he rode the escalator to the ground floor.

"It's going to take some time to get the full picture, but you'll want to know what I've uncovered so far," Gaspar replied, the sound of typing audible in the background.

Flint had reached the exit and the taxi line. Drake wouldn't arrive in Kansas City for another hour. They'd agreed to meet at the hotel.

"Still all ears," he said as he waited for the next cab. The line was moving steadily. There were only three people ahead of him now.

"Turns out, Emily Royce has deep roots with the Lymans and their company. Her parents worked on the Lyman Estate. Mother was part of the house staff. Father worked in the horse barns. She was a blue-ribbon-winning equestrian in high school and college because of the time her old man spent training her. Loves horses still. Both parents are deceased now. Emily started working for the company back in high school as a clerk in Spencer Lyman's office."

"So she'd be expected to show significant loyalty to the Lymans," Flint mused, tapping his finger on the armrest. "Which tends to argue against Anna Jones's theory about Emily's relationship with Boldo."

"You'd think," Gaspar said before he continued. "After graduating from Kansas State, she went straight back to Lyman Enterprises, working her way up through the accounting department. She's been CFO for the past five years, and from what I can tell, she's done a damned good job."

"How so?"

"Well, she hasn't been replaced and Spencer Lyman is notoriously quick on the trigger to let people go if he feels they're not performing," Gaspar said. "Not only that, he's signed off on significant bonuses through the years. Three years ago, Spencer Lyman gave her a seat on the board."

"Sounds like the chairman believes she's dedicated to the company," Flint said, his mind processing the information as he climbed into the cab and gave the driver the name of his hotel.

"Yep," Gaspar agreed. "But here's where it gets interesting. About two years ago, Emily began taking frequent trips to Chicago. And guess who else was in the Windy City during those same time periods?"

"The one and only," Flint deadpanned, unwilling to mention names that the cab driver would know.

"Bingo," Gaspar confirmed. "I can't tie it down yet. But the frequency, timing, and duration of those trips are looking like more than just a coincidence."

"Which means Anna's story could be true," Flint said. "And maybe the two are closer than Anna knew."

"It's starting to look that way," Gaspar agreed. "If there's an airtight connection between Emily and Boldo, I'll find it. Assuming they're having an affair, if Boldo's using her to take over Lyman Enterprises, disclosing the affair to Spencer Lyman might be enough to thwart Boldo's plans."

The taxi pulled up at the hotel entrance. Flint paid with cash and stepped out onto the sidewalk. "I'm at the hotel. Anything else?"

"I'll keep digging, and I'll let you know as soon as I have something more concrete," Gaspar said. Before he ended the call, he added, "Scarlett asked me to say she's looking for you."

"Thanks," Flint replied.

Inside the hotel, Flint approached the registration desk to pick up two keys to his suite. He texted Drake with the suite number. Drake was still in the air, but he'd see the message when he landed.

Upstairs, Flint stretched out on the bed and closed his eyes. He did some of his best thinking that way. He moved the pieces of intel around in his head for about five minutes before he was fast asleep.

A knock at the bedroom door pulled Flint to consciousness about an hour later.

"Come in, Drake," he called out.

Drake stuck his head into the room. "Fresh coffee and a snack just arrived from room service. You can fill me in while we eat."

"Yeah. Be right there." Flint washed his hands and splashed cold water on his face and finger-combed his hair before he joined Drake.

Room service had wheeled a table into the room and set up a feast of charcuterie and coffee. Flint's throat felt parched. He grabbed a bottle of water and drank it all in one gulp.

"Okay. What do you know that I don't?" Drake asked.

Flint filled him in on the basics while devouring meats and cheeses. He drank three cups of coffee, too.

Drake listened closely until Flint finished. "So we need a meeting with Spencer Lyman. Update him on our search for Ward and see what he knows about whether Emily Royce's loyalty runs to Lyman or Boldo."

"Since Spencer Lyman already knows and trusts me, I'll handle that part on my own. I'm not sure he'd speak freely with you in the room," Flint said, moving to a more comfortable seat and propping his feet on an ottoman.

Drake nodded, leaning forward in his chair. "So what do you need me to do while you're taking care of Lyman?"

"Dig around. If Emily and Boldo have a secret connection, somebody will know about it," Flint replied. "Gaspar says they've been meeting in Chicago. But that doesn't mean they haven't been seen together in Kansas City, too."

"So you want me to encourage gossip?" Drake said with a smirk as if he were genuinely shocked.

"And lots of it. Try to separate the wheat from the chaff if you can. But at this point, we'll take whatever gossip is floating around out there." Flint nodded. "In the meantime, I'll reach out to Spencer Lyman set up a meeting as soon as I can get it. I need to let him know Ward didn't die in the submersible. And that he's in bigger trouble now, if Boldo's after him."

"Are you planning to tell him about Emily and Boldo scheming to destroy and capture Lyman Enterprises?" Drake arched both eyebrows.

Flint shrugged. "Depends on how it goes."

They spent the next hour going over details and mapping out strategy.

After that, Flint called Spencer Lyman's private number. Spencer answered the call himself.

"It's Michael Flint. I'm in Kansas City. I've got a few things to discuss with you. Can I come out?"

"I can see you in an hour," Lyman replied curtly, as if someone were in the room with him and he didn't want to say more. "I'll send a car."

"Perfect," Flint said and disconnected. "Lyman's sending his driver."

"Guess we'd better get downstairs then," Drake replied, headed to his room to collect a jacket and the two handguns he'd brought from Houston.

He returned and gave one of the pistols to Flint. They left the suite and took the elevator to the lobby.

"I'll call you after our meeting. Keep in touch," Flint said with a nod. Drake nodded back.

Outside on the sidewalk, Drake walked toward the parking garage and Flint waited for Lyman's driver.

CHAPTER 45

THE LIMO PULLED UP a few minutes later. The same one that had taken him to the Lyman Estate the first time. Flint recognized the driver. But if the driver recognized him, he gave no indication.

Less than half an hour later, the limo pulled up in front of Lyman Enterprise's headquarters in downtown Kansas City and waited for his passenger to exit.

Flint strode into the lobby, scanning the bustling group of employees and visitors as he approached the reception desk.

"Michael Flint to see Spencer Lyman," he said to the young woman behind the desk.

The receptionist nodded, picked up the phone and spoke in a low voice. After a moment, she hung up and turned back to Flint.

She gestured around the corner to her left. "Take the executive elevator to the top floor. His office is at the end of the hall."

Flint thanked her and made his way to Spencer Lyman's office suite. Another gatekeeper was seated at a desk in the anteroom. She looked up with a smile.

"Michael Flint to see Spencer Lyman," he said.

"He's expecting you," she replied, standing to usher him through the door into Lyman's private office.

Flint was struck by Spencer's commanding presence. The tired old man he'd met before was nowhere to be seen. This Spencer Lyman sat behind a large mahogany desk, straight posture, silver hair, and piercing eyes giving him an air of unassailable authority.

"Flint," Lyman said, standing to shake hands with the strength of a man half his age. "You have information about my grandson?"

Flint sat in a client chair across from the desk. "I'm afraid it's not the news you were hoping for."

Lyman leaned forward. "What do you mean? Is Ward alive or not?"

"I don't know," Flint replied, his tone grave. "But it seems you were right. We've confirmed that Ward did not die in the submersible implosion. He never boarded the submersible at all."

Lyman slumped back in his chair as if Flint's words had punched the air from his lungs. His eyes glassed up with tears and his lips quivered briefly. Then he got ahold of himself.

"Then where is he?" Lyman demanded.

"We have credible evidence that he's been hiding out on an island off the coast of Mexico for the past two years," Flint said.

"Hiding out? From what? Why would he do that?" Lyman seemed genuinely perplexed.

"We haven't talked to Ward, but one of his buddies said Ward was absolutely paranoid about the Lyman Family Curse. He thought he could hide on the island and wait it out."

"Wait it out? You mean he intended to stay there until he turned thirty? Seven whole years?" Lyman asked, incredulously. "That's preposterous."

"Possibly. But that was the plan," Flint replied firmly.

"Well, where is this island. I'll go down there and get him, if need be," Lyman demanded, sitting ramrod straight in the chair and showing the steel spine for which he was famous.

"We tried that and failed. Ward is no longer living on the island," Flint said, and Lyman's eyes widened. The news seemed to have left him momentarily speechless. "He left two weeks ago."

"Where did he go?"

"We're not sure. Yet. We're working on that," Flint replied. Before Lyman had a chance to explode, Flint continued. "The island where Ward was lying low is owned by Anthony Boldo."

Lyman's eyes widened. Shock and anger flashed across his face. "Boldo? What the hell was Ward doing?"

Flint shook his head. "I don't have all the details yet. At this point, Ward is on the run. Probably from Boldo and his men."

Lyman slammed his fist on the desk. "I can't believe this. My grandson, mixed up with a criminal like Boldo. How can that be?"

"I understand your frustration." Flint leaned in. "When we find Ward, you can ask him. But right now, we need to find him before Boldo does."

"Yes. Of course. There must be another explanation." Lyman took a deep breath to compose himself. "Ward knows our family history. Lyman Enterprises can't be connected to Boldo in any way whatsoever. I've spent my entire life severing that connection. There are vultures out there who would destroy everything we've built if we were tied in any way to organized crime."

Flint said nothing.

Lyman spoke again, as if Flint had argued the point. "Ward is young and impetuous and maybe a little too fanciful with this curse business. But he would never hurt the family or the business. I'm sure of that. Why would he? He stands to inherit everything. He wouldn't shoot himself in the foot like that."

"When we find Ward, we'll have more answers." Flint said and then pressed on. "There's something else I need to ask you about. It concerns Emily Royce."

Lyman looked up, even more surprise evident on his face. "Emily? What about her?"

"We have reason to believe that Ms. Royce may be involved with Anthony Boldo as well," Flint said, watching his reaction closely.

"*Involved*? What the hell does that mean?" Lyman snapped. "I doubt Emily even knows who Boldo is."

"We believe she does know him," Flint said, treading carefully. "I was hoping you might be able to shed some light on their relationship."

"Relationship? What do you mean?" Lyman's famous composure was rattled. "Emily's parents worked for me for years. My wife, God rest her soul, loved Emily's mother like a sister. We've always treated Emily like a member of the family. I can't imagine her being mixed up with Boldo in any way. Makes no sense at all."

"Boldo could be coercing her in some way. We just don't know yet," Flint nodded. "But if there's anything unusual about Emily's behavior, any changes you might have noticed, I need to know. It could be important."

Lyman sighed, rubbing a hand over his face. "I'll have to think about it. Emily's always been a dedicated employee, a rising star. Ward and Emily should run Lyman Enterprises one day, just as she and I have done."

"Could you have missed something?"

"I suppose it's possible," Lyman admitted. "I've been preoccupied with Ward these past few years. Maybe I wasn't paying enough attention to Emily's activities."

"If you think of anything, call me." Flint stood, extending his hand.

"Find my grandson, Flint. Bring him back to me." Lyman shook Flint's hand, his grip firm. "And if Emily is involved in any of this, I want to know about it. I won't have my business compromised by criminal associations of any kind."

"I'll do everything I can," Flint said as he left the office and returned to the elevator to the main floor.

When he stepped outside, Flint waved the limo aside and walked toward his hotel. He pulled out his phone and punched Drake's number.

"Drake."

"I'm on my way back to the hotel. Find anything?" Flint asked.

"Yeah. But Gaspar's hot to talk to you about it first," Drake replied.

CHAPTER 46

Houston

SCARLETT SAT IN THE outdoor café enjoying the sunshine as she sipped iced coffee. Well-dressed Houston office workers, singles and pairs, hurried past on the sidewalk on the way to important meetings and court hearings and the like.

Naomi Wagner spotted Scarlett and hurried over, slid onto the chair opposite and waved to capture the barista's attention, all in one fluid movement like a graceful Olympic ice skater.

"Sorry I'm late," she said, not the least bit winded. "Traffic was a nightmare."

Scarlett waved off the apology.

Wagner leaned forward eagerly. "You said you had something. About the Preston case."

Scarlett nodded. "I do. And you're not going to like it."

Ignoring Wagner's frown, Scarlett pulled out a folder and slid it across the table. Wagner flipped it open, her eyes scanning the contents.

"What is this?" she asked, frown deepening as she skimmed.

"Those calendars Dean Taylor gave us, the ones that supposedly proved Preston's alibi? They're frauds."

Wagner's head snapped up, eyes wide. "What?"

"More precisely, the calendars are genuine. Preston wrote the entries in them. And they're the right age to have been written at the time," Scarlett explained.

"So what's the problem, then?" Wagner demanded.

Scarlett said, "I did some digging. Talked to people who attended the county fair. They remembered Preston. But not from the night of Pentwater's murder. From the week before."

"And you believe these people?"

"One hundred percent," Scarlett replied with absolute conviction.

Wagner sat back, her face pale. "But that means..."

"Preston either falsified the calendars to give himself an alibi after the fact, or he made a mistake when he wrote down the dates," Scarlett said. "Or maybe there's another innocent explanation. Regardless, Preston was not at the county fair the night Pentwater was murdered and these calendars can't be corroborated to support his alibi."

Wagner shook her head, disbelief etched on her features. "But why? Why would he do that if he was innocent?"

Scarlett's gaze was as hard as her tone. "Because he wasn't innocent. He had something to hide."

Wagner was silent for a long moment, her mind racing. "We need to talk to Dean Taylor again. Find out what he knows."

Scarlett shook her head. "I already tried. He's gone. Skipped town."

Wagner's eyes narrowed. "What do you mean, gone?"

"I mean he's disappeared. No one knows where he is."

Wagner stood abruptly and the lightweight chair tipped over with a loud crash against the concrete. "We have to find him. He's the key to all of this. Without him, I don't have a story."

Scarlett stood, tossed a twenty on the table, and grabbed her bag. "I've got some leads. Places he might have gone."

They walked out into the pleasant day with no further conversation while Scarlett gave Wagner a chance to absorb the implications.

If Preston had lied about his alibi, if he had falsified evidence, then everything Wagner thought she knew about the case was wrong. People usually had trouble accepting a mistake that big and Wagner definitely wasn't the humble type.

"I've got too much work into this project to quit now," Wagner said, breathing too quickly. "We've got to fix this. Somehow. Where do we start?"

"There's a cabin Taylor owns by a lake near Dallas. We can start there," Scarlett said. "I've got a private plane standing by."

Wagner nodded, her jaw set. "Let's go. We need answers."

They climbed into Scarlett's SUV and Wagner kept talking even before Scarlett had a chance to start the engine.

"I've got a million questions," Wagner said. "If Preston did kill Pentwater, why did he wait a full week from the alibi he established by going to the fair? That makes no sense."

"Dunno. But my guess is that he didn't intend his visit to the fair to be an alibi for the Pentwater murder. He might not have intended to murder Pentwater the next week. Could have been a crime of opportunity," Scarlett replied.

She waited until Wagner tried that theory on for a few moments before she raised another.

"I think he went to the fair for another purpose," Scarlett replied, paying attention to traffic. "Later, after he killed Pentwater, the county fair alibi didn't work for the night of Pentwater's murder, so he didn't bring it up at trial."

"While the false alibi was fresh, it would have been easy to disprove." Wagner slowly nodded her head, thinking it through. "Witnesses and other evidence and whatever happened there would have been fresher, too. His alibi could have been debunked early on if he'd tried to raise it."

Scarlett turned into the executive airport and drove to the waiting jet. She parked and grabbed her bag and a light jacket. "Come on. The pilot's ready."

Wagner stepped out of the SUV and followed Scarlett up the jet stairs. Scarlett closed the door, and they took their seats. The plane rolled toward the runway for takeoff. Soon, they were in the air at cruising altitude.

"You're sure he falsified the Pentwater alibi?" Wagner asked again through her headset.

She seemed incapable of letting it go. She'd built a whole fiction around Preston's innocence in her head. She'd probably imagined she'd win awards, be on the cover of magazines, and so on.

Scarlett replied, "Absolutely. No question whatsoever."

"Why? What makes you so sure?"

Scarlett pretended not to hear the question. She had promised to protect Eliza and she wouldn't break that promise. She retrieved a file from her bag and focused on it for the rest of the flight to discourage Wagner's next batch of twenty questions.

When they landed in Dallas and deplaned, another rental was waiting. Scarlett tossed her bag and her jacket into the back and took the driver's seat. Wagner buckled into the passenger side. A few minutes later, they were on the road.

Scarlett pulled up the navigation on her phone and fed it through the Bluetooth onto the screen in the rental. The lake was about fifty miles away. They should be there in an hour. Maybe less, with light traffic.

Wagner had finally settled down and stopped her rapid-firing questions. They made most of the trip in silence, which was just fine with Scarlett.

When they reached the turnoff for the cabin, it was a narrow dirt road winding around the lake. About a mile in, Scarlett killed the engine and let the car coast to a gentle stop among the trees.

Hikers and bird watchers and campers were common in the area. She'd seen a couple of other vehicles tucked off the road on the way in. With luck, no one would bother the SUV while they were gone.

"We'll go on foot from here," Scarlett said, reaching for her flashlight and her jacket. "Less chance of being spotted. If he sees us, he's likely to run."

Wagner nodded, zipping up her hoodie. They stepped out into the cool air, shade, and shadows.

They walked about half a mile along the gravel drive. Scarlett watched for CCTV, but she didn't see any cameras in obvious locations. Which didn't mean they weren't there.

When she spotted the cabin up ahead, she said, "There it is. Watch yourself. If he's in there, he could be armed."

The cabin was dark, unkempt. It appeared to be abandoned. Scarlett saw nothing to suggest Taylor or anyone else was inside.

They approached cautiously, Scarlett leading the way, flashlight in hand and weapon within easy reach.

The door was locked, the windows shuttered. Scarlett circled around back. Wagner followed close behind.

And then Scarlett saw it. A glint of metal in the sunlight. A padlock. Sheared clean through with one quick snap.

Someone had been here. Recently.

They exchanged a glance.

"He was here," Wagner whispered, her heart pounding. "Might still be inside."

Scarlett nodded, reaching for her gun. "Or someone else is."

They crept toward the cabin. Scarlett kept her focus on the back door and windows, half expecting Taylor to burst out. He didn't. In fact, the closer she came to the broken padlock, the more it seemed like the cabin was unoccupied.

When she reached the door, she stood aside and reached around to shove it open.

Nothing happened.

"Taylor? Are you in there?" Scarlett shouted from the porch. No response.

"He's not here," Wagner said, sounding deflated.

Scarlett pulled her gun and ducked inside, flashlight sweeping the darkness. The place was a mess, drawers yanked out, papers scattered.

Someone had been searching for something.

Wagner followed her in and swept her flashlight into the corners.

And then they heard it.

A creak of a floorboard. The rustle of clothing.

They spun around, flashlight beams falling on the man standing in the doorway.

Dean Taylor. His face pale, his eyes wide with fear.

"Don't move," Scarlett said, her voice low and steady. "We just want to talk to you."

But Taylor was already bolting for the door.

Scarlett lunged after him. Wagner, too.

They chased him out into the woods, footsteps pounding on the hard ground. He had a solid lead and the vegetation slowed them down.

And then, up ahead, the sound of a car engine. Tires spinning on the dirt.

Scarlett burst out of the trees just in time to see taillights disappearing down the road.

She swore, lowering her gun. "We lost him."

"Now what?" Wagner bent over, catching her breath.

Scarlett holstered her weapon, her jaw tight. "You find him again."

Wagner nodded, straightening up. "Where do we start?"

"Sorry, but I'm out. I checked out the alibi. It's false. I don't know why Taylor led us down this path, but it doesn't matter. He's made it pretty clear that he no longer wants to be involved in this." Scarlett turned to walk toward the SUV and Wagner tagged along. "Preston didn't have an alibi. The prosecutors proved that he killed Pentwater. The jury was satisfied and none of his many appeals changed that. We have no reason to believe he wasn't guilty as charged. Now that he's dead, let it go."

"I've got a lot of time and money invested in this thing. I can't just give up," Wagner said. "There's more to this. Why would Dean Taylor come forward with those calendars now if they were fake?"

"Human psychology is complicated."

"Yeah, but that's not it. He knows something," Wagner insisted.

"Possibly. When you find him again, you can ask him." Scarlett said when they'd reached the SUV. She slid into the seat and started the vehicle. "But as far as I'm concerned, this assignment is over. With the Pentwater alibi falling apart, there's no point to going further with the Baker case. Pentwater was a liar, a rapist, and a murderer. End of story. I'll send my bill."

Wagner didn't argue. She was unusually quiet all the way back to Houston, twisting the facts in her head trying to salvage her theories, but Scarlett barely noticed.

She had other things on her mind now that she'd managed to push Wagner away from investigating Flint's mother.

Which begged the question. Was James Preston also guilty of Marilyn Baker's murder?

Possibly. She hadn't chased down Taylor's story about Preston conducting a memorial service in another town the night Baker was killed. Because Preston was never charged with that crime, Wagner wasn't interested in pursuing it.

Which was good. Because Scarlett intended to respect Flint's wishes and leave that question to him.

CHAPTER 47

Kansas City, Missouri

FLINT WAS BACK AT his hotel room, pouring over the files and notes scattered across the small desk, when his phone buzzed with an incoming call. He glanced at the screen, seeing Gaspar's name.

"Gaspar, what's up?" Flint answered, leaning back in his chair.

"I've been digging into Emily Royce's background, and located something... odd," Gaspar's voice came through the speaker, an unusual hint of uncertainty in his tone.

Flint sat up straighter, his interest piqued. "Odd how?"

"Turns out Emily Royce submitted some DNA samples to one of those online ancestry databases a few years back. Standard stuff, you know, trying to learn more about her family history."

"That's all the rage these days," Flint said, frowning.

"The odd part," Gaspar continued, "is that she submitted two samples. One was labeled as her own, but the other was listed as 'unknown male.' And the results showed a familial match. Given the variables, the 'unknown male' is likely Emily's father."

Flint replied, "Her father? Why would she want to test her father's DNA? I thought her parents worked for the Lymans and died years ago. Is it possible Ronald Royce wasn't her biological parent? She was adopted?"

"That's what I thought at first, too," Gaspar replied. "But then I did some more digging. I ran the male DNA through a specialized database, one that can identify genetic markers specific to certain families."

Flint said, "How accurate is your genetic DNA analysis?"

"Not perfect. It requires some guesswork and confirmation, unless we have known samples," Gaspar replied, clearing his throat. "These preliminary results suggest that the 'unknown male' identified as Emily Royce's biological father is likely a Lyman."

Flint felt a chill run down his spine.

If her father was a Lyman, it meant Emily was not the lonely only child he'd thought she was. Instead, she was a member of one of the richest families in the world.

Learning something like that as an adult could stir a wide range of behavior, much of it negative.

"Before they died, there were several male candidates for the role of Emily's father. Can you narrow it down?" Flint asked, his voice low and serious.

"I ran a more detailed analysis, comparing the male DNA to known samples from the Lyman family," Gaspar said. "The 'unknown male' is most likely Spencer Lyman. We'd want to confirm with controlled samples. But my best guess? He's almost certainly Emily's biological father."

Flint blew out a long stream of air. "Question is, who knows about this? Emily? Spencer Lyman? Ward Lyman? Boldo?"

"And how are they using the knowledge," Gaspar replied. "Explosive secrets like that usually change people, and not always for the better."

Flint was silent for a long moment.

Gaspar said, "If Emily Royce is Spencer Lyman's daughter, it could explain Boldo's connection to her. He's using her to get to the old man."

"Or, assuming she knows, Emily's waiting for the right moment to leverage the truth," Flint said. "And if Ward found out, that could be why he faked his death and is hiding out from the old man."

"Why would he do that?"

"Jealousy. Petulance. Outrage. Annoyance," Flint rattled off the motives he could think of off the top of his head. "Maybe Ward didn't want to be displaced. Or maybe he thought having another possible heir would get him off the hook. Or even get both of them killed. Who knows?"

"Possibly," Gaspar replied doubtfully. "I'll keep digging, see if I can find anything else to confirm. We're not certain that the samples Emily Royce submitted were hers and

Spencer Lyman's. If we had fresh samples from both of them, we could nail this down."

"I'll work on that. Meanwhile, keep me posted."

Gaspar rang off and Flint leaned back in his chair, staring at the ceiling while he considered the implications.

If Emily Royce was the daughter Spencer Lyman never knew he had, how would that shift the family and business dynamics?

He glanced at the clock, stood up, grabbed his jacket and headed for the door. No point in speculating when he could get the intel straight from the source.

Flint drove the SUV along the winding road that led to the sprawling Lyman Estate. The air was heavy with the scent of freshly cut grass. He drove past the mansion and the pools and the gardens deeper into the property all the way to the rolling green pastures where the horses were grazing peacefully.

He pulled up in front of the impressive horse barns. Flint's work had exposed him to immeasurable wealth, but few estates he'd seen could match this one for sheer grandeur. The barns were as well maintained as the grounds. Fresh paint, neat flower beds, graded gravel. The place looked more polished than Churchill Downs on race day.

A Range Rover was parked close to one of the barns. The license plate said, "Lyman 2," which one of Gaspar's reports had identified as one of Emily Royce's vehicles on the estate. The exterior of the SUV was muddy and sported a couple of small dents, suggesting she had driven it over rough terrain.

Flint stepped onto the gravel and approached the vehicle. Quietly, he lifted the door handle on the driver's side and ducked his head in for a quick look around.

Royce was as neat about her vehicle as she was about her person. The Range Rover might have come here straight from the show room. The interior was spotless and smelled as if it had been recently detailed.

She'd left a half-empty water bottle in one of the cup holders. No way to be sure the bottle belonged to Royce, but it was worth a shot.

Flint pulled an evidence bag from his pocket to carefully collect the bottle. He closed the bag and stuffed it into his pocket.

Afterward, he made his way toward the barn, following the faint sound of movement within. The rich, earthy scent of horses and hay filled his nostrils, mingling with the sweet aroma of honeysuckle.

Royce was standing in one of the stalls, brushing a magnificent chestnut mare with long, gentle strokes. The soft swish of the brush moved against the horse's gleaming coat in a soothing rhythm like a lover's caress reflecting a deep, abiding bond between them.

Royce looked up as Flint approached, her eyes widening in surprise.

"Mr. Flint," she said. "I didn't expect to see you here."

Flint leaned against the stall door.

Emily Royce was a striking woman. Auburn hair pulled back in a neat ponytail. Riding clothes hugging her athletic body in all the usual places. But it was her eyes that drew him. Deep emerald pools that had the capacity to hold a lifetime of secrets.

"I apologize for the intrusion, Ms. Royce," Flint said firmly. "I saw a vehicle out front and thought it might be yours. There are some things I need to discuss with you. About your family's history with the Lymans."

Her hand stilled on the horse's flank and her expression shifted from surprise to wariness.

"My family's history?" she repeated, defensiveness creeping into her tone. "I'm not sure what you mean."

Flint crossed his arms, his gaze never leaving hers. "Your parents, Ronald and Beatrice Royce. They worked for the Lymans here on the estate for many years, didn't they?"

A flicker of emotion crossed her face, gone as quickly as it had appeared. "My mother worked in the house. She and Mae Lyman were incredibly close. Like sisters, really."

Flint nodded. "And your father?"

"My father was in charge of the horses." A smile tugged at the corners of her mouth and genuine warmth suffused her features. She resumed the gentle brushing. "He loved his work more than anything. Except for my mother and me, of course. He used to bring me out here when I was just a little girl, teaching me to ride, to care for the horses. It was our special time together."

Flint watched her for a moment, taking in the way her face softened as she spoke of her father with love and nostalgia.

"It must have been a unique childhood," he mused, his gaze drifting to the horse. "Growing up so close to the Lyman family, being a part of their world."

Tension returned to her shoulders, and she shrugged, maybe to loosen up.

"I suppose," she said, carefully neutral. "But I was just a child. I didn't really understand the complexities of the relationships between our families. To me, the Lymans were just the people who lived in the big house. They were always kind to me. Always welcoming. We weren't treated like servants, if that's what you're implying."

Flint raised an eyebrow, emphasizing the evasion in her words. "And what about the tragedies that have befallen the Lymans over the years? Five members of the family dead before the age of thirty, including Ward. That's quite a coincidence, don't you think?"

"The Lymans have always been risk-takers, Mr. Flint." She sighed, shaking her head, a note of exasperation in her voice. "They live life on the edge, pushing boundaries, chasing thrills. It's just who they are. And sometimes, those risks catch up to them in the worst possible ways."

Flint didn't reply.

"But if you're suggesting that there's something suspicious about their deaths, that someone is targeting them, then I'm afraid you're barking up the wrong tree." She turned to face him fully, her eyes blazing with a fierce intensity. "The Lymans' tragedies are of their own making. No one forced them to take the chances they did."

Flint held up his hands, a placating gesture. "I'm just trying to understand. To see the full picture."

"Well, I'm afraid I can't help you with that." Her jaw tightened and she gripped the brush harder. "I'm the CFO of Lyman Enterprises now. My job is to keep the company running smoothly, not to manage the Lyman family's personal lives. They handle their own affairs."

"I understand." Flint nodded slowly, his eyes never leaving hers. "But there's one more thing I'm wondering about."

He paused, letting the silence stretch between them, heavy with unspoken tension. She didn't seem to notice or react.

"You and Anthony Boldo," he said, words measured and deliberate. "You're about the same age, aren't you? Too young to have been involved in the earlier Lyman tragedies."

"I don't see what Boldo has to do with anything," she snapped, voice trembling slightly. Her eyes flashed with a sudden, scorching anger. She set the brush aside. "Ask him yourself."

"Of course," Flint said smoothly, pushing off from the stall door. He raised an eyebrow, allowing a small, knowing smile to play at the corners of his mouth. "Just an observation."

She ignored him and returned to brushing the horse.

"Thank you for your time, Ms. Royce," he said, cordial but distant. He tipped his head to her. "I'll let you get back to your work."

With that, he turned and strode out of the barn, the sound of his footsteps echoing in the sudden, ringing silence.

He felt her eyes on his back as he walked away.

CHAPTER 48

THE PRIVATE, ENCRYPTED CELL phone that connected Boldo to Emily vibrated in his pocket. The sensation was not quite as pleasant as Emily's personal touch, but he liked the feel of it, knowing Emily was there on the other end. He picked up the call.

"Are you alone?" she demanded.

"Yes. Sadly," he teased.

She was not amused. "Michael Flint was just here. He's asking questions about things he shouldn't even know."

Her breathlessness clued him in to her state of mind. She was angry, yes. But also frightened. He could tell.

"Don't worry. I'll take care of Flint," Boldo replied.

"Flint is dangerous. He's getting too close." Her fear and fury traveled through the connection. Boldo could feel it.

"I warned you," he said, his words clipped and harsh. "I told you to be careful. To keep your distance from the Lymans and their troubles."

She took a deep, steadying breath. "It's way too late for that now."

Boldo was silent for a long moment. He could feel her tension crackling through the phone line.

"Do what you have to do," she said, steady and resolute. "But be careful. We can't afford any mistakes. Not now."

She ended the call, and he slipped the phone back into his pocket.

Marino returned with Shorty and Zero, extra muscle promoted to the duties recently vacated by Romeo and Paulie. Shorty was seven feet tall and thin as a rail. Zero was a total psycho. He'd cut your throat out and eat your tongue. Or so people said.

All three stood tall in front of Boldo's desk, hands respectfully folded, awaiting orders.

"Where is that sniveling young billionaire now?" Boldo demanded.

Marino spoke for them. "We know he's left Mexico. He hired a private jet in Mexico City. No flight plan was submitted. The pilot paid local officials to cover for him. That's why we didn't find out sooner."

Boldo scowled and glared toward Shorty. "And what did you learn when you squeezed the idiot who took the bribe?"

Zero responded, "The pilot said they were headed to Texas. He claimed he had a distraught son aboard. Spun quite a yarn. Claimed the father was on his death bed and the young man was racing against the grim reaper to get there before the father died."

"Of course, he won't tell anyone else that story," Boldo said coldly.

"Definitely not," Shorty replied.

"Good," Boldo declared. "You're sure Ward Lyman was on that plane? We don't have time for another mistake. Michael Flint is getting closer. He can't find Lyman before we do."

Zero took the lead again. "We found CCTV for the private air strip. We have footage of the kid entering the jet. Ran the images through facial recognition. One hundred percent match to Ward Lyman."

Boldo was feeling better. A small grin lifted the corner of his mouth. "Where did the jet actually land? Not Texas, I'm assuming."

Shorty replied, "Emporia. Landing confirmed. We located the pilot. He, uh, volunteered the name of his passenger. Confirmed. Ward Lyman."

Boldo's grin stole across his entire face when he heard the news. "He won't share this information with Michael Flint, I assume."

Zero replied with absolute certainty. "Guaranteed."

"Excellent," Boldo said, completely satisfied with his change in personnel and the superior results achieved by the new team.

All witnesses were eliminated, and Ward Lyman located.

The situation was improving by the moment.

"Where is Lyman now?" Boldo asked, unable to contain his pleasure.

Shorty and Zero kept quiet as Marino, Boldo's right-hand man, delivered the rest. "The pilot said Ward is still spooked about the Lyman Curse. He's twenty-five, which gives the curse another five years to get him."

Boldo laughed and wagged his head. "That kid never was the sharpest knife in the drawer."

"Looks like he's working his way back to the grandfather. But he's being cautious about it," Marino continued. "The entire world believes he's dead and he doesn't want to prove them wrong. Or give the curse another chance."

"Pick him up before we lose him again," Boldo ordered. "No witnesses."

"Already on it," Marino replied. "Our guys are on the way."

"Stash him at the park. Around the clock security," Boldo demanded gruffly. "And no mollycoddling this time."

"Got it," Marino replied. "Maybe four hours, he'll be in place."

"Confirm when he's there," Boldo said, "When Lyman is secured, Shorty, Zero, bring the armored SUV around to the back. Load up the fire power. Be ready to head out on my signal."

"Yes, Boss." Shorty and Zero left the room, as directed.

"What about Flint and Drake?" Marino asked. "Want our guys to deal with them?"

Boldo scowled. "No. If we're lucky, I'll have the chance to do that myself."

Marino left the room and Boldo poured a generous slug of whiskey into one of his favorite glasses. He tossed it back and refilled the glass.

He was close now. He'd end Ward Lyman once and for all. Which would bring old man Lyman to his knees. Boldo grinned, watching the scene unfold in his head. Hell, maybe Spencer Lyman would die of shock and grief on the spot. That would be a nice bonus.

Regardless, Boldo would implement the final stages of the plan and take over Lyman Enterprises immediately. Enough of this. His patience was exhausted. Emily wouldn't like it, but he'd make it up to her. She'd be okay. Or not. He shrugged.

He grinned again, thinking through the coming confrontations. First, Ward Lyman.

The abandoned amusement park on the far outskirts of the city was one of his preferred places for what he euphemistically called personnel management. It had been a favorite spot for family outings when he was a kid, his father had owned it before him.

Now, it was closed to the public. The rides no longer functioned. The perimeter was closed by a highly effective electrified fence.

He felt comfortable at the park. More importantly, he knew every inch of the place. And the local authorities were well paid to ignore whatever went on there. All of which gave him a significant advantage over any adversary.

Michael Flint and his man Drake, if they showed up, didn't stand a chance.

CHAPTER 43

Chase State Fishing Lake, Kansas

"ALRIGHT, WARD, LET'S SEE what you've got for me," Flint murmured, a slight smile playing on his lips as he guided the black Chevy Tahoe along the winding rural highway. The GPS screen flickered, indicating his destination was just a few miles ahead.

His phone buzzed in the cupholder, and Flint glanced at it, his smile widening as he read the text from Gaspar. "Ward Lyman. Cessna landed at Chase State Fishing Lake airstrip last night at 2300 hours. Good hunting."

"Attaboy, Gaspar," Flint chuckled, tossing the phone back. "Always coming through in the clutch."

He'd been anticipating this meetup ever since Ward had pulled his disappearing act after the Key West debacle. It was just a matter of time before Flint's sources sniffed him out.

The GPS chimed, signaling a turn. Flint smoothly spun the wheel, guiding the Tahoe onto a narrow side road flanked by towering pines. Branches scrubbed against the SUV's roof and sides. With luck, Flint wouldn't need to have the damned thing repainted after this excursion.

"Three miles to go," the GPS announced in its soothing, electronic tone.

The mysteries surrounding events in Key West still nagged him. Unanswered questions lingered like wisps of smoke.

Ward's last-minute bail on the submersible mission. The chaos that followed. The lives lost.

"What's the real story, Ward?" Flint wondered aloud. "Why the sudden change of heart? And what really went down with Boldo's goons?"

The GPS chimed once more. "One mile to destination."

Flint's grip on the wheel was relaxed but assured. "Showtime."

Gravel crunched beneath the tires as Flint parked his rental at the edge of the narrow road. The dense woods surrounding Chase State Fishing Lake engulfed him with the scent of pine and damp earth.

"The landing strip is just a mile from here." He traced the route on Gaspar's map with his finger.

"The cabin is just ahead," Gaspar had said through the speaker an hour ago.

Flint scanned the tree line until he picked out the faint trail leading into the undergrowth. His boots crunched on the carpet of fallen leaves and twigs as he hiked toward the coordinates.

After he crested a third hill, he spied a small, rustic fishing cabin nestled among the pines about twenty yards from the water's edge.

Ward's bolt-hole.

A thin curl of smoke rose from the chimney, carrying with it the faint scent of burning wood. Flint checked his gun, more out of habit than necessity. Time to get some answers.

Flint's phone buzzed, and he glanced at the screen, a slight smile tugging at his lips as he picked up. "Didn't expect to hear from you so soon."

"Just checking in," Drake replied, his voice steady. "Wanted to share some intel. Park rangers confirmed a last-minute cabin rental near the airstrip. Paid in cash by someone fitting Ward's description."

Flint nodded, moving silently around a curve in the path. "Aligns with Gaspar's info on the flight. What else you got?"

"A couple of other rentals in the area, but this one stands out. Remote, isolated, and close to where Ward landed."

"Yeah, I'm looking at the cabin now. Looks like someone's in there. With luck, Ward Lyman will be alone."

"Copy that," Drake confirmed. "Need backup?"

"Negative. I've got this handled. Just be ready if things go south."

"Copy that. Watch your six, Flint."

"Always." Flint ended the call.

"Why'd you bail from the submersible excursion, Ward?" Flint muttered under his breath, his eyes scanning the cabin's exterior for any signs of movement. "Something tipped you off?"

The video footage from that night played in his mind's eye, showing Ward confronting Boldo's men, a brief scuffle, Ward running away, and then the sickening sound of gunshots before Ward was dragged off camera, leaving a trail of blood in his wake.

"And how did Ward Lyman go from being Boldo's prisoner to his guest?" Flint wondered aloud, his brow furrowed in concentration.

But perhaps the most haunting question was whether Ward knew about the sabotaged submersible. The five lives lost weighed heavily.

If Ward knew Boldo's plan and let it happen, this wouldn't end well for Ward. He had to know that. Which made him not only a fugitive but a dangerous one.

Flint's jaw clenched and his grip tightened on his gun. He approached the cabin cautiously.

The weathered boards creaked under his weight as he climbed the steps to the porch.

He knocked on the door.

The sound echoed in the stillness.

For a long moment, there was no response. Then, slowly, the door swung open, revealing a haggard and wary Ward Lyman.

"I suppose it was only a matter of time before someone tracked me down," Ward said, his voice rough with fatigue

Flint offered a smile, keeping his posture relaxed and nonthreatening. "Your grandfather sent me. I'm here to help."

"And who are you?"

"Michael Flint." He glanced past Ward into the cabin's dim interior. "Can I come inside? We don't want anyone to see me standing at the door talking to you."

Ward hesitated, his gaze flickering past Flint to the woods beyond, as if he were seriously thinking about running again. But then his shoulders slumped, and the fight drained out of him, leaving him exhausted and pliable.

"I didn't know where else to go," he admitted, stepping back to allow Flint entry. "After Mexico, I just needed somewhere I could think."

Flint followed Ward into the cabin, taking in the sparse furnishings and the crackling fire in the hearth. The air was thick with wood smoke and the scent of musty old furniture.

"And this place holds good memories for you," Flint said easily, as if he were gentling a fawn.

Ward nodded, sinking into a chair by the fire. The orange glow played across his face, highlighting the worry etched there. "Some of the best memories I have. Fishing with Grandpa, listening to his stories. Those were the only times I felt free from the weight."

"I'm sure the Lyman legacy feels like a burden. But it doesn't have to be." Flint took a seat across from him, leaning forward intently. "You have a chance to make Lyman Enterprises something new, something better."

Ward's laugh was bitter, the sound grating in the quiet of the cabin. "There won't be time for that. I'm twenty-five now. What can I accomplish before the curse gets me?"

"The curse is just a story," Flint said firmly. "But you have real power. The power to lead, to inspire, to build something great. The question is whether you have the vision. And the guts to do it."

CHAPTER 50

WARD WAS QUIET FOR a long moment, staring into the flickering flames. The fire popped and hissed, sending sparks dancing up the chimney.

"I'm scared," he whispered at last, his voice barely audible over the crackling of the fire. "Scared of failing, of becoming another victim of the curse. If I could be just a plain Joe, no one would want to kill me, you know?"

"Come back with me. To the Lyman Estate." Flint placed a comforting hand on Ward's shoulder. "It's time to stop hiding and start living. It's time to face your destiny head-on and make your life your own."

Ward took a deep breath and said nothing.

"I can help you, but you've got to fill me in," Flint insisted. "I need answers if we're going to keep you alive another eighty years like old man Spencer."

Before Ward could reply, breaking glass shattered the stillness. Flint dove for cover, pulling Ward down with him as a hail of bullets tore through the cabin's walls and windows.

The sharp scent of gunpowder and splintered wood filled the air, along with the barrage of bullets.

"Boldo's men," Ward gasped, his eyes wide with fear. "They must have followed you."

"More likely, they followed you. Just like I did." Flint cursed under his breath, adrenaline flooding his system as he drew his gun.

His eyes scanned the room, searching for a better defensive position.

"Stay down and stay quiet," he ordered.

The gunfire paused, creating a sudden, eerie silence.

Flint used the momentary lull to dash toward the window, keeping low. He peered outside. He caught a glimpse of movement in the tree line. One of Boldo's soldiers, no doubt, armed and ready for a fight.

"Alright, you bastard," he muttered. "Let's see what you've got."

He motioned for Ward to stay in place. Then he crept toward the back door. As he neared the exit, he heard footsteps crunching outside, drawing closer.

Flint readied his pistol.

The door burst open, and he was in motion.

He fired a round toward the intruder, diving to the side as the man's gun barked return bullets directed at Flint's first location.

Rolling to his feet, Flint fired back, his shots precise and lethal. The man staggered, then fell. His gun clattered to the ground.

Flint approached cautiously, kicking the weapon away before checking for a pulse. Nothing. The immediate threat was neutralized but more would follow.

He turned to Ward, who had watched with a mixture of awe and fear.

"We've got to go," Flint said, calm but firm. "Boldo's not going to stop until he gets what he wants. There'll be more coming."

Ward's face paled, trembling as he pushed himself to his feet.

"You don't understand," his whispered voice shaking. "Boldo... he's not like anyone you've ever faced. He's relentless, ruthless. He'll stop at nothing."

Flint met Ward's gaze with steely determination. "Then it's time we put an end to this. We find Boldo and take him down."

A hysterical laugh bubbled from Ward's throat. "Take him down? You can't be serious. Boldo's untouchable. He's got men, resources, influence. He's an absolute psychopath. We'll be dead before we even get close."

"Listen to me. I've faced men like Boldo before. Men who believe power and a willingness to use it as they wish makes them invincible." Flint placed a reassuring hand on Ward's shoulder. "He's wrong. Simple as that."

"No. He's not. You don't know the half of what he's done." Ward shook his head, eyes the size of basketballs.

"It won't be easy, and it won't be safe." Flint's reply brooked no further argument. "But we'll get it done."

Ward took a shaky breath. Softly, he said, "Okay. Where do we start?"

Before Flint could respond three more of Boldo's men burst through the cabin's front door, guns blazing.

Flint dove for cover behind the cabin's rustic wooden table as bullets splintered the walls around him. He returned fire and the first man was down.

Flint rolled to a new position, narrowly avoiding a hail of gunfire. From his new vantage point, he aimed at the second thug and squeezed the trigger, dropping him.

As Flint turned to face the third intruder, the man released a shot that grazed his bicep, throwing off his aim.

Seeing the opportunity, the man fired three more times. Under cover of the gunfire, he grabbed Lyman by the hair and dragged him toward the door.

Flint crouched and aimed the pistol, but he didn't have a clear shot. The third man held Ward between them, using his hostage as a human shield.

"Drop the gun, Flint!" the man snarled, pressing his own weapon to Lyman's chin as he continued backing toward the door, Lyman barely resisting. "I'll splatter his brains all over this damn cabin!"

Flint hesitated, his finger hovering over the trigger. The standoff stretched out, moments feeling like hours. Finally, seeing no alternative, Flint lowered his revolver.

A wicked grin spread across the goon's face. Keeping Lyman positioned between them, he backed out of the bullet-riddled cabin and disappeared into the woods.

Flint jumped to his feet and ran outside, but they had already slipped into the trees.

He heard a helicopter landing nearby. They'd be gone before he could reach them.

Flint slumped back against the cabin, his wounded shoulder throbbing, the taste of failure bitter in his mouth. He picked himself up and hurried through the woods to the Tahoe. On the drive back to the airport, he called Drake with instructions.

CHAPTER 51

Kansas City, Missouri

FLINT AND DRAKE HAD waited outside Boldo's building. It was near dawn when he came out, he climbed into an armored SUV. The driver rolled into traffic, and Drake followed.

The SUV traveled through Kansas City streets headed west out of town. If the driver was aware that Drake was following, he seemed unconcerned about the tail.

"Where are they going?" Drake mused aloud.

"With luck, they're headed to wherever they're holding Ward Lyman," Flint replied.

"I suppose you bought a Powerball ticket this week, too?" Drake grinned.

"And I bet the winnings on the ponies," Flint replied good naturedly.

Twenty minutes later, the SUV turned off on a gravel road leading away from the highway. Boldo's vehicle went over a slight hill and Flint lost visual contact briefly.

When Drake crested the same highpoint, they could see the specter of celebrations and laughter up ahead.

Flint's car rolled to a stop at the rusted gates of the abandoned amusement park. Boldo's car had disappeared through the gates minutes before, leaving a trail of dust.

Flint and Drake left the SUV parked in the shadows, approaching the gates on foot. Up close, Flint could see the thick chain and heavy lock that had secured the gates had been recently snapped with a bolt cutter.

"You sure about this?" Drake's voice was steady, but Flint heard the undercurrent of tension. "We don't know that Ward Lyman is here."

Flint nodded, his jaw set. "We do know Boldo's in there."

They stepped through the gates onto the dusty grounds. Flint imagined he could smell old popcorn and hear the carnival barkers. The decrepit park was a sprawl of rusted rides, decaying booths, and overgrown pathways.

In the distance, the skeletal remains of a roller coaster rose against the dawn sky. Across from it the rusted Ferris wheel stood, with half a dozen buckets hanging askew.

Flint touched his earpiece, the small device nestled securely in his ear. "I'll take the coaster. You head for the haunted house. Keep your eyes open and your weapon ready."

"Always do," Drake said to check his earpiece.

They moved through the gates and split up. Flint crept toward the roller coaster. Drake melted into the shadows headed toward the haunted house.

Flint's earpiece crackled. Drake's voice came through with a hint of static. "Two goons near the coaster entrance. Shorty and Baldy."

"Copy that. I'll find another way up." Flint's lips twitched when he spotted them. Shorty stood seven feet tall, a mountain of muscle and menace. Baldy was exactly as described.

He skirted the perimeter, sticking to the shadows. The coaster loomed above him, a rusted behemoth from another era. The metal was pitted and worn. Definitely not strong enough to support his weight.

He found a maintenance ladder around the back. The metal was cold beneath his hands as he climbed. The only sound his ears picked up were his own breath and the creaky ladder.

Each step took him higher until he reached the top. He paused to scan the park below. The Ferris wheel cast an eerie shadow with carriages swaying gently in the breeze.

There. A dark shape moving purposely through the shadows. Boldo?

Flint started along the coaster track, his feet sure on the narrow metal. The structure groaned beneath his weight. Each step was a calculated risk as he danced with danger high above the ground.

From below he heard a shout. Marino, Boldo's second-in-command, stood pointing up at the coaster to Flint.

Flint cursed and quickened his pace.

Marino pulled a gun, took aim, and fired.

Bullets pinged off the metal around Flint, causing sparks to fly.

Flint picked up the pace, moving as quickly as he could, ducking low, leaping across gaps in the track. The coaster twisted and turned, a dizzying path through the air.

His heart pounded and his breath came in sharp gasps.

But he didn't stop, didn't falter, even as Marino's bullets continued to land around him and ricochet in all directions.

Drake's voice crackled in his ear, grunting with exertion. "I'm in the haunted house. Traps everywhere. Boldo's work."

Flint vaulted a broken section of track, his muscles screaming with the effort.

"Boldo's heading for the Ferris wheel." He forced the words out between breaths.

He heard Drake grunt and then the sound of gunfire, loud even over the earpiece.

Marino had stopped shooting. What was he doing now?

Flint found a low spot in the coaster rail and dropped to the ground, rolling to absorb the impact. The hard earth was unyielding beneath him. He felt the jolt through his bones.

He stood and dusted himself off. Before he had a chance to sprint toward the Ferris wheel, he saw Marino running away.

A moment later, a section of the roller coaster exploded behind him, propelling him forward and knocking him off his feet.

Flint landed hard on the gravel. He scrambled away, putting distance behind him. The roller coaster had been blasted apart. Flying debris was everywhere.

He kept low and ran, weaving between the faded and peeling game booths. Marino's explosion had sent sparks in several directions, starting small fires that were growing every second.

Ahead, Boldo had reached the base of the Ferris wheel. He started to climb, his movements quick and agile, like a spider ascending its web, a move he'd probably perfected in childhood.

Flint followed Boldo. The metal frame was slick beneath his hands. The wheel creaked and swayed. They climbed higher and higher as the ground fell away beneath them.

At the top, Boldo waited, a vivid silhouette against the lightening sky

"You shouldn't have come here, Flint." His voice was calm, almost amused.

Flint hauled himself onto the platform. He could feel the cold metal beneath his feet and wind tugging at his clothes.

"It's over, Boldo. You've got nowhere to run."

"Who's running?" Boldo spread his arms, a mocking gesture.

Boldo lunged. The knife blade in his right hand caught the sunlight, a deadly flash.

Flint dodged and the blade whistled past his ear. While Boldo was still leaning forward, Flint struck out. His fist slammed into Boldo's jaw. The impact reverberated up his arm.

Boldo staggered briefly and regained his balance. Instantly, he came again, slashing the knife. Flint caught his wrist, twisting hard.

Bones ground together, tendons straining.

The knife clattered to the platform.

They grappled while the wheel swayed beneath their feet. Boldo was strong and his muscles coiled with power.

But Flint was faster.

They traded blows, fists and elbows, knees and feet. Each impact produced a dull thud, or a grunt of pain or exertion.

Absorbing a hard blow to the ribs and knee to the gut, Boldo grunted, doubling over.

Flint pressed his advantage, punching Boldo over and over. His knuckles split and blood spattered the rusted metal.

Boldo seemed to be shrinking under the assault. Until his hand scrabbled at his waistband to pull out a pistol.

Flint saw the gun too late.

Boldo squeezed off the first round.

The shot was deafeningly close. Flint felt the heat of the bullet as it grazed his shoulder, a searing line of pain. Blood ran down his arm, hot and sticky.

He didn't hesitate. He drew his weapon and fired in one smooth motion.

A lifetime of training and instinct guiding his hand.

Boldo jerked back, eyes wide with shock. A dark hole appeared in his forehead. A trickle of blood ran down his face.

For a moment, Boldo teetered on the edge of the platform. Then his limp body plummeted to the ground below.

He landed with a sickening thud and all four limbs splayed at unnatural angles.

Flint stood, breathing hard, his gun still trained on the spot where Boldo had stood.

The wheel creaked a mournful sound in the sudden silence and the night wind tugged at Flint's hair, cooling the sweat on his brow.

Drake's voice crackled in his ear, tense and urgent. "Flint? What's your status?"

Flint touched his earpiece, still breathing hard. "I'm here. Boldo's dead."

"Marino, too. Got him just after he exploded the coaster." After a brief pause to breathe, Drake said, "I've got Ward. He's not in great shape."

"Bring him with you," Flint said, breathing hard.

"Three goons and Boldo down. Cops are on the way. ETA three minutes. We need to move," Drake reported. "Meet you at the gate."

"Copy that." Flint climbed down from the wheel, muscles aching, body battered and bruised.

At the bottom, he looked down at Boldo's broken body, eyes staring sightlessly at the sky, frozen in surprise. He spent a full second staring before he turned and hustled toward the front of the park.

Drake waited in the driver's seat at the gate. "Ward's conscious, but severely beaten. Carried him from the holding room and dumped him into the SUV."

Flint climbed into the passenger seat. "Go."

Flashing lights of the approaching police were visible in the distance. The sirens were growing louder.

"Hell of a morning," Drake said, his face grim as they sped away. He had a bloody cut above his eye but seemed otherwise unharmed.

"And it's not over yet." Flint nodded, holstering his gun. "The board meeting begins in a few hours."

They slipped away leaving the wailing sirens behind them.

CHAPTER 52

THE DNA SAMPLES FLINT had sent to Gaspar came back as expected. Emily Royce was Spencer Lyman's biological child, which gave her a strong motive to push Ward Lyman aside.

Curiously, even though she'd teamed up with Boldo to get Ward out of the line of succession, it was Boldo who tried to harm him. Flint hoped that meant Emily wasn't a cold-blooded killer.

He planned to confront her first and then inform Spencer Lyman. He could do both after the Lyman Enterprises board meeting. But he was running late. The meeting would be over soon. He wanted to be there when they finished.

Flint parked his SUV in the underground garage and hustled up to the main entrance. He burst through the revolving doors into the Lyman Enterprises headquarters in downtown Kansas City and raced across the lobby, footsteps echoing off the polished marble.

The elevator doors stood open and he lunged inside, jabbing the button for the top floor.

When the elevator car eased to a stop and chimed, the doors slid open. Flint stepped out into the plush corridor. He could hear muffled voices from the board members behind the closed conference room doors. The meeting was still going on.

Suddenly the doors flew open. Emily Royce emerged, eyes wild with panic. She spotted Flint and froze. Her expression morphed into pure rage.

"You!" she snarled, turning to an athletic security guard. "Get him out of here."

The security guard pulled his weapon and lunged toward Flint, knocking him to the ground while Royce sprinted toward the private elevator at the end of the hall.

Flint grabbed the guard's pistol and shoved him aside, scrambling to his feet, and giving chase.

He reached the elevator just as the doors were closing, allowing him to catch a glimpse of Royce's triumphant smirk.

Without hesitation, he turned and raced for the stairs, taking them down three at a time.

When he reached the parking garage, Royce's car was already peeling out, tires squealing against the concrete.

Flint leaped into his SUV, gunning the engine and tearing off in pursuit, tires squealing as he rounded the pylons inside the garage.

Both vehicles launched onto the streets of Kansas City like rockets.

Royce's sporty convertible weaved through traffic at reckless speed. She had several advantages. She knew the city. And her car was made for precision driving.

Flint followed as close behind as he could get, knuckles white on the steering wheel of the boxy SUV.

Royce swerved around a corner, sideswiping a parked car and sending sparks flying.

Flint gritted his teeth, slowed for the corner, and sped up trying to anticipate her next move.

She was heading for the highway, no doubt intending to lose him on the high-speed lanes where she could race ahead.

Flint wasn't about to let her get away. He pushed the accelerator to the floor and the SUV surged forward.

Up ahead, Royce's vehicle swerved again, narrowly avoiding a head-on collision with an oncoming semi-truck.

She over corrected and almost missed the turn onto the bridge.

Flint's heart pounded in his chest as he watched her careen close to the bridge's edge while weaving between the lanes.

He accelerated harder until he could pull up alongside her and buzzed his window down.

"Move over, Royce!" he shouted, barely audible over the roar of the engines. "You'll kill yourself!"

She jerked the wheel hard to the right, slamming into the side of his SUV.

The SUV rocked more than he expected, but her shiny red convertible barely seemed to notice the blow.

Which was when he realized her muscle car must have been armored.

Flint fought for control of the SUV, tires screeching as he swerved to maintain his position.

Royce rammed him again. He felt the top-heavy SUV lurch into the guardrail and lean toward the water.

He slammed on the brakes, dropping back just as Royce made another attempt to force him off the road.

But this time, given only the open air to collide with, she lost control.

Her spiffy little convertible swerved violently. The wheels slid up and along the curb at high speed.

The sports car rose into the air and sailed over the guardrail. The car seemed to be flying for a full second before it plunged off the bridge.

Flint saw the car tumble through the air and crash into the churning waters of the Missouri River below.

He brought the SUV to a screeching halt.

Leaving the engine running, he leaped out and raced to the edge of the bridge.

Traffic backed up behind him. A few horns blasted against the delay.

He scanned the water desperately, searching for any sign of Royce.

Suddenly, he spotted her, clinging to a piece of wreckage and struggling to keep her head above the waves.

Flint didn't hesitate.

He kicked off his shoes and dove into the river, swimming toward her with powerful strokes.

The strong current threatened to pull them both under.

Flint eventually reached Royce and grabbed her by the collar.

He pulled her toward the shore.

She fought against him all the way, clawing at his face and screaming obscenities.

But Flint held on tight and kept swimming.

When they reached the riverbank, he dragged her out of the water and tossed her to the ground, breathing hard. The gunshot wound to his bicep burned like a hot poker.

Royce glared up at him, her eyes filled with hatred.

"You think you've won?" she spat, her voice dripping with venom. "You have no idea what you're up against."

"I know enough." Flint said breathlessly as he looked down at her.

The sound of sirens filled the air.

He pulled her upright and marched her up the embankment, where a swarm of police were waiting.

CHAPTER 53

THE NEXT DAY, FLINT leaned against the wall near the window of Ward Lyman's hospital room. Boldo's goons had worked him over. He was lucky that he came out of it with only a few broken bones and serious bruises. Spencer insisted on a full physical examination complete with every medical test on the planet, to reassure himself that Ward was fit for life.

Ward simply didn't have enough energy to fight about it.

Spencer Lyman and Jeffrey Connor, Ward's new security detail, flanked the bed. They'd been talking for an hour and Flint had a plane to catch.

He cleared his throat and spoke during a brief pause in their conversation. "Ward, tell us what happened at the submersible. We need to hear it from you."

Ward closed his eyes and swallowed hard, as if the memories were painful. Which they probably were.

"No one was supposed to die," he whispered. "The plan was for the submersible to reach the galleon and all of the crew to head out for the planned exploration. While they were diving, I would pilot the submersible remotely to a safe distance and implode it. Rescue teams would collect the four divers, but not me. I'd be declared lost and presumed dead."

Flint had guessed most of this already. But there were still a couple of issues niggling his brain. "So you did intend to get on the submersible at the dock. Why didn't you?"

"Boldo's men told me Frankie, the alternate, was going in my place." Ward shook his head, and his lip quivered a bit with emotion. "They said it was too dangerous for me to go down and Frankie would handle my part."

Flint nodded. "Why did they shoot you in the back?"

"I argued with them. I said the implosion was tricky. I didn't think Frankie could do it. I demanded they let me go, as planned. They refused." Ward coughed a bit to regain his composure, shrugged, and stated the rest in a flat monotone. "So I ran. I'm fast. They weren't. They leveled the playing field with gunshots."

"Were you wearing a blue shirt that night?" Flint asked, as an easy cleanup point.

Ward's eyes widened. "How did you know that?"

"We saw you leaving the area on CCTV," Flint explained. "After they shot you, they loaded you into a van and whisked you away. I gather the next thing you knew you were on that island convalescing."

Ward swallowed hard and whispered, "It was a long time before Lucky told me what happened to the submersible. I still can't believe they killed my friends."

Silence enveloped the room for a few minutes before Spencer turned to Flint. "When did you figure out that Emily Royce was my daughter?"

"Emily put that in motion herself," Flint replied. "She submitted your DNA and hers to one of the online database sites. Once we found that report, we confirmed with fresh samples to our own labs. There's no doubt about it."

Spencer closed his eyes and seemed to be absorbing the idea that he'd had another daughter all these years.

"I was a young man. Emily's mother worked in the house. She flirted with me, and I flirted back," Spencer murmured, reminiscing. "I had no idea she'd become pregnant. I went off to college and Beatrice married Reacher Royce. When Emily was born, I didn't even know about her until I came back to live on the estate years later."

A brief silence filled the room while the other men, and probably Spencer, too, realized they all could have fathered children they didn't know existed. How would they have a handled the knowledge? Different times.

"I can't wrap my head around it," Ward murmured to Spencer. "Emily is my aunt and your daughter. But she aligned herself with Boldo? She was helping him to take over our company? Makes no sense."

Flint had a different view.

Emily believed she was the sole and rightful heir to Spencer Lyman's fortune after her half-siblings died. She had a good relationship with Ward and believed she could control him. He'd never shown any interest in the family business. Emily thought he never would.

She'd intended to cut Boldo out and keep Lyman Enterprises under her total control, once Spencer was out of the way. A gross miscalculation that would have eventually cost her her life. Boldo had never released total control over anything. Which was one reason he was dead.

None of which Flint said in front of the clients. The situation was a family matter now, so Flint kept his opinions to himself.

"Emily let hurt and jealousy consume her. She wanted to punish me for abandoning her mother and my child. If she took control of Lyman Enterprises, she could break me." Spencer's hands clenched into fists at his sides. "That's what she wanted. Revenge."

Ward frowned and scrunched his face into a quizzical expression. "Doesn't sound like Emily, does it? I don't believe she wanted to kill me. Or you. And where did Boldo fit into her plan, then?"

"Boldo probably told her she could have everything she wanted, and he'd help her to get it," Spencer said, shaking his head. "He would never have followed through on those promises. He'd have thrown Emily under the bus as soon as he had the chance. He wanted Lyman Enterprises for himself. Always has, just like his father did."

Flint faced the others. "The Boldos have engaged in a quiet vendetta against your family for years, Spencer. It started with Big Tony. If we continued to investigate, I believe you'd discover that he was the one who orchestrated the deaths of the four Lyman heirs and created that nonsense about a curse."

Spencer closed his eyes as if the suggestion pained him. "Nothing will bring them back. I'm an old man now. I'd like to live the years I have left in peace. Let it lie."

"Why didn't Big Tony Boldo get caught when he killed my dad?" Ward asked, bewildered. "Surely there were investigations into those deaths, too."

"Because Big Tony was very, very well connected. He was the head of one of the biggest criminal organizations in Kansas City, and he wanted to broaden his influence," Flint replied.

"He always had way too much untraceable hard money lying around," Spencer said wearily. "He used cash to bribe and coerce others to do his bidding."

"The son picked up where his father left off," Flint continued. "Emily saw an affair with Boldo as an opportunity to gain power and she took it. Pretty simple plan."

"And the plan almost worked, too." Ward shook his head, eyes flashing. "But Emily didn't want me dead. It was Boldo who tried to have me killed in Key West and kept me on that island for years. He probably kept me alive to control Emily, too. If it wasn't for her, I'd have been dead long ago."

Connor shifted his weight. "What about Lucky Jones? I've run across him a couple of times. He always seemed out of his element to me. Wasn't he on that island with you?"

"Yeah," Ward replied. "After I survived the gunshots and was able to move around, Lucky was good to me. The situation was great for a while. Perfect weather. Privacy. No one hounding me about anything. For the first time in years, I was able to avoid the threat of dying young. We played chess, tennis, talked for hours. I would have gone absolutely stir crazy without him."

"Why did you leave, then?" Connor asked.

"Two years is a long time," Ward shrugged. "I guess I just got bored. Or maybe too cocky. I mean, I'd been shot in the back and survived. I figured I could survive just about anything after that. I asked Lucky to get me a plane ticket home. That's when he told me I couldn't leave."

Spencer chuckled. "Guess he didn't know you very well, did he? You have never done what you're told. Not once in your life."

Ward had the grace to look sheepish and not argue the point.

"Lucky Jones is probably dead, but we haven't found his body." Flint's eyes narrowed. "I suspect Boldo killed him for allowing Ward to escape. And to tie up loose ends."

Flint had asked Gaspar to tip off the Justice Department about Boldo's crimes and they'd been only too happy to jump in.

"The feds have tried to destroy Boldo's criminal organization for years. They've got a solid chance to do that now," Flint told them. "They will dismantle Boldo's posse, and someone will talk to save their own skin. Nature abhors a vacuum. His organization will rise again. They always do. But it'll be different and Boldo will no longer be in charge."

"I should have seen the signs," Spencer ran a hand over his face. "I've treated Emily like my own daughter for years. Why didn't I see that she was capable of such betrayal?"

Flint placed a hand on Spencer's shoulder. "You can't blame yourself. Her jealousy and ambition blinded her."

"She is my daughter, though. I can't abandon her," Spencer said quietly. "What will happen to her now?"

"The feds will probably make a deal, if she'll testify against the rest of the Boldo organization," Flint explained the realities of criminal prosecution. "Emily's not the kind of person who will do well in prison. She'll agree to almost anything to avoid a long sentence."

"We'll get through this, Gramps. We'll rebuild Lyman Enterprises, make it stronger." Ward pushed himself up, ignoring the pain. "We'll get back on track. You'll see."

Flint nodded, a small smile tugging at his lips. Youthful exuberance was a wonderful thing.

"You're a survivor, Ward. You escaped that island without any help of any kind. You'll overcome this. The Lymans will come out on top," Connor said.

"You're completely right, of course. If this didn't break us, nothing will." Spencer's eyes glistened and he cleared his throat. "Flint, I've deposited your fee as requested. And added a handsome bonus. There's no way I can ever thank you enough."

Flint shook hands all around and glanced at his watch. He'd promised to meet Scarlett at his place in Houston tonight. Time to go.

"If you need me, you know where to find me. But you've got this handled."

With a final nod, Flint strode out of the room. His footsteps echoed down the hospital corridor and to the parking lot.

He stepped out into the bright sunlight and slipped his Aviators on. Families could really screw people up. He never wondered what his life might have been like if he'd been born into different circumstances. If the Lymans were an example of family solidarity, Flint was happy not to have one.

Besides, his hardscrabble upbringing had given him many advantages, including Scarlett and eventually, Maddie. Which was plenty. Way more than most people had.

CHAPTER 54

Houston, Texas

FLINT'S HOUSE WAS QUIET when Scarlett arrived. She made her way inside, following the dim lights and the smoky welcoming scent of a fire burning in the hearth.

She found Flint in the living room, nursing a glass of whiskey as he stared pensively into the crackling flames. A matching glass filled with a couple fingers of amber liquid waited on the coffee table for her.

Flint looked up as she entered, his expression inscrutable.

Scarlett slipped off her jacket and sank into the buttery leather armchair across from him. She scooped up the glass, letting the whiskey's familiar burn coat her throat as she sipped.

An unusual silence stretched taut between them.

Finally, Flint broke the tension with a weary sigh. "Did you come here just to drink my booze?"

"Definitely. Why do you think I bought it for you?" Scarlett grinned and threw a pillow at him. He ducked and her soft missile hit the floor.

"How's Maddy?" he asked as she settled in. He hadn't seen the little imp in a while, and he missed her. "Thought I'd take her and Whiskers to the park tomorrow."

"She's pissed as hell at you for being gone so long," Scarlett replied. "But she'll forgive you when you buy her ice cream."

Flint grinned and shook his head. "You women are all the same."

"Damned straight. Let's get to it. I need to get home," Scarlett said and took a sip of the whiskey.

"We can skip right over your obnoxious habit of doing exactly what you want with my life, whether I want you to do it or not." Flint's teasing tone was less harsh than his words. "Before you get all huffy, just tell me what you've uncovered about Marilyn Baker's murder."

Scarlett ignored him and set her glass down, leaning forward with both elbows on her knees. "Where do I start? It's turned into one hell of a rabbit hole, that's for sure."

"Begin at the beginning. If I get bored, you can fast forward to the good parts," Flint said dryly.

"Solid plan," Scarlett replied, taking a swig and then a breath before she started. "Naomi Wagner approached me at Maddy's soccer game. She wanted to hire my team to dig into potential new evidence."

"New evidence about what?"

"James Preston's alibi for the murders of June Pentwater and Marilyn Baker."

"He had a solid alibi and he never raised it?" Flint's expression was both astonished and appalled. "He let himself be executed for a crime he didn't commit?"

Scarlett gave him a glare to squelch the interruption. "If true, this new evidence would have exonerated Preston for the June Pentwater murder and possibly Marilyn Baker's murder, too."

Flint's brow furrowed deeper with each new detail, but he didn't speak again until after Scarlett explained about Dean Taylor and the former prison chaplain's relationship to Preston and the calendars he claimed he had secretly preserved.

"Wait, wait. This dude Taylor is *just now* revealing evidence that contradicts the entire prosecution case against Preston? After all this time?" He shook his head in disbelief. "What, Taylor had the truth stuffed under his mattress for thirty years?"

"I know, I pushed back on that too," Scarlett replied, refilling her glass. "Taylor claimed Preston gave him strict instructions not to release the evidence publicly until after Preston's death. According to Taylor, Preston was certain prosecutors would bury the evidence or the judge would refuse to consider it or somehow the evidence would disappear if anyone got wind of the facts before he died."

"That's possibly the dumbest excuse I've ever heard." Flint shook his head slowly. "He must have had another reason."

"And here's the kicker." Scarlett took another fortifying sip of the whiskey. "The alibis were recorded in Preston's own handwriting on his personal calendars. Back when people wrote things like that down in a daybook and kept the book in a pocket."

Flint stared at her like she'd sprouted a second head of wild and curly brown hair.

"We had those calendars subjected to every authentication test under the sun by the best forensic teams. The vinyl covers, the handwriting of individual entries, even the ink on the charred pages," Scarlett said, as if she really couldn't believe the evidence herself. "It all checked out. The calendars are legitimate, and the entries were created by Preston himself, at or about the time those events occurred."

Flint dragged a hand down his face, suddenly feeling decades older. "Jesus...so what you're telling me is these calendars prove Preston simply could not have been there. He couldn't have been in two places at once. Which means he didn't kill Pentwater. And attempts to link him to Baker's murder were completely bogus?"

"Almost," Scarlett shrugged. "The calendar entries provided potential alibis for Preston that directly contradicted the state's case against him. He'd have had no opportunity to commit two murders four years apart if he was miles away when they happened."

A tense silence fell again, punctuated only by the crackle of flames. Flint's jaw worked as he processed everything. Scarlett could practically see the storm of emotions rolling through him.

"This is a lot to take in," he said at last, clearing his throat. He reached for the whiskey decanter and sloshed a generous pour into his glass.

Scarlett waited for him to wrap his head around it all.

"I knew the Baker case against Preston was controversial. There was never enough evidence to charge anyone, including Preston. But the Pentwater case seemed airtight," Flint murmured. "There were plenty of doubts and disputes over the years, sure. But documented proof of credible alibis that were never presented or pursued? That's just crazy, isn't it?"

He trailed off, shaking his head again.

"We always had more questions than answers when it came to Marilyn Baker," Scarlett said quietly. "If this calendar business had held up on the Pentwater case, it could have forced prosecutors to find out who really killed both women."

Flint's gaze bored into hers then. "And what makes you think I'd want that to happen?"

"Don't you want answers? Shouldn't Marilyn Baker finally get the justice and peace she deserved? If nothing else, so that you can move on." Fiercely, she insisted, "We'd deal with it together, like we always have."

Flint didn't reply.

"Turns out, the calendars were genuine, but the alibi for Pentwater's murder was not. Preston fabricated the alibi. Then, he couldn't offer it as a defense because it would have proved he'd committed another crime," Scarlett explained because she'd kept him in the dark long enough. "He was guilty. Not just for the Pentwater murder, but sexual assault on a minor, too."

"What about Marilyn Baker? Did he actually have a valid alibi for her murder?" Flint asked.

"I didn't get that far." Scarlett shrugged and sipped the whiskey and savored it on her tongue before she swallowed. "I persuaded Wagner that Preston had lied about the Pentwater alibi and if he'd lied about one, he couldn't be believed on the other."

"Why'd you do that?" Flint wondered aloud.

"Because you made it pretty damned clear that you wanted to handle the matter on your own terms. Even though you're dead wrong. It's still your decision and I need to respect that," Scarlett said, which was as close to an apology as he was going to get.

"Okay. Tell me everything. I want to know the good, the bad, and the ugly," Flint offered a stoic nod. "I've put this off for too long. Time to face the music about the mother I never knew."

"And then what?" Scarlett asked.

"One step at a time, Katie Scarlett," Flint grinned and raised his glass. "First, we find out who murdered her. Then we'll figure out how to deal with the killer."

Scarlett raised her glass in return. "It's about damned time, Flint."

ABOUT THE AUTHOR

Diane Capri is an award-winning *New York Times, USA Today*, and worldwide bestselling author. She's a recovering lawyer and snowbird who divides her time between Florida and Michigan. An active member of Mystery Writers of America, Author's Guild, International Thriller Writers, Alliance of Independent Authors, Novelists, Inc., and Sisters in Crime, she loves to hear from readers. She is hard at work on her next novel.

Please connect with her online:
http://www.DianeCapri.com
X: https://x.com/DianeCapri
Facebook: http://www.facebook.com/Diane.Capri1
http://www.facebook.com/DianeCapriBooks
Instagram: https://www.Instagram.com/dianecapri/